MINNESOTA
NOT SO NICE

MINNESOTA
NOT SO NICE

EIGHTEEN TALES OF BAD BEHAVIOR

An Anthology Edited by

**BARBARA MERRITT DEESE, PAT DENNIS,
MICHAEL ALLAN MALLORY, AND TIMYA OWEN**

Twin Cities Chapter of Sisters in Crime, LLC
Saint Paul, Minnesota

This is a work of fiction. Names, incidents, and locales are the product of the authors' imagination or are used fictitiously, and any resemblance to any actual persons, living or dead, or actual locations is entirely coincidental. First edition.

This anthology is a product of the Twin Cities Chapter of Sisters in Crime. Sisters in Crime is a national organization founded to promote the professional development of women crime writers and to help them achieve equality in the industry. Membership is open to both women and men, as evidenced by the stories in this collection.

Interior Design: Sherry Roberts, The Roberts Group
E-book Design: Doug Dorow

While every effort has been made to provide accurate Internet addresses at the time of publication, neither the publisher nor the authors assume any responsibility for errors, or for changes that occur after publication. Further, the publisher does not have any control over and does not assume any responsibility for author or third-party websites or their content.

ISBN: 978-0-9994371-2-4

Library of Congress Control Number: 2020906309

*To our families and friends who have supported
each of us on this journey.*

CONTENTS

ACKNOWLEDGMENTS

Many thanks to Judy Kerr, Sherry Roberts, and Fay Dubois Wallin without whose invaluable assistance this anthology would not have been possible. Special thanks to Doug Dorow for his work on the ebook version of this anthology.

FOREWORD
By Brian Freeman

When I talk with readers and booksellers around the country, I hear the same question over and over. What is it about Minnesota that produces so many amazing mystery writers?

Because, with all due respect to the kids in Lake Wobegon, we really are above average here. Way above average. I can't think of any other state with a more talented collection of writers whose stories make us check the locks on our doors, peer under our beds, and make sure no one's hiding in the closet.

What's really puzzling about all these great Minnesota crime writers is that Minnesotans themselves seem to be . . . well . . . so gosh-darn nice. We smile at strangers. We wave to our neighbors. We say please and thank you. Heck, Minnesotans don't need to take numbers at the bakery. "Oh, were you here first? You go ahead."

Even when you squeeze a couple hundred thousand of us together at the State Fair, we line up politely for our cheese curds and fried pickles. No pushin' and shovin', ya know? The most popular booth at the fair is Sweet Martha's cookies . . . Sweet Martha's! I mean, how nice is that?

Hmmm. Then again. Perhaps that's what we want you to think.

Maybe, just maybe, Minnesotans have been fooling you all along. Maybe we've been keeping dark and dastardly secrets at the bottom of our ten thousand lakes. Be honest, haven't you wondered how Minnesotans can put up with long winter months of twenty-inch snowfalls and twenty-below-zero nights and still keep those annoyingly cheerful smiles on our faces? Come on, nobody can be that nice!

I think our mystery writers are on to something. Underneath all those Minnesota smiles may well be a whole lot of pent-up mayhem. Murder. Crime. Greed. Revenge. A hotdish bubbling over with vice and depravity.

That's what you'll find in this anthology. In the stories ahead, eighteen of our state's masters of mystery will do their best to convince you that Minnesota Nice hides a much darker reality . . . Minnesota Not So Nice. This is a side of our state that you've never seen before . . . from haunted sanatoriums to secret societies . . . from cats on the street to cougars in the bedroom . . . from murderous minnow shots to millions in missing gold. These stories are all about Minnesotans behaving badly. We steal. We betray. We cheat. We kill.

Nope, we are not nice at all.

Okay, okay, I'm just kidding. Really, we're just as nice as everyone says. Which is what makes our fictional body count so impressive—and entertaining.

So sit back and savor these twisted tales of mystery and imagination, brought to you with an unmistakably Minnesota flavor. You'll soon discover why readers can't get enough of our state's rich community of writers.

THE CAT WHO LOVED BELLS
By Sherry Roberts

The cat was drawn to the sound of bells, and it wasn't particular about the denomination. It had been chased out of church by the Catholics, the Lutherans, even the Unitarians. Father Murphy at the Basilica of Saint Mary had gone so far as to post a not-wanted poster. Although he could use the help with the mice, Father Murphy was afraid the cat would get into the Holy Communion hosts so he had made a sign for the tall front doors: "Please do not let in the cat." On it was a drawing that looked nothing like the cat. Father Murphy was a lousy artist.

The churches were warm, had such lovely nooks, and created a pleasant reverberation, an attribute not taken lightly by a purring creature. But the ginger cat's favorite stop was on Hennepin Avenue in Uptown, where a woman rang a bell with such joy the cat felt a kindred spirit and a slight envy for beings with opposable thumbs.

Maritza the bell ringer called the cat Bella Whiskers. "Merry Christmas, Bella Whiskers," she said as the cat trotted up one Saturday morning. She reached into the pocket of her coat and pulled out a handful of cat kibble. "Today is tuna. You'll like. Eat, eat." She bent over and poured the nuggets on the snowy sidewalk beside her worn boots, the ones with bells tied to the laces.

This was the best time of all for the cat. And the best time of all for Maritza.

Although life had physically worn down the woman, it had not touched her spirit. She often laughed, her breath puffing into the cold air, and she was always polite. Mr. Svenson, the man who owned the hardware store on her corner and who insisted on bringing her cups of hot cocoa on chilly afternoons, said she had a "good soul."

Tightening the purple and gold Minnesota Vikings scarf she'd found in the alley by her apartment, she said to the cat sitting at her feet, "Bella, you are the one with the good soul. You are my lucky charm. When you visit me, people open their wallets wide."

When the day was done, after the Salvation Army driver picked up her red kettle, Maritza would say, "See you tomorrow, Bella," and then walk the seven blocks home, jingling with every step as she climbed over the snow banks and slid on the icy patches. Maritza didn't know it, but many nights the cat followed her right up to her door but didn't slip in. Instead, it leaped onto the building's snowy broken fire escape and sat outside Maritza's window, where she kept a bowl of kibble for "all God's creatures," she said. The pigeons often visited the bowl to snatch pieces of food.

Sure, the cat thought, the food was nice, but the best stuff was on the other side of the window. For Maritza had a collection of bells, of all sizes and sounds, and when she took them from their case and played them, the tintinnabulation was a symphony that belonged in the stars.

❂

One day when Bella Whiskers was sitting calmly at the woman's side on the corner, looking up at her as she made beautiful music with the bells in her mittened hand and on her tapping feet, a photographer from the *Star Tribune* took their picture. The man interviewed Maritza. The next day, the newspaper printed a story about Maritza the bell ringer and Bella Whiskers, the cat who loved bells.

And that was how Coyote found her.

Coyote was the type who believed he had the right to other people's money. It didn't matter how hard they worked for it or that they needed the money to feed their family. He was a man with eyes that scared children and big, muscled arms, perfect for persuading people to give him what he wanted. He thought his strength was God's blessing and surely meant to be used.

On Monday, while Maritza stood on her usual street corner, ringing and wishing a joyous season to all, Coyote lounged in the shadows of a doorway a few buildings down, watching her. They had history. Hadn't he smuggled her into this country? Yes, she had paid his usual fee, in full and then some. But, he figured, now she could pay more. Look at the money people gave her every day.

He watched the cat from the newspaper approach, rub against her leg, and then sit patiently by her side. She fed the cat, which was so typical of soft-hearted Maritza. Back when they were bumping along dark roads making their way to America, she'd given her small portion of food and water to the whining children in the truck. So what if they were hungry and crying? he'd told her. How will they learn this is a tough world if you pamper them all the time?

At the end of the day, quite a lucrative one from what he could see, Coyote followed Maritza home. It was hardly difficult; with those bells on her boots, anyone could hear her coming, even with the city buses roaring by and impatient drivers laying on their horns. Then, like a cat himself, he climbed the fire escape, slipping and cursing. At Maritza's window, he kicked over the bowl of food and tapped on the window. Too startled to think, Maritza let him in.

"What do you want?" she asked, stepping back. "I paid you. We are even, Coyote."

He filled the small space, taking its air away. Looking around the pitiful one-room apartment, he said, "You got a nice thing going, Maritza."

When Maritza's glance flew to the purse lying on the table, he lumbered across the tiny apartment, his steps making the small Christmas tree on the table tremble. He snatched up the purse, pawed through it, and came out with two wrinkled dollar bills.

Flinging the purse to the floor, he demanded, "Where is all the money you got today?"

"That money is not mine. It is for the needy, Coyote."

He slapped her, hard, and she fell. The cat watched it all from the window.

"You didn't keep any of what you got today?" growled Coyote. "Stupid woman."

Maritza scrambled up on her old knees. "Please, Coyote."

He stepped toward her, hand raised. "I am the needy one, Maritza," said Coyote. "Or have you forgotten?"

Maritza remembered exactly the brutal ways of Coyote. Desperate, she covered her head and began crying. "Please, please. I have something else of value. A fine collection of bells."

Coyote stopped. "Bells?" he laughed.

"Golden bells," she said. "The best bells in the world. Take them. Sell them." She quickly rose and fetched a suitcase from behind the lumpy couch, which also served as her bed. When she opened it, he stepped forward and saw golden handbells nestled in soft velvet. Maritza kept them clean and polished, so much so that they glowed.

Coyote's eyes grew wide at the sight of the golden bells. "How did you come by such things?" he hissed.

"I am in a bell choir. The good women of the church gave them to me. They say I have a special talent."

"Talent," sneered Coyote.

In the end, Coyote took the bells. At the door, he warned, "And don't think you can tell anyone about this, Maritza. Or immigration just might get an anonymous tip."

The cat at the window watched the woman sink into a wobbly chair and sob.

The next day, Maritza was back on her corner, ringing the Salvation Army bell, the one that always stayed with the kettle. Now, it was the only handbell she had. It wasn't as pretty or as lovely sounding as her bells, but that didn't seem to matter. That day Maritza greeted everyone with her usual smile and a "Merry Christmas."

When the cat appeared, Maritza reached into her pocket. "Chicken today. It is good to vary one's diet." Stroking the cat's head, she said, "Enjoy, Bella Whiskers."

That evening, Coyote was waiting for her on the fire escape. When she refused to let him in, he broke the window and came in anyway, filling the apartment with cold air and menace. Then he hit her twice and tossed all the food from her freezer until he found the cash hidden in an orange juice container. All of Maritza's savings.

He shook his finger in her face. "Tomorrow night, you bring home the red bucket, Maritza."

"I can't; that is not allowed."

Coyote kicked her in the ribs. "See you tomorrow."

After Coyote left, the cat at the window watched the woman crawl across the floor, pick up a frozen bag of peas, and hold it to her bruised cheek.

Finally, Maritza had had enough. Had she not come to a new land so she could stop being afraid? The next evening, before she made her way home, she told the kind Mr. Svenson that she needed a baseball bat but that she had no money. Mr. Svenson, eyeing the bruises on Maritza's face, gave her the bat. "Pay me when you can," he said.

Maritza had decided that if she were ever to have a good life here in Minnesota, she must kill Coyote, strike him down as the drug cartel had struck down her husband of thirty years. Her heart cried when she thought of her Juan, a gentle man who had wanted no trouble. Yes, Coyote must go. She made the sign of the cross. She just hoped God would understand.

That night, when Maritza heard a commotion on the fire escape and knew Coyote was back, she was ready for him. She flung open the window with cardboard taped over the broken pane and raised the bat. But she couldn't believe her eyes. The cat and Coyote were struggling on the narrow grate. The cat was clawing at Coyote's face, and Coyote was trying to fling off the cat. Suddenly, the rotten rail of the fire escape gave way, and they both plunged over the edge.

Maritza cried out, dropped the bat, and hurried out of the apartment. She dashed down the stairs, flung open the outer door, and raced around the corner to the alley. There lay Coyote in the dirty slush and snow, his head at an awkward angle. And beside him was the cat.

Ignoring Coyote, she picked up the cat's limp body and brought it back to the apartment. There she wrapped it in the Minnesota Vikings scarf and held it through the night, praying. When morning came, Maritza awoke to a nudge at her arm.

She looked down and smiled at the ginger cat. "You used one of your lives last night for me. *Gracias.*"

Maritza leaned over and untied the lace of one of her shoes. Then she gently secured the lace with the bell around the cat's neck. Stroking its head, she said, "*Feliz Navidad.* Now, you will hear the sound of bells wherever you go."

And the cat did, but it still made the rounds of the churches and visited Maritza's corner. After all, what would Father Murphy do without a cat to chase and what would Maritza do without a cat to look after her.

END

SHERRY ROBERTS is the author of award-winning mysteries and fiction. Four of her books are Library Journal Indie Author Project Select titles: *Down Dog Diary, Warrior's Revenge,* and *Crow Calling* (Minnesota mysteries with a yoga spirit) and *Book of Mercy,* in which a dyslexic woman fights a North Carolina town banning books. Sherry has contributed essays and short stories to national publications such as *USA Today* and anthologies including *Saint Paul Almanac* and *Dark Side of the Loon.* She lives in Apple Valley, Minnesota. Sherry's author website is at sherry-roberts.com. Her essays can be found at The Hearth: hearth.sherry-roberts.com.

JUDY WITH THE RED HAIR
By Pat Dennis

Cigarette ashes floated downward, landing on both the threadbare beige recliner and Tyrone's head. Louise continued her circular pace while blurting out, "I just don't understand why you refuse to renew our wedding vows! Why won't you make me happy?"

"I don't like you," Tyrone answered simply, lifting the latest copy of *Fins and Feathers* over his face, shielding his eyes from his wife's ice-cold glare of continued resentment.

"Don't give me that crap. You love me," Louise insisted, reaching under her tight, size 3X Vikings T-shirt to adjust the thick bra strap that dug into her shoulder. "Husbands and wives love each other. Period. It says so in the Bible."

Tyrone didn't bother to dispute Louise's faulty biblical interpretation. He muttered, "You've been acting crazy since you started watching that stupid show about people renewing their wedding vows. It's worse than when you were saving up for a butt implant because of the Kardashians."

"Stupid? *Say I Do Again and Again* is one of the top rated cable shows in Minnesota. Everyone watches it."

"Not anyone that counts," Tyrone answered, pulling himself up before heading to the front door. He grabbed his camo hunting jacket and slipped on his Green Bay Packers knit cap. They couldn't even watch a friggin' football game together without calling each other names like *traitor* or *idiot*.

Louise announced, "If you're worried about the cost, I already have a wedding dress, picked it up at the Goodwill last week. With my senior discount, it only cost eleven dollars and thirty-seven cents. The mold on the hem is hardly noticeable."

"Why the heck would you waste money like that?" Tyrone sputtered, not bothering to turn around. "Do you really think I'd actually marry you a . . ."

Louise interrupted, "There's money involved and a casino, the new one in Miracle."

Tyrone's salt-and-pepper unibrow edged up into a question mark. He let go of the doorknob and swerved around. "Tell me more."

Money and gambling were the two things Tyrone loved unconditionally. Well, there were three things, but now was not the time to bring up Judy with the red hair.

Louise plopped loudly on the plaid sofa, particles of dust sparkling in the beams of sunlight streaming through the windows. She patted a cushion. "Come sit next to me."

Tyrone immediately sat across from her. His feet planted firmly on the carpet, as if preparing to bolt at a moment's notice. Stoically, he crossed his arms in front of him, waiting for an explanation.

His wife began. "Here's the deal. *Say I Do Again and Again* is teaming up with Miracle Casino to find the perfect couple to air on the show's third anniversary."

"And you think the perfect couple will be us? You've got to be kidding. We don't even talk."

Louise shrugged her shoulders. "We don't have to . . .well, except for a couple words, I guess."

"Like *I do*?" Tyrone growled.

"Exactly. See, that wasn't that hard. I knew I could get you to say them." Louise giggled. "Plus, it's a heck of a deal. The total cost for the vow renewal is only fifty-nine dollars and ninety-five cents."

A grimace invaded Tyrone's face. "It's gonna cost money?"

Louise's hand shot into the air. "Hear me out. The price includes a one-night stay, a ten-minute video of us renewing our vows, a ten-dollar gas credit, two seafood buffets, a bottle of champagne placed in our room . . ." She paused for effect. "And four hundred dollars in free slot play."

A flicker of a life willing to be lived came back into Tyrone's eyes.

Louise continued, "You can have the slot play. All of it. And, for your cooperation, your wedding present from me will be an extra five hundred dollars in cash, given to you the moment we arrive."

Tyrone's shoulders slumped in despair. "Does that mean I have to give you a . . ."

"Of course not," Louise replied. She already knew he wouldn't give her a gift. He never had. On every birthday, Christmas, and anniversary he'd repeat the same old wisecrack. "I'd give you a gift, but you already have one . . . *me.*" He'd laugh. She never did.

Tyrone did the math . . . even with the hotel cost, he'd still be at an eight-hundred-and-forty-dollar profit and more if he managed to turn the slot play and cash into a jackpot or two. Maybe he'd even hit the million-dollar progressive a few Minnesota casinos offered. He could leave his life and wife behind.

Besides, it had been years since he'd been a high roller. After filing for bankruptcy four years earlier, Louise kept a tight grip on their purse strings. She had the gall to put him on an allowance, like some snot-nosed kid.

True, as far as Louise knew, their financial problems were caused solely by his out-of-control gambling. Even Tyrone admitted it was kind of true—that, and bad luck. But keeping a forty-some-year-old ginger on the side cost a bit of dough as well. And if he knew Judy, she'd insist on a room for herself at Miracle casino. On the plus side, it would be a room Tyrone could easily slip into once Louise reached her mandatory 9 p.m. bedtime.

Tyrone managed to display a sixteenth of a grin. "I guess I'll do it."

Now it was Louise's turn to jump up and grab her coat. "If we're leaving tomorrow, I have to get to Great Clips today, and The Dollar Tree. Can't be remarried unless I'm sporting new makeup and smelling like lavender soap."

The shiny brass doors at the hotel's entrance opened automatically. Yet Louise, dressed in her thrift store bridal gown and a puffy orange parka to ward off the below zero temperatures, struggled to step inside. It wasn't her voluminous, size 24 ensemble or the floor-length lace veil that made her stride difficult. It was the fact that Tyrone insisted she pull their wheeled luggage while carrying a six-pack of Miller Lite.

Tyrone stopped his quick pace and glared over his shoulder. "If you hadn't worn that stupid outfit you wouldn't be having so much trouble."

"I wore it because I knew we wouldn't have a lot of time when we got here," she lied.

Time wasn't the reason she'd donned satin and lace for their three-hour journey. Louise needed the attention. It had been decades since she'd received any. Nothing made a person take notice like seeing a bride, especially a sixty-year-old one. Even the Kwik Trip cashier not only mentioned she was a beautiful bride, but worried Louise might splatter gasoline on her gown when she filled the car tank.

Louise reminded her husband, "We're scheduled to be at the chapel no later than 7:20 p.m. There are over fifty other registered couples. The instructions said we had to be prompt."

Everyone in Minnesota wanted to be on television, it seemed.

"That soon?" Tyrone barked, looking around the crowded casino filled with thousands of blinking slot machines and yelping players. "That only gives me three hours to gamble."

"What about the buffet?" Louise whined, a bad feeling taking root in her gut. She chose to ignore it. True, Tyrone usually disappointed her, but she had gotten him this far. There was still a chance everything would turn out perfectly.

"I ain't got time to eat stupid crab legs. I'll meet you at the chapel." Tyrone stretched out his empty hand, palm side up. "Where is it?"

"Where's what?" Louise asked.

"The money you promised me."

Louise sputtered, "You're not checking into the hotel room with me? Don't you want to take a shower, or get dressed in something other than . . ."

Tyrone pushed his hand out further until it poked into his wife's belly. "I don't have time for that. Just give me my money, now."

Unzipping the side pocket on her jacket, Louise pulled out a stack of currency held together with a paper clip. Tyrone grabbed the stash and walked away, heading toward the table games.

Louise followed the signs to the hotel check-in. Her spirit brightened when she noticed people smiling or giving her a thumbs up. Dozens of women were dressed in similar attire while the men next to them wore tuxedos. Louise couldn't decide if the scene looked incredibly romantic or simply like Halloween, where everyone pretended to be something they were not, just to get a treat.

⚜

"I'm sure my husband will be here any minute," Louise pleaded with the irritated, twenty-some-year-old production assistant. She didn't dare look at her watch. The last time she did, it read 7:41 p.m. Behind her was a line of anxious couples chatting away about how exciting it would be if they were the ones chosen.

Inside the chapel, a camera crew filmed the twenty-fourth pair of love birds. An officiant, dressed as a priest, stood in front of the octogenarian duo. Not a good choice, Louise decided. Especially when the other option was an Elvis impersonator. Louise knew one thing for sure. If you want to make good television, always go with a dead rock star.

Scratch them off as potential winners.

Rolling his eyes in frustration, the P.A. said, "I'm sorry but your husband's a half hour late. It's not fair to the other participants."

"Please," Louise begged. "I'm one of your show's biggest fan. I've watched every episode a dozen times. It's always been my dream to . . ."

The assistant interrupted with a quick wave of his hand. "Fine, you've got twenty minutes to find him and get back here. Not a minute more."

Louise swirled around and lifted up the skirt of her frock slightly and began sprinting to the casino floor. She rushed past hundreds of penny slots, then rows of nickel, dime, and quarter machines. Eventually she raced by dollar slots, heading towards the high stakes table games. It wasn't hard for her to determine where her husband would be. But it was her fault he hadn't shown up. Why in the world did she give him the money before the ceremony?

Rushing through the narrow aisles, her protruding elbow crashed into a seated, slot player's bald head. "Hey lady," he hollered after her. "You friggin' hit me!"

"Sorry," she answered back, not slowing down for a millisecond.

"What's your hurry?" another young man yelled out. "I'd ask if it was a shotgun wedding, but you're like a million years old."

"A million and a half," she responded in a voice loud enough to create a wave of chuckles and snorts coming from the most diehard gamblers.

Louise's anger catapulted her at rocket speed. Tyrone wasn't going to destroy the only dream she had left. It wasn't that she wanted to be on television or be famous. Not at all. It was only she wanted proof that she existed. Perhaps, when she saw her image reflected on the screen, she'd realize she wasn't invisible after all.

And if she found Tyrone, Louise wouldn't care if he was waiting for a ten-thousand-dollar hand pay to be delivered. She'd grab him by his flannel shirt collar and drag him to the Miracle Chapel of Love.

With the help of her rubber-soled sneakers, Louise slid to a halt as soon as she reached the table gaming area. Her lungs felt like they were about to explode in pain. She rested her hands on her waist and bent over, inhaling slowing, allowing her chest to stop burning. Finally, when she was calm and the pain had subsided, she scanned the room. Immediately, Louise understood why Tyrone had forgotten all about her. Even she could tell he was on a roll, a winning streak, a grand slam. Seated at the one-hundred-dollar minimum bet blackjack table, Tyrone's hand was high in the air, his palm opened wide as he high-fived the gambler sitting next to him—Judy with the red hair.

❊

The swirling red and blue lights filtering through the glass balcony doors bounced around the hotel room ceiling and walls.

"Looks like a disco," Louise mumbled out loud, before dipping a Cheeto into her fourth glass of champagne. Sitting back against the tufted vinyl headboard, Louise's wedding dress puffed around her like a parachute in flight. She grabbed the television remote and clicked on the closed captions feature. The station was running an all-night marathon of a reality show she'd never watched. And though it was the most fascinating show Louise had ever seen, it was time to mute the sound. She wasn't exactly sure when the police would begin to pound on the door, but she wanted not only to be totally wasted, but passed out.

Why officer, she'd announce while rubbing her eyes, *I didn't hear you knock. I've been asleep for hours after drinking all that free champagne. Where did you say my husband was? Splattered all over the parking lot? He fell off the balcony? My God, was it suicide? My sweet, sweet husband's been so depressed lately since the Packers lost. . . .*

Or she could claim he simply fell off the balcony because he was clumsy. Didn't Tyrone once break his toe after dropping a bowling ball on it? Certainly, that would be in his medical records.

Of course, it wasn't death by self-choice. And surprisingly, it was fairly easy to do. A filled ice bucket helped. And the fact the balcony easily turned into a slippery nightmare when covered with cold water and melting ice cubes.

Tyrone had entered their room around midnight, shocked to find Louise still awake. He'd begun his apology by saying he didn't want to do a vow renewal anyway. He'd said *I do* once and he didn't need to say it again, ever. Louise agreed.

Even seated yards away from Tyrone, she could smell Judy's cheap perfume lingering on his clothes, just like she had from day one of her husband's affair. The moment Tyrone lit his cigarette, she insisted he not smoke in the room. When he stepped outside, Louise immediately followed. One quick shove, and all of her problems disappeared.

Louise could hear footsteps rushing down the hallway. *Crap!* There would be no time to finish the episode, but at least she had written down the show's call-in number for later. Of course, she'd have to wait a while . . . maybe a year before she'd be eligible to be a featured guest. Or perhaps just a few months? In fact, she could be featured on the very next season. She'd want to lose a few pounds first, maybe get a makeover, but it could be fun. It would be fun. Fun was something she hadn't had for a long, long time.

As soon as she heard the knocking, Louise clicked off the television and lay back on the bed. She closed her eyes while wondering how in the heck she'd never heard of such a fantastic reality show? She struggled to hide her smile when she realized it was all meant to be. That, like her mother said, everything always turned out okay in the end. And besides, who wouldn't want to be on a show called *The Happy Widow*? Life is good, Louise decided. And sometimes, death is better.

END

PAT DENNIS is the author of the short story collection *Hotdish to Die For.* Her memoir *Fat Old Woman in Las Vegas: Gambling, Dieting and Wicked Fun* reached #1 on Amazon. She authored the popular adult coloring book *Kill Me! My Husband's Retired!* Her Betty Chance mystery series includes *Murder by Chance, Killed by Chance,* and *Dead by Chance.* Pat's work has appeared in numerous publications including: Anne Frasier's *Deadly Treats, Once Upon a Crime Anthology, Writes of Spring, Cooked to Death, Silence of the Loons, and Resort to Murder, Minnesota Monthly, Woman's World, The Pioneer Press,* and more.

GRANDMA'S RULES
By Karl W. Jorgenson

Elle saw the customer appear at the far end of the racetrack, the main aisle that looped around the home-improvement warehouse. Mid-day, the store was slow and her department—kitchen design—dead, so she had nothing better to do than watch people. He looked right at her, so maybe he was going to ask her about the cabinets, countertops, sinks, and appliances upon which she earned a 2 percent commission to supplement her base wage. Grandma's first rule was to work a regular job. The cops knew they had their perp when they found her unemployed but living in Edina and driving a Lexus.

She guessed the man was about her age—twenty-nine. He appeared to be of Somali descent, so her estimate could be way off. For one thing, Somalis didn't seem to add the five pounds per year so common among last century's white immigrants.

In two years on the job she'd never helped a Somali plan a kitchen. He passed the wall of granite samples and stopped in front of her desk. Neatly dressed in a polo shirt and sleek slacks, his apparent affluence raised her hope for a sale. On the other hand, he was too young for the mid-life-crisis-master-chef kitchen remodel, the kind of sale that would earn her four or five hundred dollars. And he was committing the rookie mistake of so many young husbands: he had not brought his wife.

"How can I help you?" She smiled up at him.

"Eleanor Fine?" He returned her smile and seated himself in a client chair.

Her smile wavered. Her nametag said only "Elle." She hoped he wasn't a process server. Was her previous landlord suing her for the collapsed bathroom? That was hardly her fault. Putting up with the leaking pipe had been a minor inconvenience, until the tub supports rotted. "I'm Elle."

He offered his hand and she shook it, his skin cool and smooth. "Your grandmother is Henrietta Fine?"

So that's what he wanted. Somebody missing their family heirloom and looking for a scapegoat. Grandma Fine's reputation had spread and grown until she was suspected of every crime involving jewels, precious metals, or artwork.

"My name is Salah. I have a business proposition for your grandmother." Then, leaning forward and lowering his voice, he said, "Your neighbor told me you worked here."

Elle leaned back and shook her head. "She's retired. Living in a senior community in Naples, Florida." Where Elle suspected an occasional diamond-studded bauble vanished without explanation.

Salah pouted. "That is unfortunate. It's an excellent opportunity. Does she visit you? It must be hot down there."

"I probably won't see her until Thanksgiving." Unless Grandma needed help. It had been a year since the last job, a shipment of gold to a jewelry manufacturer. That had been worth sixty thousand dollars: forty for Grandma, twenty for Elle. Now that she thought about it, she had spent the last of her share a month ago. Both of her credit cards were approaching their maximums, and she had been forced to hold her rent payment until her end-of-month paycheck cleared.

She leaned over the desk, bringing her face within a foot of his. "Maybe I can help you."

Salah laughed, the warm, inviting laugh of someone who sees only good luck, sunshine, and hazelnut-infused-Italian chocolate in his future. "No, it definitely has to be your grandmother. I need someone with her experience."

Elle nodded her acceptance. "I have assisted my grandmother several times. I'm an attentive student."

He appraised her. "I don't know you. Anyone can brag."

She smiled smugly. "Tell me about the project. Perhaps I'll see a solution."

Salah looked around. The only person in sight was a workman dressed in paint-spattered jeans and faded T-shirt looking at the end cap of towel holders, thirty feet away. "There is a *xawaala*, a money transfer business."

"You can't rob a bank," she said.

"Listen. The first of the month, everybody gets paid. They cash their checks and bring the money to the transfer bank to send it to their families in Mogadishu. These are people who don't use regular banks, so most of it is cash. Monday, Wednesday, and Friday mornings, a Brink's truck makes a pickup."

"You want to take an armored?" She almost laughed. Her dim-bulb brother Rick had tried that once in Colorado and barely escaped with his freedom.

"No. When they bring the money out. It's two guards with a kind of luggage cart, carrying a metal box."

"What's the name of the bank?" This didn't sound so promising anymore. She wasn't about to shoot it out with private guards.

"International Equity. In the mall on Lake Street. When the first of the month falls on a Friday, the pickup is extra big on Monday. Maybe fifty thousand dollars or a bit more."

Elle checked her phone. Friday, September 1, was two weeks away. Labor Day weekend; the pickup would be on Tuesday. For a chance at half-a-share of fifty grand, she could take a look. "I'll talk to you in a couple of days."

"All right. Every morning I'm in the Kabbasho Café on Cedar. Do you know it?"

"I'll find it."

He nodded. She held out her hand and he met it with his own, lifting it gently to his lips for the lightest of kisses. She felt her neck and cheeks grow hot.

Grandma's second rule was to case. Study the target, know the people, learn their routine. More burglars were caught by late-working bookkeepers than by alarms.

International Equity was inside a block-long building that must have been a huge store, maybe a car dealership, back in the days when people rode buses to shop and nobody had yet dreamed of surrounding a mall with sixty acres of asphalt. The building had two hallways that crossed in the center of the structure, one going from the main front door to a rear service door, the other running lengthwise, terminating at store entrances. The walkways were lined with small, mom-and-pop retail. At 8:30 a.m., the only open businesses were the bank and its neighbor, a nail salon. The nail place was entered through an alcove, from which the smell of acrid chemicals wafted. On the opposite side, closer to the street, was an African-clothing boutique. Across the hall was a jewelry store with a showcase featuring flashy gold necklaces and earrings so bulky and ornate an elephant would find the weight uncomfortable. One glance was all she needed to dismiss the place. The entire inventory might be worth ten large.

Elle wore a shapeless sundress, a floppy hat as wide as a seat cushion, and dark glasses to obscure her identity for any CCTV. As she pretended to study the costume junk in the jewelry store's window, a pair of Somali women came down the hall and entered International.

Stealing the hard-earned money of immigrants went against her principles. But that wasn't what Salah was talking about. Once the bank mixed a customer's cash with other currency, it became the bank's property. They sent an electronic transfer somewhere and banked what they had taken in. If the money was stolen it was their loss, or more accurately, their insurance company's.

The mall's front door opened again and two security guards came in, the first pushing a handcart, more or less like the lumber carts where she worked. A low, steel-mesh platform and four wheels, the back two on swivels. She turned away and walked to the rear exit. She had seen what she could. The inside of International would have more and better cameras.

The rear door was exit only, self-locking and closed by a hydraulic arm. It thumped shut behind her, and she blinked against the bright sun. She was in an alley running the length of the block. On the opposite side from the mall was the light-rail station, a brightly lit, glassed-in fishbowl of white tile and posters forbidding smoking and encouraging bus passes in English, Spanish, Somali, Vietnamese, and Hmong, the big five languages of the Twin Cities.

She followed the alley south to the cross street, passing the entrance to the transit terminal and the associated array of bike lockers. The lockers were gray metal, like high school lockers but three times as wide and five feet deep. It was a sad comment on society that cables, chains, and U-locks were insufficient to protect bicycles from roving thieves.

She settled in her Nissan, but didn't start the motor. The two guards from the Brink's truck were armed. They had probably received at least some training and would reach for their weapons at the first sign of trouble. There would have to be a distraction, something spectacular, something worthy of P.T. Barnum.

In Grandma Henrietta's time, the bars and cafés on Cedar Avenue had been sanctuaries for student revolutionaries who rallied against the draft in the Sixties, marijuana laws in the Seventies, disco in the Eighties, and finally, and most heart-felt, against the march of time, against the day when they must leave their ivory towers and make payments on their student loans. Now the avenue was lined with shops serving East African immigrants.

The Kabbasho coffee house occupied the ground floor of a narrow, two-story brick building that stood shoulder to shoulder with two larger buildings. To the north was an electronics store selling phones, tablets, laptops, and every other device that could communicate with the web. A banner across the front offered "PAY AS YOU GO PLANS!! LOWEST INTL. RATES!!!" To the south a chiropractor promised to accept most insurance, the message pasted unevenly across the glass, like a ransom note cut from newspaper.

Inside Kabbasho, the scent of clove and cinnamon embraced her. The café had a dozen small tables, most occupied by groups of Somali men. In the back was a corkboard layered with business cards and flyers for Realtors, immigration lawyers, and Amway distributors. Salah was having an animated discussion with three other men, seated in a nook at the front.

As she considered whether to interrupt, two older men stood from their table, spread prayer rugs in an open space, and knelt to pray. She gave them a wide berth, uncertain of their customs, and approached the counter, where she ordered a vanilla-flavored latte.

Salah joined her at the end of the counter. "I'm a little surprised to see you again."

She nodded. She had a plan for International Equity, a plan for herself and three others. Salah didn't have to be one of them, but she felt an obligation to include him since he had brought the idea to her. Grandma Henrietta used to say, "Treat your partners fairly, but be ready to burn them if they twitch." That was one of her top rules.

"I had a look at the place we discussed. There is a way."

A young Somali woman with luminous skin, wearing a green-and-gold hijab, stood a few feet away, watching them with obvious discomfort. Elle was about to confront her when Salah spoke in Somali. The woman answered in a rush of words, her face softening. They discussed back and forth for a minute, and then the woman dipped her head and gushed what could only have been fervent thanks.

"What was that about?" Elle asked when the woman had left the café.

"Oh, she's a cousin, related to some other cousins on my mother's side. Her landlord has threatened to evict her because she has too many people living in her apartment."

"That's terrible. What did you tell her?"

Salah shrugged. "I'll call the landlord. He said he wouldn't evict her if she agreed to a four-hundred-dollar increase in the rent. This tells me he doesn't really want her out, he just sees an opportunity for more money."

"Are you going to help her pay it?" If it were her, she would skip her last month's rent and move without warning. But it probably wasn't as easy for an immigrant to find another apartment, especially if she was providing for an extended family.

"Pay it? No." Salah's eyes twinkled. "My father taught me the fine points of bargaining. I know the building where she lives. Some of the apartments have cockroaches. There are mice in the basement. I will help the landlord keep this shameful problem a secret, in exchange for renewing her lease without an increase."

Elle couldn't help grinning. "Blackmail."

Salah made a clucking sound with his tongue. "That shows you do not understand bargaining."

Elle picked up her coffee and followed Salah to the table in the nook. The three men were standing, exchanging final words before departing. Salah spoke to them and Elle understood one word: *nabad,* peace.

"We need a driver," she said when they were seated, and she was satisfied that nobody could overhear them. "And another man to act as a decoy."

"You have a plan?" Salah looked skeptical.

She told him how they would surprise the guards and more importantly, how they would escape when the alarm was raised.

Salah thoughtfully sipped his milky *shaah*, which gave off waves of fragrant cardamom and nutmeg.

"You need me," she said. He seemed to be an amateur, and amateurs tended to overestimate their abilities, leading to foolish solo attempts. "It can't work without a woman."

"Maybe."

She could almost see him thinking. Was he contemplating a double cross, or trying to assess the risk? "You can think about it, if you want. But it's five days to Labor Day."

Salah nodded and stared into his mug.

"We need an untraceable car and two men to drive it."

"I know a couple of brothers." Salah grinned and she wasn't sure if he had decided to go along or had found a way to cheat her.

Labor Day was a big day at the home-improvement warehouse. She volunteered to work the afternoon shift and even sold a set of cabinets that earned her a $124 commission. What she liked about working holidays was that the bosses were always absent. Some junior-assistant manager was in charge, twenty-five years old, a pimple on his forehead and nervous sweat staining his polyester uniform shirt as he jogged from department to department, certain that everything was falling apart.

It was simple to get into the security office and use their computer. Security video was stored on-site for two months in an array of hard drives. She couldn't do what she thought of as the Hollywood Hack, where the video would be edited to add her to a scene. What she could do was make a copy of an existing file and set up a simple routine to copy it over a newer video at midnight tomorrow.

She picked the file from August 16, two and a half weeks ago. She had been at work early, a little after seven, and left at lunch. It wasn't a perfect alibi since a careful examination of the file's history would reveal its age—it was beyond her skill to change that—but the name of the file would be correct and someone looking at the video would see her and the timestamp and should conclude that she worked Tuesday morning.

The cops were only going to catch her through luck or Salah's help. One of Grandma Henrietta's top rules: plan your alibi before the job.

✿

Tuesday morning Elle clocked in at the store just after they opened. Her area was quiet, as it always was until late morning, though the back of the warehouse bustled with contractors, loading trucks with lumber, wallboard, roofing, pipe, the raw material for their day's work.

She slipped out through the back, retrieved her car, and drove to the light-rail station.

She left the train one stop early, half a mile from her target. In the restroom of a McDonald's she transformed herself. A short blond wig with streaks of gray, layers of makeup to age her skin, and a Harley-Davidson-logo tank-top to show off temp-tattoos on her back and arms. Now she was an aged biker momma, toughened by years of hard living. She hoisted her backpack and went to meet Salah.

Salah was dressed as instructed in jeans, a long-sleeve yellow shirt, and a Twins ball cap. Grandma's rules said a disguise should present an alternate identity, not just obscure the truth. Salah looked like a rube. Good enough.

They strolled into the mall. Salah pulled away when she reached for his hand but she persisted, determined to make a show for the CCTV. They stopped at the jewelry window and waited.

"They'll be here soon," he said.

"Relax. It will work. Even if something goes wrong, we'll vanish."

The front door swung open and the first guard came in, holding the door for the second, who pushed the empty cart through. Elle gave the guards a few seconds to observe them—Somali man with yellow shirt, biker-chick with tats.

She turned her face to Salah and said, a little too loud, "I *saw* you. She was hanging all over you."

Salah, forgetting his role, as she knew he would, said, "What?"

She poked his chest. "That bitch Naomi."

"Oh," he said. "*Oh.*" He puffed out his chest. "Don't be gettin' all up in your biz-ness."

She started to correct him, then realized that, just like any live performance, it was better to ignore mistakes and keep going. The guards were at the door to the bank. She glared at them, then lowered her voice so he had to lean in. "Okay. Now we whisper. They have the picture." Projecting anger and self-righteousness, she shouted, "Right!?"

The door swung shut at International Equity. The guards were in.

A minute later, the lead guard emerged, checked the hallway, then held the door for the cart, now laden with the metal strongbox. Elle took a deep breath and screamed. She crumpled to the floor.

"You must this not do," Salah snarled.

A tiny sigh escaped from Elle. They should have rehearsed. She rolled out of the way as Salah's kick bashed the wall just past her head. She scuttled on all fours toward the nail salon's alcove, using the archway to pull herself to her feet. Salah slammed into her from behind, carrying them both into the recess, where she spun away into a corner and screamed her best scream of anguish.

Salah waited, his back to the hallway, one fist raised as though he intended to punch the door that announced "Full Set 29.99." Elle set her backpack on the carpet and drew her gun. Where were they? She kicked the wall and screamed again, pressed tightly into the corner.

A guard appeared in the door. He pointed his gun at Salah's back and said, "Don't move, asshole."

Elle placed her pistol gently against the man's ear. "Same to you, buddy."

Salah took his gun and motioned for him to kneel. Elle stepped into the hallway. The other guard was talking on his phone, gun holstered. "Drop the phone," she said, her pistol pointed at his chest.

With the guards lying in opposite directions in the alcove, Salah zip-tied the first guard's wrist to the second's ankle and then the second's wrist to his partner's ankle. Maybe they could move as a six-limbed spider, but not easily, or fast.

Salah held the back door as she pushed the cart through. To the right, a silver Camry waited at the end of the alley. Elle turned left, trotting behind the cart.

"Hey," Salah said. "He's over there."

"Change of plan," she panted, exactly as she'd planned. "Car could be searched."

She stopped in front of the bike lockers, pushed a debit card in the slot, pulled the key, and swung the door open. The box weighed seventy-five or eighty pounds, but she lifted with her legs and heaved it into the space, slamming the door shut.

Elle pressed the locker key into Salah's sweaty palm. "Wipe the cart handle and leave it in the street. We'll meet here tomorrow, at ten." She grabbed his arm. "A friend is going to follow you, to make sure you get away cleanly." She could see he understood. She'd know if he returned early.

Salah looked at the bank of lockers, opened his hand and looked at the key.

"Go," she said.

He spun the cart around and hustled down the alley.

She tucked her wig in her backpack and extracted a windbreaker to cover her skin art. Then back the way she had come, six blocks to the next rail station, where she boarded and rode to her car and drove to her job. Inside, she spent ten minutes removing the tats and makeup with rubbing alcohol, changed back into her white blouse, and sauntered through the store to her sales desk. Across town, Salah would have removed his yellow shirt and been dropped by the Camry's driver a few blocks away, behind a bar, where a different man would replace him and put on the yellow shirt. The two men would drive main streets through the heart of Minneapolis, stopping at coffee shops and cafés.

At 12:15 p.m. she punched out and drove home, matching the pattern on the August 16 video.

✿

Eight o'clock the next morning she parked on Lake Street, a block from the bike lockers and the cash box. She was sure Salah was not going to wait until ten as instructed. If he believed she had an accomplice watching him, he would appear just early enough to dismiss the timing as a mistake if she caught him.

It was not yet nine when a government sedan stopped next to the bike lockers. Salah emerged from the rear seat. Two white men in sport coats and polyester slacks who could not have been less plainclothes if they had "POLICE" in yellow letters across their backs stepped out, leaving their doors open.

She used a new burner phone to call Salah, who answered immediately. "I see you brought some friends." She watched from inside the rail station, concealed behind a head-height poster urging caution around trains.

Salah walked away from the car and the cops. He looked around, settled for staring at the back door of the mall, as though she'd be dumb enough to go in there. "Eleanor? My apologies. I've been working with these gentlemen for a while. The *xawaala* is washing money for criminals. There's probably $200,000 in there, but it's dirty money."

So that was it. "You're a CI?" Salah was an informant. "They don't have enough evidence for a warrant. But a robbery . . ."

"Yes. Sorry."

The older detective had the locker key. He opened the door, and they transferred the cash box to the trunk of their car.

"I won't mention you," Salah said and returned to the car, which sped away.

Elle drove into the alley. The other bike-locker key was in the center cup holder. She opened the locker next to the one the cops had just emptied and moved the second cash box, grunting with the effort to clear the trunk's lip. The box in the cops' trunk had cost her $285 on eBay, plus a ridiculous $68 for expedited shipping. Salah would change his mind and rat on her after it was opened. The police would come straight to her job. She would act surprised, but be helpful. That was Grandma's rule too: always appear to help the police.

Yes, she remembered Salah, the handsome Somali. He had stopped by two weeks ago, said he was planning to buy a house that needed some updates. Security video would confirm their meeting.

Video from the day of the robbery would show her at her desk with customers passing by, a solid alibi. The cops would conclude Salah had used a tattooed, gray-haired biker momma to divert the money. She felt a little sorry for him. *Nabad,* Salah, *nabad.*

END

KARL W. JORGENSON is a member of the Minnesota Bar, having graduated from an actual law school and passed the bar exam. He finds writing fiction more fun than writing law, perhaps because he is allowed to make stuff up. He and a cowriter are currently seeking an agent for their just-completed international thriller, which is set in Somalia.

TOE BREAKER
By C.N. Buchholz

I wanted to wrap my hands around the woman's throat and squeeze until her red-painted lips turned a permanent blue. I clenched and unclenched my fists. *Breathe.*

After weeks of playing private eye, I knew the con woman's routine. Every morning at 6:30 a.m., my 70-year-old father drove Luella Lopez' 40-year-old ass to work at St. Cloud's Loon State Senior Living Center. Immediately following her shift, she would skedaddle across the street to Rowdy Red's—a friendly rival to Minnesota's largest honky tonk, Rollie's—for after work pick-me-ups. And pick-men-ups.

My father, blinded by "true love" for a whole two months, twiddled his farmer thumbs in the living room until—hours later—the queen bar fly beckoned him for a ride back to our homestead. "She's the one," he told me and anyone else within earshot. "As soon as Luella's divorce is final from that no-good-lying cheat, I'm gonna marry her."

Never mind that the no-good-lying cheat was Luella.

It took me awhile, searching through the crowded bar, before I found Luella. She had swapped her scrubs for tight denim shorts, a plunging V-neck T-shirt that boasted breasts the size of Minneapolis-Saint Paul, and knee-high diamond-studded cowboy boots. I stomped over and stood behind her. By the empty shot glass in her hand, it was clear Luella had already slammed drink number one.

"Another whiskey, Jonny darlin'," Luella cooed to the bartender, batting Tammy Faye Bakker eyelashes. "My throat is simply parched."

Jonny smiled and tipped his cowboy hat. "You betcha."

I tapped Luella on the shoulder. "Ahem."

She turned with a start. Her eyes opened wide and her hand fluttered to her chest. "Why, Kelsey Kaye. What're you doing here?"

"I'd like to ask you the same question." I nodded toward the refresher shot Jonny was placing in front of her. "Thought you were court-ordered to be on the soda pop wagon. At least that's what your husband says. You do remember your husband, right?"

Luella tossed her long black hair over her shoulder. She turned to stare at the couples on the dance floor, two-stepping to the beat of Stifle, a local band of four brothers. "Well, you heard wrong. My soon-to-be *ex* is just pissed and spreading lies because I've finally found a man who truly cares for me."

I grabbed her arm and twisted her back around to face me. "You mean a lonely old man who owns rich farmland and believes your line of bull crap."

She shoved my hand away. "I don't have to listen to you." She tossed back her drink and slammed the glass on the bar. "Jonny, call security. This woman's harassing me."

"You needn't bother, Jonny," I said. "I'm leaving." I stared into Luella's dark eyes. "Don't play me for stupid. I'm on to you."

❖

The smell of hamburger hotdish met me at the door. Dad stood at the kitchen counter, stirring leftovers in a microwave bowl. He frowned. "Luella called. Says you've been stalking her and caused a scene at Rowdy Red's." He set down his spoon. "What's gotten into you?"

"I wasn't stalking. I stopped at the bar to check this week's events. One of my friends is flying in."

"Well, you should go to Rollie's. Tanya Tucker's s'posed to be in town." He picked up the spoon and started stirring again. "And for gosh darn sake, quit bothering Luella. She's a good person."

I leaned forward and gripped the counter's edge. "Really, Dad? She's thirty years your junior. Red flag. She's still married and causing problems with the law. More red flags. And she not only invited herself to live in our house but brought along a mini bar. Big red flag. Need I go on?"

Dad shoved the bowl into the microwave and slammed the door shut. "Aw, bean sprouts. Age don't matter. And that loser she married has everyone from the Cities to the Boundary Waters brainwashed into hating her. Luella's got no place to go. Anyway, she loves me and I love her. That's what counts."

I shook my head. "Fine. Believe what you want."

As I stomped downstairs to the grown-daughter-still-living-at-home basement apartment, Dad shouted after me, "Luella and I are going to be together. Forever. Till death do us part."

⁕

I stared at Mom's picture. She was thirty-five in the photo, beautiful, vibrant, and with a mind no one questioned. When she reached her "golden years," her personality shifted and her memory slid away. Only a few years ago, I had helped care for her as the dementia shuffled through her brain. If Mom was still Mom and alive today, she'd kill Dad. And Luella.

"He's gone crazy," I exclaimed, looking at the clear focused eyes I once knew. "All that penny pinching over your health care, and now Dad doesn't think twice about bailing that bitch out of jail every other week." Tears welled in my eyes. "If Dad goes through with this marriage, Luella will legally become my stepmother. Hell, she's barely older than me!"

Dad was a homegrown farm boy. He had been an avid collector of guns, antiques, and all things John Deere his whole life. His parents gifted him and Mom the farm long ago. "If anything ever happens to Dad, this will all go to Luella."

Mom smiled back at me as if to say, "*Then do something about it.*"

⁕

Around noon the next day, still dressed in a nightgown, I sat at my downstairs kitchen table, eating breakfast. Working from home as a cozy crime writer could be a luxury. But not so much lately with Dad and his gal pal carousing above me night after night.

The basement door squeaked open and heavy footsteps clomped down the steps. Dad rounded the corner. The lines on his forehead and dark bags around his eyes had doubled in the past few weeks. He cleared his throat, his hands trembling and mouth twitching,

and stared at an invisible spot above my head. "Luella and I talked. I want you to go to the courthouse and take your name off the
deed."

My stomach churned. I pushed the cereal bowl away. "What? You
and Mom were the ones who added me to the deed in the first place.
This farm has been in our family for generations."

He scratched his head and stared at the floor. "Well, we only did
that in case something happened. You don't need to be on there anymore." He turned and hurried up the steps.

In case something happened. I'd make something happen all right.

I picked up Zoa from the Lindbergh Terminal and filled her in on the
Dad and Luella saga during the hour plus drive back to St. Cloud. Zoa
was Mom's closest friend and like an aunt to me. She didn't give a lick
about style or fashion and always shot her words straight from the hip.
"If I ever trade my jeans for polyester grandma pants, you better put
me in a home," she liked to say. "It'll have meant I lost my marbles. Or
at least my favorite toe breaker."

Zoa wasn't kidding about her marbles. She owned numerous jars
filled with vintage glass marbles and carried her favorite shooter or "toe
breaker" in her pocket for good luck. Her collection meant the world
to her and consumed her spare time since she retired.

I glanced over at her in the passenger seat and half-smiled. "This
would've made a great story for my next almost best seller if I wasn't
living it."

She nodded and adjusted her glasses. "And Luella a hellion of an
antagonist." She fumbled with the A/C. "Lord knows why I agreed to
visit durin' an August scorcher."

I laughed. "Because I'm going crazy and you're here to verify why."

"And put a horse's halt to it," Zoa added. She gazed out the window
at the stop-and-go traffic heading out of the Cities. "I can't believe what's
happenin' with your fool of a father. Makes my blood boil. He always
seemed so levelheaded accordin' to your ma. To be that stupid now—"

"People do stupid things when they're in love."

"In lust, honey. Pure lust."

A car darted into my lane, and I slammed my foot on the brake. I
jerked my middle finger in the air and let loose a string of expletives.

"Whoa. Easy girl," Zoa said, her hands braced on the dashboard. "Where's your Minnesota Nice? Save them words for that evil stepma-to-be."

I grimaced. "She deserves worse than that. I've got a plan."

It was close to 5 p.m. by the time we arrived at the farmhouse. From the snores emitting from Dad's bedroom, it was obvious he was resting up for another late night. Two place settings, complete with wine glasses and cloth napkins, sat on the dining room table. Mom's favorite vase displayed a dozen red roses.

"You weren't kiddin'," Zoa said, peering around the room at the framed photos of Luella. "Old man's got it bad."

I sighed. "I have to admit, I feel mostly at fault."

Zoa turned and faced me. "What're you yakkin' about?"

"I'm the one who encouraged him to get out of the house after Mom died. He said he was lonely."

"Lonely can be the shits."

"So I introduced him to the book club at the St. Cloud library. 'Them ladies are too old,' he had complained, although they were all around his age give or take five, ten years."

"Too old, my ass," Zoa said. "I swear, women get wiser and men get dumber as they age."

"Well, my dumb move was helping him sign up for dance lessons at Rowdy Red's. I figured the exercise would do him good. The music. The socializing. I didn't know I was sending him into Luella's lair." I choked back sudden tears. "If only I had let him wallow in his grief at home, there would've never been a Luella."

Zoa patted me on the shoulder. "You've been a good daughter, Kelsey Kaye. To both your ma and pa. You did what you thought was best. Sure you don't want me to knock some sense into his noggin?"

"No. He gets angry at anyone who tries." I sniffled and then jerked my chin toward a twelve bottle case of wine on the counter. "Tuesday is Senior Day at the liquor store. Dad's their favorite customer. Cheap wine all in the name of love."

"Lust, remember?"

"Yeah, sure."

Zoa shook her head. "That woman has no shame. Can't believe she can hold a job."

"I've discovered through my sleuthing Luella's been caught with alcohol on her breath at work. But you know how short-staffed senior living centers can be."

"Speakin' of work, when do I earn my detective badge?"

"Tomorrow. Luella works until 4 p.m. and then heads to Rowdy Red's for happy hour. If you can catch an Uber early afternoon from your hotel to the farm, I can lend you my old winter beater behind the barn for reconnaissance. Luella has no idea who you are, so you're free to get up close and personal. And remember, stick to the plan."

Zoa flashed her dentures. "You betcha."

❃

I woke the next morning to Dad's footsteps pacing back and forth above me. I stood by the ceiling vent and listened to a one-sided conversation.

"Like I said, my lady friend and I are gonna get hitched and want this place to ourselves . . . Yep, you're darn tootin' . . . So if my daughter decides to cause trouble, can I get her evicted?"

My jaw dropped open. Who the hell was he talking to?

"What about a restraining order? She's been stalking . . ."

I slapped my hands over my ears. No more. If Dad wanted to throw me to the garter snakes and screw up his life with that hussy, so be it.

When Dad left for his daily look-see of the back forty, I bolted up the steps. His .22 Marlin was missing from behind the front door. "Good," I muttered. "Extra snooping time while he gopher hunts."

I entered his bedroom. A framed photo of Luella and Dad holding hands sat on top of Mom's dresser. An array of Luella's over-the-counter pill bottles, perfumes, and body lotions stood on Mom's nightstand. A black negligee was draped over a bedpost.

I glanced at Dad's dresser and noticed legal papers. I peered out the window to make sure Dad's four-wheeler was still gone and then rifled through the papers. His will was marked up with red lines and scribbles in a woman's handwriting. Luella was now named his sole heir. I stared at the picture of the two of them, glaring into Luella's eyes. "You're sure not wasting any time considering you're still married to someone else."

I wanted to rip the will to shreds. Along with the negligee. Damn that woman. It took all my energy to control my anger and not throw everything of hers out on the front lawn and set it ablaze.

Next to the will was a small jewelry box. I pried it open. A one-carat diamond ring gleamed back at me.

I spent the next hour scheming of ways to kill Luella. I had been a pretty good shot with a BB gun as a kid. Maybe I could rustle up some rat poison to mix into her next tater tot hotdish.

While I waited for Zoa to arrive for the car hand-off, I searched the internet for famous unsolved murders.

⁎⁎⁎

Around 8 p.m., Dad's cell phone rang. I listened through the ceiling vent and heard him say, "On my way. Love you, sweet thing."

The front door slammed. I grabbed my phone and texted Zoa. *Any luck?*

Affirmative. I'll swing by. We can then maneuver to hotel to discuss.

⁎⁎⁎

We pulled two chairs up to the table in her room and hovered over her phone. She scrolled through the pictures she'd snapped at Rowdy Red's. "This man, here, with his paws all over her, is some rodeo cow-poke named Shack."

"Some of the cowboys who compete at Rowdy Red's are the world's best professional bull riders. It's a pretty intensive sport. Even here in the Midwest."

"Pshaw. I'd rather watch the rodeo clowns." She swiped to another picture. "Luella and lover boy dancin' and pantin' out on the floor. Definitely two clowns. Instead of boots, they both shoulda wore over-sized floppy shoes. And red rubber noses."

I laughed. "This is great stuff. When Dad sees what his ladylove is up to, he's sure to dump her like a sack of rotten potatoes."

Zoa swiped her finger across the screen to reveal the two sweethearts drinking at the bar, smiling and laughing. Luella was sitting on the man's lap. "Gets even better."

"And you're sure they never saw you photo snapping?"

"Sure as cow shit. I used utmost discretion. And a menu for cover. Now looky here." Zoa pointed to a picture of a motel with chipped paint, missing siding, and weeds growing through cracks in the pavement. "Huskies Motel. It ain't The Foshay, but apparently it does the trick. Or rather, she does."

"Huskies is on Division Street, right? Close to St. Cloud State University?"

"Yep. And just a two-step from Rowdy Red's." She zoomed in for a close up of the cowboy helping Luella out of his pickup truck beneath the motel's neon sign. The next shot showed the two hand in hand entering room six on the ground floor. In the final picture, the cowboy was closing the curtains.

"Well done, Dr. Watson," I said, pulling my laptop out of a computer bag. "Now, it's time to do some online damage."

Zoa leaned forward and watched me log onto the social media website Mybook. "How often does your father look at his page?"

"He and Luella are always posting kissy-face pictures. You're still a friend of his, aren't you?"

"I s'pose so. I haven't been on that time-waster site for eons."

"Well, Dad and Luella and all their friends are gonna enjoy your photography. Hopefully it'll open Dad's eyes."

"Honey, let me post the pictures and do the damage. I don't mind takin' the heat from your father. He's angry enough at you."

I pushed the computer toward her. "Have at it. Forward them to my phone, too, so I can share them with Luella's husband. I'm sure they'll come in handy for divorce court. Then I'm gonna head home. Hopefully, Dad hasn't changed the locks."

Zoa read out loud as she typed beneath the group of pictures. "Beware of bar tramp. Luella Lopez is currently in the throes of divorce, speed datin' any man who'll bull ride her—includin' one who's almost twice her age—and cheatin' on all of them. The boozin' bitch is known to love 'em and leave 'em. Penniless and broken-hearted, that is. What this master manipulator needs is a good ass-kickin' followed by a toe breaker to the temple. Or better yet, a bullet between the eyes."

"Oh, my God," I said.

"What? Too much?"

"No. Perfect. I just hope Mybook doesn't remove it."

❂

I spent the next day working on my latest crime novel while Zoa searched antique and thrift stores on St. Cloud's east side for prize marbles. "Never know what you're gonna find and where you're gonna find it," she had said.

The house was unusually quiet. I couldn't tell if Dad had seen the post as he kept to himself in his room. He didn't even go outside for his daily tour of the property.

Luella's husband sent me a text in the afternoon. *Thanks for photos. Might pay Huskies Motel a surprise visit.*

That would be something to see, I thought.

Zoa showed up at 5 p.m. in rumpled, sweat-stained clothes. "This heat's a bitch," she said. "Just walkin' from the air-conditioned car to the store a body can lose ten pounds in water weight."

"I could lose ten pounds."

"Ha. Maybe in your little toe." She pointed at the ceiling, displaying a couple long scratches on her forearm. "Any word from the Great Oz? Did the scarecrow get a brain yet?"

"Not a peep."

"Huh. Well, his truck is MIA from your driveway. I s'pose he went to pick up the tramp."

"Hmm. Didn't even hear him leave." I closed my laptop. "Guess I was engrossed in my work." I gestured to her forearm. "What happened?"

"Oh, this? Got in a tussle with an old broad over a couple onion-skins." She held two speckled marbles in the air and grinned. "I won."

I shook my head and glanced at the clock. "Hungry?"

"As a feral pig. Marble hunting tends to work up my appetite."

❖

In the middle of dinner at Sven's Tavern on St. Germain Street, my phone chirped. It was a text from Luella's husband. *They're dead. Both of them. Never should've gone to motel.*

I bolted out of my chair, dumping my plate of walleye fingers onto the floor. "Oh, my God."

Zoa stopped in mid-bite. "What the hell's wrong?"

"We gotta go. Holy effin' crap. Hurry up." I dug in my purse and threw enough bills on the bar to cover the cost of the half-eaten food.

"But I ain't done with my Swedish meatballs."

I glared at her. "I'll discuss in the car."

Zoa stuffed another forkful in her mouth and hurried after me. "Damn cellphones," she muttered.

I sat behind the wheel in the parking lot, my hand trembling as I held up the phone for Zoa to read.

She grabbed the phone and deleted the text. "Well, guess that's that."

I threw up my hands. "Are you serious? Luella's husband just killed her and my dad at that motel. We're accomplices. You pretty much asked someone to commit murder in that post. And I forwarded the pictures to him." My eyes darted left and right. "I didn't know the man was . . . violent. What if he comes after us to cover up the crime trail? We're dead. We are so dead."

Zoa grabbed my arm. "Get ahold of yourself, girl. You been writin' too many murder mysteries. We ain't dead, and we surely didn't do anything wrong." She buckled her seatbelt and stared straight ahead. "Let's mosey back to your house and act like we don't know nothin'. Oh, and throw back a few Old Fashioneds while we wait for the coppers."

"But my dad . . . That man killed—"

"Hush. We need to find out what happened first. Put on your big girl britches. No grievin' until you're properly notified by the authorities. And no admittin' nothin' to nobody."

I swallowed the lump in my throat and pulled out of the parking lot. Dad didn't deserve to be murdered by a jealous husband. This was all my fault. I only wanted to save him from Luella's true self. Dear God, what had I done?

❁

We entered the driveway. Dad's truck was parked in its usual spot. "Wonder how that got back here?" My eyes opened wide and I turned to Zoa. "Maybe Luella's husband drove it here after he killed them? Maybe he's on the property somewhere waiting—?"

"And maybe I'm the Grand Poobah." She opened the door and began to climb out. "Let's get that drink."

My phone chirped again. "Wait." I opened another text from Luella's husband. *Turn on news. I'd be worried if I were you.*

Zoa grabbed for my phone. "Stop consortin' with the enemy. You're gonna get us both in deep cow dung."

I twisted away and searched the internet on my phone for the local news. "Look," I said, pointing to a newscast taking place at Huskies Motel. I put the phone on speaker and increased the volume.

"Sources say they heard loud voices and then what sounded like two gunshots twenty seconds apart. A witness to the aftermath reported a woman's body with a marble-size entry wound between her eyes and a man's body with a similar wound to the temple." The newswoman leaned into the camera. "No weapon has been found at this time."

I shifted in my seat, thinking about Zoa's fresh scratches and her lucky toe breaker. Had she really spent the day at thrift stores or instead in her hotel room concocting some type of homemade PVC pipe marble shooter? I shook my head. For God's sake, where was my mind going? I wrote too many crime stories.

I focused back on the newswoman.

"Authorities are searching the vicinity for suspects, and the University has cancelled all evening classes. The victims' names will be released pending notification of the families. If you have any information about this investigation, please contact the police." The woman flashed a smile. "Reporting live in St. Cloud, this is Alexa Marquise."

"Ready now?" Zoa asked, her arms folded.

I nodded and then crawled out of the car and shuffled after her. On the front step, my phone chirped again. I groaned. "Why doesn't the man just turn himself in?" I reached for my phone but Zoa stopped me.

"Drink first, converse with killer later," she said.

I unlocked the door, and we entered the foyer. Dad's keys hung from their usual hook on the wall. His boots sat on the mat, freshly polished. The kitchen light shone into the hallway and we heard a low voice muttering. Zoa and I looked at each other, our brows furrowed. Zoa reached into her pocket and pulled out her toe breaker. She motioned me forward. We crept toward the kitchen.

Dad sat at the table, cleaning his old musket. A box of lead balls and a framed picture of Luella sat across from him. He looked up, his expression sour. "I guess it really was till death do us part."

END

C.N. BUCHHOLZ is a freelance writer and former anesthesia technician. Her writing has been featured in *Cooked to Death: Volume II, Festival of Crime, Tonka Times* magazine, and *Murmurs of the Past: An Anthology of Poetry and Prose.* In her spare time, Ms. Buchholz dabbles in the art of belly dance, performs karaoke, and plays guitar. She is currently working on a series of suspense novels, set in the Twin Cities, with her cohort in crime, William J. Anderson. Ms. Buchholz lives on a hobby farm in Central Minnesota with her husband, a vision-challenged dog, and five house cats.

THE BEQUEST
By C.M. Surrisi

The first time he appeared to us we were not in the safety of our Brooklyn Brownstone. I think I could have borne it better had we been there, between the thick walls, with plush oriental carpets beneath our feet to ground the experience.

But no, we were in Minnesota attending the funeral of Edgar's second cousin Karl R. Swenson. We'd never been to the Midwest. Hell, we'd never been west of Pennsylvania. What did we know of the land of ten thousand lakes? We were New Yorkers through and through. We guzzled Red Eyes and ate up the *Sunday Times*. We were writers. I was a poet; Edgar wrote commercial fiction.

As we boarded the flight for Minneapolis/St. Paul, I noted that our attire—black jeans, black leather jackets, and dark glasses in July—was not entirely out of the ordinary. We encountered the comforting sight of two tall, slender women whose black duster coats and Beaujolais lips contrasted sharply with their milky white skin. Their goth presence comforted me in a way.

We found our rental car and launched on our two-hour drive "Up North" as they say here. I listened to a podcast on mid-century lyricism, and Edgar drove with that intense brooding demeanor that meant he was deep into solving a plot problem in his newest detective screed.

About an hour out of the metro area, with crops of some sort on either side of us, we experienced a strange splattering of crow crap from a flock of black demons that had followed us for several miles, swooping back and forth and casting dark shadows over the sunroof. Edgar had the presence of mind to pull the car safely off the road, and we were obliged to scrape thick white avian feces from the windshield with the ice scraper handily provided in the trunk.

Our GPS failed us in the last few miles, so we pulled into Jo and Lou's Gas and Grocery in Marfield to ask for directions. Two men and a woman who'd been talking near one of the gas pumps wandered over to inspect our white encrusted car.

The woman, who wore jeans and a faded purple sweatshirt with *Go Vikings* across her chest, shook her head slowly and said, "Never seen anything like that. How far are you going?"

I said, "We're going to Pederson's mortuary in Stenville. Our GPS crapped out."

She laughed. "Good one." Then she turned and pointed up the road. "You go up this way about six miles, you'll see a sign to Stenville, then turn right and go about three miles, and when you get into town turn right on Main, and there you are. It's a block past Flakey's Bar. If you get to Bums Park, you've gone too far."

"Thanks," said Edgar. I imagined he was thinking, *Bums Park. How enticing.*

All we needed to do was endure the visitation, attend the reading of the will the next day, and be on our way with whatever precious item Edgar had been bequeathed. Whatever it was, the letter from the lawyer had been insistent that Edgar appear in person to receive it, and it would be worth his while. Edgar had initially tossed the letter into the trash, dismissing it as probably a meager amount of money. I had speculated it was an old watch or a family Bible. Later that night it was back on his desk.

When we emerged from the station after paying for our gas, the locals were scratching their chins and pointing. I gasped. Our rental car was now a roosting post for at least fifty crows whose slick feathers glistened deep purple in the afternoon sun.

"What the hell?" Edgar yelled.

The Minnesota trio shrugged in unison.

"That's a lot of crows," one of the men said. He dug his hands in his khaki pants pockets and rocked back on his heels

"No kidding," I muttered.

Edgar pulled the fob out of his pocket and popped the hatch. A dozen or more crows rode the hatch as it rose.

"Edgar, don't let them get in the car!" I yelled.

Too late. Two particularly ominous looking birds lifted off, dove through the opening, and settled on the back-seat headrests. The rest of the crows took off in a thick cloud of darkness. Neither of us made a move to shoo the crows out.

"You could use a broom handle, I suppose," said one of the men.

"Is there a broom around here?" asked Edgar.

"Don't know," the man replied.

The other man went into the station, emerged with a giant push broom, and handed it to Edgar.

If there is one thing I know about my husband, it's that he will display his manliness when it is called for. I could tell immediately that he would not shrink in the presence of these Minnesota characters. In fact, he would tackle this crows-in-the-car problem with Brooklyn bravado.

First, he opened the passenger door and lowered all the windows. I admired this as an excellent first move. This way he could poke the crows, and they would fly out any available exits.

"Just nudge them in the belly," said one of the men.

"I'd tap the claws," said the other. "But be careful. Them things can be meaner than a bee in a jar."

Edgar studied the situation and then said, "I suppose I could rest the tip of the broom handle on their tails. A weight on the tail might do it."

The woman, who was working a piece of gum in her jaw, offered, "Put the handle in front of them like a perch and see if they climb on. Then you can pull out the handle and shake them off."

Edgar and I looked at her with new respect. This was an excellent idea, especially since it was not likely to provoke the crows.

Edgar carefully slid the broom handle through the open window and poised it in front of the crows' claws. We all leaned back, prepared to run if the crows flew out in our direction.

Instead of climbing aboard the handle, the crows seized it in their powerful beaks and snapped it in thirds, spewing wood splinters. The nearest crow gave Edgar the most disdainful look as if to say, "Seriously?"

An hour later, the crows were still in the car and everyone was losing interest. Including Edgar. "Ceil, let's get going. We're going to be late. I'll close the hatch and leave all the windows open. Maybe they'll fly out once we're on the road."

The three locals nodded and chorused a round of "yeps" as if this were the Minnesota way to go.

I elected to tie a plastic bag around my hair, in case the crows went berserk and attacked us as we drove. Edgar rolled his eyes like he thought I was being overly dramatic. Perhaps I was, because they didn't waver during the rest of the drive. They made low *tck tck tck* sounds occasionally, and when I turned to look at them, they each met my gaze without a flinch. Oddly, I was becoming accustomed to them.

Edgar repeatedly checked the rear-view mirror. "Damnedest thing. What do you think they want?"

"I don't imagine they want anything. I think they're disoriented."

It wasn't long before we were turning right on Main and cruising up to Pedersen's where there were about ten cars in the parking lot. As we got out of the car, the crows lifted off and flew to the ridgeline of the mortuary's roof.

I looked at Edgar, and he said, "Maybe they just wanted a lift?"

"Ha. Ha. Maybe they're coming to Karl's visitation."

"Very funny."

Inside the low stone building, a discreet sign directed us to the Swenson Visitation where a closed coffin sat at the front of the room. Next to it on an easel was a photograph of the deceased, a weathered man with thinning hair, large ears, and a pronounced Adam's apple.

A man with an Izod golf shirt stretched over a medicine ball-sized belly sidled up to us. "You must be the New York relations?"

"Brooklyn," I replied.

"I've never been there. Never really wanted to go."

"Then I guess we're even. We never imagined a trip to Minnesota, yet here we are."

"You knew Karl?"

"No," said Edgar. Then after a couple beats of awkward silence, he added, "Sorry to say."

The man raised one eyebrow. He turned his head and called out, "Joanie, come meet Karl's New York relatives. Came all the way here and didn't even know him."

I had the odd feeling he was insulting us, but perhaps this was an expression of Minnesota Nice.

Joanie's head was tipped to the side and her smile was tight. "You must be the writers? I heard there were writers coming from far away. What do you write? How was your trip?"

Edgar latched onto the question he liked to answer. "I write contemporary fiction."

"I'm a poet," I said. "We had a fine trip until we were followed by a murder of crows and shat upon. Two of them got into the car and rode with us here. Dreadful things are on the roof right now."

"You must be Karl's relatives, then," Joanie said, patting my arm. "That man never went anywhere without a couple of crows following his pickup and perching on the box. That barn out there is filled with 'em."

What? I was expecting alarm, but I got a yawn and the apparently old news that Karl Swenson was a well-known crow magnet.

Edgar continued to work our crow story. "Did you know they call a group of crows a murder?"

Joanie didn't blink. "Well, no I didn't, but that's not surprising, what with the murders that have occurred out at the Swenson place over the years."

I blinked. "Murders?"

"Joanie, don't go telling tales about the deceased," said her husband.

She leaned in. "I can honestly say there has been only one in my lifetime, but my granny told me that the Swenson farm was no place for drifters." Joanie crossed her arms. "Some say it was a murder, some say that poor girl was attacked by some wild animal. I'll tell you, I don't know any wild animals that drain the blood out of a corpse and clean up after themselves."

"Phooey," said her husband. "Was wolves. That's all. Now shut up about it. Let Karl rest in peace."

A young fellow joined us. He reached out to shake Edgar's hand with Ichabod Crane-like fingers. "Hello, you must be Edgar Waterman. I'm Ted Larson, of the Larson Firm. I'm the administrator of Karl Swenson's estate. I wrote you?" The pitch of his voice went up at the end of the sentence, seeking Edgar's confirmation that he recognized him.

"Yes. Sure," said Edgar as he extended his hand.

In a lower voice, Larson said, "I don't know what your plans are, but if you would like to come by my office after this, I can disburse the bequeathed item to you. If that would be agreeable?"

I was surprised by this. It was almost as if he was eager to get this *bequeathed* item off of his hands, out of his office, on its way out of the county and state.

Edgar shrugged. "Sure."

Ted Larson's shoulders relaxed. "Great. Let me know when you're ready to go."

An hour later, we were sitting in his office over Dun Right Dry Cleaners. The Larson Firm turned out to be a one-man show in a small office overflowing with crooked stacks of bulging accordion files, loose papers, and a stale sandwich. His framed law degree from the University of Minnesota leaned against a lamp.

He offered by way of explanation, "I took over from my father who passed away recently."

"I'm sorry for your loss," I offered.

"Wouldn't have had anything to do with crows?" Edgar smiled.

I gave him a look. *Seriously? Don't joke about his father's death!* But I could tell the Brooklynite had had enough of Minnesota.

Cheers for Ted Larson, though. He laughed. "No, those crow murder stories are limited to the Swenson estate. I've got to admit, there're a lot of crows around that farm and those folks."

Larson shuffled through a fat folder and then shoved a multipage document in Edgar's direction. "All you'll need to do is sign here." He handed Edgar a pen. "Right down there on the bottom, acknowledging receipt and completing the conveyance."

Edgar put the pen down without signing. "What is it?"

"It's acceptance of the bequest and a deed to the farm."

Edgar's head jerked back. "He left his farm to me?"

Larson leaned back in his chair, and it creaked like it was about to break. "Not by name. He left it to the youngest male in his family line of descent, and that, Mr. Waterman, is you."

Edgar reached for the pen as he asked, "He has no sons?"

"No. He was a Norwegian bachelor farmer."

I put my hand on Edgar's arm to keep him from picking up the pen. I couldn't imagine what we would do with a farm in Minnesota.

He moved my hand away and picked up the pen. Then he pressed the point to the designated line and scratched his signature. "I'd appreciate if you would drive us out there."

My anger radiated in the dingy room. What the hell did Edgar think he was doing?

Larson handed him a packet of documents in a marled, stiff brown envelope. "I'll record the deed for you and send you a copy. You can follow me out there."

I had no idea what had gotten into Edgar, but a few minutes later we were following a silver sedan out of town. Edgar drummed his fingers on the steering wheel. I glowered. We turned on to a narrow strip of unpaved road heralded by a beat-up metal mailbox on a weathered post. The two crows rode on the roof rack.

I had a hard time resisting a plunge into a knock-down, drag-out fight with Edgar over his decision to accept this farm without consulting me. The only thing that kept me from unloading my dissatisfaction was the glazed look in his eye and the urgency with which he tracked Larson's cloud of dust. Something about the farm had ignited a fire in him. Something about his intensity pushed me away. I tried to blot out the afternoon's revelations about murder.

Larson didn't turn off his car. He held onto the open door as he tossed the keys to Edgar and said, "If you decide you want to sell it, I can hook you up with a good Realtor. She handles a lot of farms."

This was hopeful. "Do farms sell fast around here?" I asked.

"Sure, but like anywhere, it's all about curb appeal."

Larson tried not to look like he was in a hurry, but he beat it out of there, leaving us standing in front of a charmless farmhouse and a faded red barn.

Edgar stepped toward the barn.

"Hey, don't you want to go in the house first?" I asked.

He didn't answer.

I reluctantly followed him. The two crows dive-bombed low over my head, causing me to duck in the middle of the farmyard.

For an old structure, the barn's door opened easily on its rusted hinges. The dark interior smelled of must and an acrid odor that burned my nostrils.

"I'm going back to the car." I turned to leave, but the barn door closed in my face. SLAM. I tried to push it open, but it resisted.

"Edgar?"

"Quiet."

A thump in the hayloft sent my heart racing.

"Edgar!"

The response was another thump, this one louder.

White wispy smoke swirled like a tornado in the rafters above us. The two crows perched on a timber, barely visible in the murk.

I tried to say, "Edgar," again but my throat could not produce a sound. Then I grabbed him to keep from sinking to my knees. My breath came in short rasps.

The white wisps, accompanied by the sound of rapidly flapping wings, swirled into a vision of black and red silk, as though unfurling from a bolt of fabric.

When the spectacle subsided, a man with wrinkled but creamy white skin, wrapped in an ebony cape with an arched collar, sat quietly on the edge of a bale of hay.

Edgar's jaw moved silently.

A chill crawled up my arms.

"Relax. I am Count La Plasma. And yes, I am a vampire." Apparently to prove this, he yawned revealing fangs that could use some brushing.

Edgar stood up straight. "What do you want?"

"I said, I am Count La Plasma. What do you think I want?"

Edgar and I clutched each other and backed against the door. I hoped this was Minnesota humor.

Edgar laughed. "Vampires? La Plasma? A little hokey, don't you think? The crows are a nice touch, though."

"I beg your pardon?" The man turned to the crows. "Ladies. Reveal yourselves."

In a flurry of wings, the crows transformed themselves into none other than the two New Yorkers from the airplane, black duster coats, deep red lips and all.

I shrank deeper against the door, my stomach pressing against my spine. Edgar whimpered.

The Count continued. "I need something from you . . . something other than your blood. I've waited over 1000 years for someone in this God forsaken family to have a literary bent."

Edgar perked up. "Literary bent?"

I blinked. Did he say literary bent?

"You have no idea how I've suffered," the Count whined.

"Suffered?" Edgar asked.

"Oh, you know, the standard tortures of the damned. But more importantly, not a one of you has been able to tell a decent story. It's been one farmer after another for centuries. From the Viking village to this lonesome place. Not a spark of literary creativity." He suddenly jumped up, dove into the stall, grabbed a giant roach, and popped it into his mouth.

I screamed.

The Count stretched his neck. "You have Count La Plasma and his two Valkyrie berserkers in your presence and you scream over a roach snack?"

I shook. "I'm not making rational choices at this moment."

Edgar summoned some courage. "Why this farm? Why this family?"

"Simple. I was turned into a vampire in the year 1001 in a Viking settlement. I was able to grow my haven and protect it with a Golem which I hid in the animal shelter. Everything was fine until—"

"Wait. You were a Viking?" Edgar looked awestruck.

The Count opened his cape to reveal a blousy shirt, shearling vest, leather pants, and a large buckled belt. "Sadly, yes. I have to wear this ridiculous outfit for eternity."

Edgar began to seriously engage with the Count. "Wait. Let me catch up. You had a Golem. A clay statue to protect your . . .what did you call it . . . ?"

"Haven. Yes. All was well until 1888 when Olaf Swenson up and moved here, taking my Golem with him."

"Why don't you just take your Golem and go wherever you want?" Edgar asked.

Count La Plasma rolled his eyes. "Because that diabolical fool hid it somewhere in this barn and I can't find it."

"So, you're tied to this barn?" I asked. "Is that why . . . the murders here?"

"In the beginning. But we don't feed in this county anymore."

"Anymore?" asked Edgar.

"You've heard the expression, *don't mess the nest?* Just saying."

This was becoming comically surreal. Something fluttered near my hair. I raised my arm to brush it away. My hand came in contact with the cheek of one of the berserkers. I screamed for the second time.

"Relax," she said. "I'm just smelling you."

I put my hand on her chest and pushed her back. Cold seeped through to my bones.

She actually looked hurt by the disgust in my eyes. "I have no control over my proclivities," she said.

I looked at the Count with his vulnerable arrogance. "What does this have to do with our being writers?"

"I have to sleep every day in this god forsaken barn and all I really want is for people to know my stories. My nights have been fantastical, glorious, globe-trotting extravaganzas—nights to remember. I want you to write the stories I tell you. The stories of my eternal life."

"You've been waiting centuries for a writer to inherit the land upon which you keep your haven so your stories can be told?" Edgar asked.

"Yes, and I wish them to be *New York Times* best sellers."

"Good luck with that," I said.

The Count replied, "I have my persuasive ways."

Edgar stepped forward. For a second I thought he was going to extend his hand for a shake, but he hesitated and then slipped it into his pocket. "Well, then. I guess you have a deal," he said. "When will you tell us the first story?"

"Tonight, of course. After dinner. In your modest farmhouse parlor."

Edgar cleared his throat. "Er. About the name."

"What about the name?"

"La Plasma sounds a bit, you know, hokey."

"I don't know what you mean. I changed it when plasma was finally discovered. It has haute cuisine panache. Before that, it was Malgahr. Dreadful. Arcane."

"Malgahr. Now that has a Bram Stoker ring to it."

The Count raised his hands to his chin, entwined his slender fingers, and passed judgment on Edgar's suggestion. "My name is and will remain La Plasma."

Edgar didn't argue.

The barn door opened by itself, and Edgar and I walked outside. My mind replayed the consummation of the deal. Was Edgar going to write these books alone? *Could* Edgar write these books alone? Not that he wasn't a credible writer, but that was the extent of his craft. The project cried out for the pen of a poet. I began to feel the task demanded my input.

Dozens of crows pecked about on the ground and roosted on the tree limbs. A chill rain fell, and I looked at the old farmhouse in a new light. I began to mentally organize the details of the move. I'd be packing and shipping the things we held dear: the oriental rugs, the Stickley lamp, the books—so many books. Then I let my thoughts drift to the first title. *Count La Plasma: The Crows Will Come. . . Count La Plasma: The Stiffening Wind . . . Count La Plasma: Prairie Longing . . .*

I imagined our names appearing over and over on the *New York Times* best seller list. Maybe it wasn't so bad that the Count couldn't find his Golem. All around me, the sky stretched forever, the crops drank the rain, and the dense woods had a subtle, soft roll to them. Minnesota was starting to look pretty damned good to me, too.

END

C.M. SURRISI is the author of the Agatha nominated middle grade mystery series The Quinnie Boyd Mysteries, including: *The Maypop Kidnapping, Vampires on the Run,* and *A Side of Sabotage*; and short stories, *You Know How Actresses Are,* in Malice Domestic's 2020 anthology, *Mystery Most Theatrical,* and *The Bequest*. She practiced law for many years before pursing an MFA at Vermont College of Fine Arts. She is a member of Mystery Writers of America, The National League of American Pen Women, and is the current president of Minnesota's Sisters in Crime chapter.

RANDOM HARVEST
By Michael Allan Mallory

The wild violet was pretty. Angelina paused to appreciate the dainty purple flower before yanking it out by the roots. A weed was still a weed. She tossed the offender into a wicker hand basket and scanned the tomato bed again for invaders. Satisfied the row was clean, she grabbed her pruning shears and deftly snipped newly formed suckers from the vines.

At the koi pond she paused to talk to the colorful swimmers before moving on to the strawberry patch. Kneeling on the terra cotta pavers, she plunged both hands into a plastic bucket and pulled out a heap of mulch and spread it across the bed. "There you go, my lovelies. Stay comfy and grow for Mama—"

She stopped. Was that mold on that strawberry leaf? Her mouth turned down. She pinched off the leaf stem.

Problem solved.

Angelina's lips pulled into a satisfied smile. Nothing beat tending her vegetable garden, the pleasure of nurturing a seed into a vibrant plant and later enjoying its edible bounty.

"You're hard at it on a hot day."

She looked to the side. Her neighbor Warren stood by the chain-link fence that separated their yards, one hand resting on the top fence rail, the other holding a large pair of hedge loppers. Angelina struggled to her feet. Geriatric knees didn't appreciate being asked to work.

She adjusted her straw sun hat and ambled along the pavestone path to join him. "It's tough work some days, but the end result makes it worthwhile."

Warren, sliding gracefully into his sixtieth year, was a roundish, doughy, sweet cinnamon roll of a man with a pleasant face more used to listening than talking. He smiled back broadly. "Your garden is the envy of the neighborhood. Our geraniums are timid, like they're afraid to bloom. Your flowers burst open like they want to please you."

"That's nice. I like that."

Warren sniffed the air. "Hang on. Why do I smell coffee?"

"That's me," Angelina chuckled, displaying her cotton-gloved hands. "The mulch I was spreading is a blend of pine needles and coffee grounds."

"Seriously?"

"It's great for acid-loving plants like strawberries. Makes them grow."

"See! That's what I'm talking about. Plants thrive around you. Your vegetables are prize winners. The cucumbers, bell peppers, tomatoes, they're picture perfect and full of flavor. The most luscious garden I've ever seen."

"Luscious?" Her eyebrow sat up.

"I mean it."

She shrugged. "All living things need encouragement. Plants too."

"It's more than that. You give them love and your plants respond to it."

Angelina grinned. All this praise made her blush. She drew closer to the fence. "How're you, Warren? Goodness, I can't remember the last time I saw you."

"Been workin' my tail off," he said as if sharing a confidence. She knew he'd been pulling extra shifts at the Duluth Port Authority where he labored as a shipfitter. Hoisting heavy metal and tack welding brackets to bulkheads all day had left their mark. His face looked more careworn than the last time she'd seen him, and new strands of iron gray streaked his thinning hair.

"I'm sorry. Hope things get better soon." She glanced furtively toward the drab Tudor-framed house behind him. "How's Edna? Did she have another stroke?"

"Yeah, last month. Touch and go there for a while but the paramedics did wonders. Kept her stable all the way to the hospital."

"Isn't this the third one?"

"Yeah."

"She doing okay?"

"Good, she's doing good."

Something about that "good" rang hollow. The big smile that had first greeted her went out like a smothered campfire. Warren glanced over his shoulder, checking they were alone. "Edna's on nitroglycerin tablets for her angina. Under doctor's orders to take it easy. But you know how she is."

Angelina knew all too well. Taking it easy was an alien concept to Edna, an unrepentant fusspot of a woman with impossibly high standards who didn't give a damn how they impacted others. Like three winters ago. Duluth was blasted by eight inches of lake effect snow. Warren fired up the snowblower and cleared the driveway, despite a raging fever that should have kept him in bed. That didn't matter to Edna, who'd insisted the sidewalk and path to the front door also be cleared, something Warren had planned to do in the morning. Edna made him go out again at night in subzero temps, his temperature of 102 degrees irrelevant.

Angelina sighed at the memory. Poor Warren, he put up with so much without complaint. "Edna's lucky to have you to look after her."

"Yeah," Warren agreed with a hangdog expression.

It bothered her to see him like this. Edna had never been the easiest person to live with, even before her first heart attack, and judging by Warren's reaction, her temperament hadn't improved since. Hoping to lighten his mood, Angelina brought up a topic dear to his heart. "Whatever happened with the bank people?"

"Um, nothing."

"Too busy? I suppose with all you have to do now with caring for Edna—"

"I canceled the meeting."

"Oh, no. Why?"

His gaze fell away. "Edna didn't approve."

"I don't understand."

Warren cleared his throat. "She doesn't think I should waste my time and our money on a silly side business." Callused fingers closed on the fence rail.

"Wait? She doesn't like your baked goods? Your artisan breads? Your fruit tarts are to die for."

"Oh, she likes the stuff I bake. Just thinks the idea of me opening a specialty bake shop at my age is foolish."

The disappointment in his voice was heartbreaking. "Warren, I'm sorry. You were so excited for this. The bakery was your dream!"

He nodded once in a single leaden gesture, as though his spirit had been beaten down for so long that it didn't know how to get back up. Embarrassed for him, Angelina berated herself for bringing up a touchy subject. She slipped off a cotton work glove and rested her delicate hand on top of his in silent commiseration.

"*War-ren!*" screeched a bone-jarring voice from the depths of hell. "The hedge won't clip itself!"

Angelina felt his fingers tighten beneath hers. He withdrew his hand and made his goodbye. With the loppers at his side, Warren trudged off to his hedges, where he aggressively cut through gnarled branches.

SNIP.

SNIP.

SNIP.

What her neighbors did behind closed doors was none of Angelina's business, yet she couldn't help feeling sorry for Warren. She liked him. He was a good man, one of the nicest people she knew. In all the years she had known him, she'd never heard him utter a negative remark about anyone. Angelina had her garden to comfort her. What did he have? she wondered. She watched him trim the hedge, soldiering on without complaint, the way he always did, now with the extra burden of caring for an ungrateful harpy of a wife. Okay, Angelina conceded, Edna did have her kind and funny moments. However, they were few and far between. What stuck with you was the ferocity of her temper, stuck with you like a knife in the chest.

Angelina could only imagine what Warren was feeling. Watching him survey the job he'd done on the side hedgerow, she wondered if he'd ever be able to pursue his dream. A minute later, he trundled off to the other side of the house and out of sight.

The afternoon sun warmed Angelina's face and helped revive her sense of calm. The call of a chickadee drew her attention back to her vegetable plants. Her sandaled feet shuffled along a dirt row. She knelt, set down her weeding basket, and peeled back the cover cloth to inspect the spinach and broccoli for bugs and damage.

"*Angelina!*"

Angelina swung round. By the front yard fence gate stood a crusty-looking woman with skin the color of old putty and a sour face ready to chew nails. Edna. Angelina gave an inward groan. Now what?

"Angelina!" The voiced erupted again. Not a greeting, it was a summons.

Forcing herself to be cordial, Angelina got to her feet with effort and smiled at her visitor. "Edna, nice to see you out on a sunny day. I hope that means you're feeling better." Angelina had been brought up to be polite, to always give her best. "There's already too much strife in the world," her mother had said, "for you to contribute to it. Be kind to people and they'll reflect your kindness." Only that never seemed to work with Edna, whose flinty demeanor never lost its hard edge.

"Would you like some iced tea?" Angelina offered with a nod toward her patio table and the pitcher sitting on it.

"I didn't come for tea. I came to talk."

Not talk. Lecture. Angelina already felt the energy draining out of her. Edna clanked shut the metal gate and tromped across the flagstone path like a guided missile locked on target. For a frail-looking woman she walked with purposeful strides, eyes fixed on her objective and oblivious to the world at her feet, a casualty of which was a tender, wayward cucumber vine crushed beneath her shoe. Angelina witnessed the atrocity with a pang of annoyance.

"I want you to stop putting foolish ideas into Warren's head," demanded the plant abuser.

Angelina's brow darkened as she reviewed the conversation she'd had with Warren, unable to recall any ideas she'd put into his head, foolish or otherwise. "I don't follow. What d'you mean?"

"You know damn well what I'm talking about, this bake shop idea of his." Edna, dressed in a white blouse, purple skirt, and black pumps, leaned in slightly for emphasis. A pendant dangled around her neck, a narrow aluminum cylinder on a matching chain that caught a glint of the afternoon sun. "Warren has no head for business," she went on, "and he's too old to start over, for another thing. Total waste of money. Might as well flush it down the toilet."

"Gee, that's harsh, don't you think? Warren's a wonderful baker. His pastries are so light and flavorful. His rhubarb breakfast cake was the hit of the rhubarb festival last year. People couldn't get enough of it."

Edna huffed out a breath, hands on her bony hips. "It's one thing to bake as a hobby, another to make a living off it."

"You're right. It won't be easy. But I saw how people kept after him to go pro, not just friends, strangers too. Haven't you seen how his face lights up whenever he talks about a new bake he's perfected?"

Edna snorted. "Doesn't matter how good a baker he is; he still has to sell the stuff. Let me tell you, Warren's not tough enough to start a business. And for you to put ideas like that into his head only encourages him."

Angelina ignored the rebuke. She came from sturdy Iron Range stock and could take a few insults. In a measured tone she replied, "For the record, I didn't put any ideas in his head, but if I'm enthusiastic about his baking, how is that a bad thing?"

"I just told you, he'll fail. If Warren thinks he'll succeed, he's also a fool."

Angelina drew in a deep breath. It took will power to hold her tongue against this dark cloud of a woman who rained on everyone else's picnic. "Don't you want Warren to be happy?"

"Happy?" Edna practically choked on the word. "Squandering money and time won't make him happy."

"Oh, dear." Angelina shook her head. What a bleak, colorless world this woman lived in.

Edna saw her reaction and took offense. She jabbed an accusatory finger. "You know what's wrong with you, Miss Mary Sunshine? You see things through rose-colored glasses. Everything's bright and cheery in your fantasyland. Maybe instead of giving people advice you should mind your own damn business!"

Angelina's cheeks burned. She really wanted to fire back with both barrels but knew no good would come from it.

Her silence served only to aggravate the prickly pear cactus in human form. "You're a meddler, sticking your nose where it doesn't belong, filling people with crazy ideas and false hope."

"Disappointment is part of life. It can't be avoided. We all fall down from time to time. What matters is that we get back up." Hazel eyes blazed with conviction. "The only way to avoid getting hurt is to never do anything risky. And what kind of life is that?"

Edna's hand jerked back into a fist. "God, you're so full of crap!"

Angelina rubbed the back of her neck as she struggled to maintain her civility. The sheer negativity spewing from this woman dismayed her. "Has life been that hard on you?" she asked, trying to understand.

"What do you know about anything? You live in this artificial world where everything is protected behind your fences."

"That's why my plants mean so much to me. In life you look for the simple things you find dear and hold them close. That's where real happiness comes from."

Edna rolled her eyes as if this was the stupidest thing she'd ever heard.

Angelina sighed. The woman was a lost cause. Toxic. She waved her off. "You need to go. Talking to you is a waste of time."

Edna stood her ground. "I'm not finished."

"Then say your piece and go."

With three quick steps Edna drew close, uncomfortably close. Her sickly sweet perfume made Angelina nearly gag. Edna shot her a warning look. "Stay away from my husband."

"Pardon?"

"Stay away from Warren."

Stay away? Angelina barely saw Warren as it was, maybe two or three times a month in passing, the way neighbors do. Once in a while she might actually stop to engage him in a little conversation. She did not mask her confusion well.

"You think you're so smart, missy. I know what you're up to. I know you've got your hooks into him."

Angelina's jaw dropped. "Excuse me?"

"Don't play coy with me. I saw you holding hands with Warren earlier."

"Holding hands? Oh, Edna, that was nothing. Warren was feeling a little down and I was being a good friend. That's all."

"So *you* say!"

Angelina shook her head. "Good grief, you're a hard woman." Paranoid might have been a better description, but she held back, not wanting to make matters worse.

Not to worry, Edna did that all by herself. Her voice poured with acid. "Don't you dare judge me! You don't know a thing about me!"

The frayed threads holding together Angelina's good manners finally snapped. The words, when they came, tumbled out in a torrent.

"Really? I know you're a woman who can't stand to see joy in another human being. I know you're a woman who takes pleasure in criticizing others, in finding fault. You always find fault. Never offer encouragement. I think you can't stand to see anyone else happy; you want them to be as miserable as you. Then you don't have to change." As good as that felt to get off her chest, Angelina immediately regretted saying it, seeing its effect upon Edna, who looked as if she'd just been slapped in the face.

Edna shook with rage. "How dare you talk to me like that! How . . . how . . ."

Angelina retreated a few steps, concerned her neighbor was about to take a swing at her, which she had once done during a shouting match with Warren's sister. Edna had ended up shoving her onto the sofa. Angelina was taking no chances.

"I've had enough of you!" Edna came back, her forefinger jabbing each word. "You're—y—" She wheezed in a breath and jammed shut her eyes for a second before they flew open in alarm. She gasped for breath and grimaced. Her trembling hand grabbed the pendant around her neck, fumbled to open it.

Her nitroglycerin pills, Angelina realized, as Edna struggled with the cap.

"Let me help."

"No!" Edna rasped, slapping away her hand.

Angelina jumped back. The pigheadedness of the woman was unbelievable! Arthritic fingers struggled to open the aluminum cylinder. Finally, in frustration, she ripped the chain off her neck. Edna doubled over in pain and collapsed to the ground, where the tube flew from her grasp and skittered across the pavestones out of reach, inches away from her twitching fingers.

Concerned, Angelina stepped closer and bent down, extending her hand toward the lifesaving pills.

Then stopped.

Her better nature had made her reach out to help. Conflicting emotions made her hesitate.

One second passed.

Two . . .

Three . . .

Her eyes narrowed onto Edna, who still writhed on the ground, hand desperately outstretched. Their eyes met. It startled Angelina that, even now, behind Edna's contorted face there was nothing but contempt for her.

That did it.

With grim resolve, Angelina straightened to her full height and, after a moment's indecision, nudged the aluminum tube with her sandaled foot. The cylinder bounced off the pavestone, rolled across the narrow strip of grass, and sank to the bottom of the koi pond.

Angelina wrapped her arms around herself and anxiously watched Edna. Waiting. Thankfully the end came in less than a minute. Edna passed quietly. Angelina shuttered her eyes and uttered a prayer for forgiveness. Uncomfortable with what she'd done, she was nonetheless resigned to having done it. And on that fragile peace, she opened her eyes with a new resolve, contemplating the Tudor house across the yard with a heavy heart. Time to raise the alarm. Time for Warren to have his day in the sun.

END

MICHAEL ALLAN MALLORY is the co-author of two novels featuring mystery's first zoologist sleuth. Lavender "Snake" Jones first appeared in *Death Roll* and returned in *Killer Instinct*, which *Mysterical-E* called "a tale that will enchant you and even keep you guessing." Michael's short fiction has appeared in numerous publications. His most recent story "The Man Who Wasn't There" was published in the Bouchercon 2019 anthology, *Denim, Diamonds and Death*. He has co-edited two previous crime fiction collections. He is a member of Mystery Writers of America, Twin Cities Sisters in Crime, and the Mystery Short Fiction Society. Find him at snakejones.com.

FOR LOVE OR MONEY
By Marcia Adair

Miranda Finn slowly circled her husband's Toyota Highlander and frowned. Two canvas Duluth packs, a fishing pole, paddles, life jackets, and more filled the back. The Winona canoe was strapped on top.

"So . . . you're going camping?"

"Not me," Carl said. "We. A week of wilderness camping in the Boundary Waters. We leave on Saturday. Surprised, darling?"

"Surprised is hardly the word—darling. You know I hate camping. No thanks." She spun to walk inside.

"Remember that camping trip we took when we first started dating?" he called after her. She stopped.

"It was so much fun. I thought this trip would take us back to the good times. Before, you know . . ."

Before you made all that money and became a philandering social climber, she thought. Before you decided it was beneath you to have a wife who's a diner waitress. Before you humiliated me with all those women.

She turned to face him. "This is really strange, Carl. What are you up to?"

He gave an awkward laugh. "Miranda, it'll be great. You won't have to do a thing. I've packed everything we need. I took the SUV in last week, and it's ready for a road trip. You already have next week off work, and I can take some time, too. And I'll do all the work—portaging, everything. It'll be a real vacation for you. You can sit back and be the Goddess of the Lake."

"Goddess my foot. We'll be living like animals. Where exactly do you propose taking me?"

He smiled. "Let's go inside; I'll show you the route."

They entered the marble foyer and crossed to the formal dining room. Carl made coffee and brought two piping mugs to the table. "How about that? I'm the one waitressing today. Be sure to give me a good tip, Sugar." He wiggled his butt flirtatiously and winked. "Be right back," he said and headed for his study.

Miranda flipped him the bird. She'd lost count of the demeaning jokes she'd suffered from her husband. When he was a clerk at the hardware store working his way through community college, he'd admired her work ethic. After they married, he got his real estate license and made it bigger than they'd ever dreamed possible. What a difference a decade made.

Carl returned and spread his McKenzie Boundary Waters maps on the mahogany expanse. Miranda stirred her coffee with her finger and gave him a gaze as deep and cold as a northern lake.

"Ahem. Okay. Here's the plan. We'll leave St. Paul at 6 a.m. and go up I-35 to Cloquet. That's only a couple of hours. From there, we'll zip over on Highway 33 to Highway 53, and bang! We're in Ely by 10 a.m. Plenty of time to paddle to our campsite for the first night. A million acres of pristine wilderness and gorgeous fall colors waiting for the two of us. The weather forecast is even good." He traced his finger along the route to their put-in at Snowbank Lake and a loop through Parent and Disappointment lakes.

"You've got to be kidding me. Parent and Disappointment? After all our failures to conceive? Do you really need to rub my nose in the fact that you don't even want children?"

Carl smacked himself on the forehead. "Oh, man. I'm such an idiot. I didn't even think of that. I picked a route that would be fairly close to get to and an easy trip for you. I swear. Forgive me?"

Miranda glowered. "I still don't get why you want to do this," was all she said.

Carl reached across the table and took his wife's hands. "To end all the tension between us," he said solemnly. "It's killing us. Don't you agree?"

✕◯✕
❈
✕◯✕

Not much was happening at Schmidty's Lube Stube at seven o'clock the next morning. Miranda parked her car on the side of the building and slipped in the back door. She crept up behind the mechanic as he reached for a new fan belt from the display on the wall.

"Stick 'em up."

He jumped. "Yo, babe. Scared the crap outta me. Whatchu doin' here?" Dennis Mulberry stepped back, scowled, and crossed his arms.

She laughed, and her face lit up at the sight of his dark hair and blue eyes. It was true, she thought: You never get over your first love. If he hadn't spent a couple of years in Stillwater State Prison for aggravated robbery back in the day, she was sure they would have married.

"I thought we weren't seein' each other 'til after your old man went to work."

"I'm pretty sure he's off with that gold digger Pepper he pretends he's not seeing anymore. What's good for the gander, right?" She kissed him hard, proud of him for having made something out of himself. Another two or three years and he'd have enough money to buy Schmidty's.

"Whoa. You gonna make me wait 'til after work for more o' that?" He grinned wolfishly and teased at her skirt.

"Behave," she scolded with a playful finger wag. "Besides, I got something serious to talk to you about. Can you meet me behind the diner? About three?"

"Um, sure, I guess. Any hints?"

"Three o'clock."

✕◯✕
❈
✕◯✕

Miranda was leaning against a tree when he arrived. She wasted no time getting to the point.

"Okay, are you ready for this?"

Dennis nodded.

"You know what a rat Carl is, right? How he cheats on me and puts me down? How I don't fit in with his rich-boy life? Well, I think he's trying to get rid of me."

"So? Is that the good news or the bad news? I mean, you'll get half his fortune, maybe even the house, right? And be rid of the jerk. Sounds like a good deal to me."

"You're not getting it, Dennis. He's trying to get *rid* of me." She slit her finger across her throat.

"Huh? Nah, where'd you get that crazy idea?"

"I overheard him talking to someone on the phone about finally 'getting free.' Then yesterday he sprang a wilderness trip on me where I'll be totally dependent on him. Heck, I can barely swim, let alone set up a tent. He says it's to bring us closer, but something's not right. Plus, I peeked in his pack, and he has a murder kit in there."

"A murder kit."

"I know what I saw. There's a rope. And a hatchet and saw, too."

"Geez, Miranda, isn't that typical camping gear?"

"Trust me. It's not." She tried another tack.

"Look, I been thinking. You love me, right, Dennis?"

"Aw, come on." He shifted his gaze and shuffled his feet.

"Me, too. Listen, why shouldn't you and I get some happiness?"

He shrugged.

"I've got a plan to beat him at his own game."

"What are you talking about?"

She drew a deep breath. "You and I are going to kill him first."

Dennis's jaw dropped. Finally, he spoke. "Are you out of your freakin' mind?"

"Do you hear me, Dennis? Carl is planning to *kill* me. I gotta protect myself."

He started to protest, but she held up a hand.

"Listen. It's like pre-self defense—with a bonus. It'll end all the humiliation he's heaped on me; best of all, you and I can get married. We'll be millionaires. You can buy Schmidty's right away if you still want to."

"What if you're wrong? What if he's only planning to divorce you?"

"Only planning to divorce me? And Pepper gets his dough? Over my dead body."

Miranda thought Dennis seemed intrigued, but he shook his head. "Nope. I ain't going back to Stillwater."

"You won't, babe. There's no way anyone will know. We'll make it seem like a camping accident. He falls from a cliff or something. Happens all the time."

Dennis shifted his weight to one leg and brought his hand to his chin. "What if someone sees us?"

"Carl says no one will be up there."

"How do I know you'll marry me and share the wealth? I mean, you could be using me to do your dirty work."

Miranda cheeks burned like she'd been slapped. "How could you even say that? You know what? Fine. Forget it. Forget you." She shoved past him and stormed toward her car.

Dennis ran after her. "Okay, okay. I'm sorry. It's just, I'm taking all the risk here. You should totally get everything you deserve. I mean that." He took a deep breath. "All right. I'm in. But I'm going to plan it and do it my way. No questions."

Miranda threw her arms around his neck and kissed him. "We leave tomorrow. Here's our route." She took a piece of paper from her pocket and pressed it in his hand.

"It's still dark," Miranda grumbled Saturday morning as Carl backed the SUV out of the driveway.

"You're crabby because you haven't had your coffee yet. We'll stop in Hinckley for some of those amazing caramel rolls at the truck stop there. It's only an hour. Sun'll be up by the time we get there."

"I'm crabby because I don't want to go. Did you bring the DEET?"

"It's September, Miranda. Bugs won't be a problem."

"Yeah, well, what about bears?"

"What about them?"

"They could attack us in our sleep."

"We'll hang all the food in a tree where they can't get it."

"What if it rains?"

"We'll get wet."

"Don't get snotty with me, Carl."

"All right. I'm sorry. But you're worried about nothing. Trust me. I've planned for everything. If it rains, we'll put on our rain gear or we can stay in the tent if you want."

"It'll be cold."

"I brought all the warm gear we'll need. And we'll have a campfire every night. It'll be beautiful. We might even see the Northern Lights."

"The only lights I want to see are a neon VACANCY sign at a nice hotel," she muttered.

Miranda glanced at her husband's profile as they merged on to I-35.

Even though she was mad at him, she melted inside a little. A smile flirted on her lips, but it faded quickly as the thought of Pepper Hixon intruded like a thief.

Fresh out of college, with no credentials other than her 38C cup, the little witch had made herself indispensable to Carl in his real estate business last year. All those odd hours, every day of the week, for supposed house showings. Miranda wondered how she'd been so blind. So stupid. A cool drizzle started to fall.

"Hey, there's that place with the caramel rolls. Let's stop," Carl said cheerfully. "You never know when we'll get here again."

At 11 a.m., Carl pulled the SUV into Entry Point 27 on Snowbank Lake. The rain had stopped. The parking lot was empty.

"Guess we won't have to compete for a camping spot. We have the place to ourselves," he said.

Wanna bet? Miranda thought as she got out of the car. She watched Carl untie the canoe and carry it to the dock.

"You gonna give me a hand?"

"You said I wouldn't need to do anything. Goddess of the Lake and all that, remember?"

"Did I say that? You might have to do a few things. Grab the paddles."

Miranda pouted and watched him fetch a Duluth pack and put it in the canoe. She wandered over to the bulletin board and read the postings. "Hey, did you get a permit? It says we need one to enter."

"Nope. I shoulda. It's not very busy this time of year. I don't think it's a big deal."

"Yeah, but it says they're required. How else is anyone going to know we're in there?"

"C'mon. We need to launch before we lose any more daylight. The portage to Parent is a mile away, and we still have to set up camp. Let's finish unloading the car."

Miranda watched him carefully, wondering why he hadn't gotten the permit. She reached into the SUV and pulled out the other pack.

"Um, what's with the hatchet and rope?" She tried to sound casual.

"Just stuff I'm gonna need. Keep unloading."

"In a minute." She surreptitiously checked her cell phone. No service—and no sign of Dennis. No permit. And a murder kit. She scanned the miles of open water before her and frowned at the light chop rising on the lake.

"Maybe we should forget this trip, Carl. It's getting late and the wind is coming up. We could get a permit and go tomorrow."

"Not a chance, Miranda."

Her gut clenched.

In short order they finished loading gear into the canoe. Carl locked the SUV and swept his arm gallantly toward the Winona. "Your coach awaits."

Miranda stood on the dock, unsure of what to do.

"I'll take the stern, you take the bow," Carl said. "That's the front."

Miranda bristled. *How stupid did he think she was?*

The canoe wobbled as she stepped in. Miranda yelped and flailed her arms.

"Stay in the midline," Carl shouted. "Unless you want us to swamp."

"Don't yell at me. You know I haven't done this much."

They finally settled in. Carl pushed off, and they slipped into the clear, deep water of Snowbank Lake.

Miranda took a steadying breath and dipped her paddle into the water. There was no turning back.

Burnt Island came up on their right. "Isn't it beautiful?" he called. "Not a soul to be seen."

Or to see us, she worried.

It was calm in the shelter of large islands as they headed for a distant stand of pines. Without warning, Carl turned the canoe further into Snowbank, where the wind was roiling small white caps into rollers.

"Are you trying to kill us?" Miranda shrieked. She stabbed the blade of her paddle into the lake. Her arms ached with every stroke, straining against the wind and waves to avoid swamping. Fear splashed at her heart as she felt the power of the elements. She wished she'd worn her life vest instead of tossing it in the middle of the canoe.

She paddled harder, her breathing increasingly labored.

"Our porridge is apparently late," she heard Carl's wind-twisted voice cry. "Gopher mint."

"*What?*" Miranda hollered back at the nonsense. If he answered, it was swallowed by the wind.

After an eternity, Carl directed the canoe to a small weedy bay protected from the wind. He hopped out and started unloading the gear.

"What are you doing?" Miranda asked incredulously. She rubbed her arms, grateful for a break from paddling.

"Didn't you hear me before? I said we're skipping the portage to Parent Lake. We're gonna go for Disappointment. It was a risk to keep us on the big water in this wind, but I think it will be worth it in the end."

Miranda blanched. She'd sent Dennis to Parent.

"Let's hustle. Everything comes out of the boat. We have a 130-rod portage. I'll carry the canoe. You grab what you can handle."

She reluctantly picked up the paddles and trailed behind him on the forested path. At the end of the portage, Carl set the canoe down gently on the shore of Disappointment and turned to his wife.

"That's it? That's all you portaged?" He shook his head. "Let's get the rest," he ordered. "Trees are whipping up in this wind. I think a front is moving in. I want to make camp as soon as possible."

Half an hour later, the canoe was reloaded and they pushed off into Disappointment toward a small island on the south end of the lake. Eventually, Carl headed toward a rocky point. "Home, sweet home," he said. "Grab the gear and let's make camp."

Rain held off long enough to get the tent up, gear stowed, and dinner cooked and eaten. It was only freeze-dried fare, but after a stressful afternoon, Miranda thought it was delicious. Carl had scarcely packed the food away and strung the food pack high in a tree when the sky opened.

"You said the weather would be gorgeous," she complained as they huddled in the tent. "You said I'd be warm enough. You said we were going to Parent. You said I wouldn't have to do any work. What other lies have you told me?"

Carl shook his head. They changed into their fleece and settled in for a cold, silent night.

An hour passed. Miranda heard rustling outside the tent and startled. "What's that?" she mouthed.

"Probably nothing."

Miranda knelt by the tent door and slowly pulled down the zipper on the flap.

"Hello, there." A man's face peered in, backlit by a flash of lightning. Miranda gasped.

Carl scrambled up. "What the—?"

"Now calm down everyone. I didn't mean to scare you. I'm the ranger from the Ely station. Erickson's my name." He remained crouched under the fly, his large frame filling the space. Miranda suppressed a giggle at Dennis's ruse.

"Creeping up on people at night? In the middle of a storm?" Miranda put a convincing edge of indignation in her voice.

Erickson chuckled. "I see your point, ma'am. Fact is, I'm in pursuit of someone. We had a tussle down the lake earlier and, I'm embarrassed to say, he cold-cocked me and stole my canoe. I'm stranded and wondered if there might be room at the inn. And maybe a bite to eat?"

"You want to sleep in here with us," Carl clarified.

"That's right, Mister."

Miranda cut to the chase. "No, there's no room here. For heaven's sake. Total stranger wants to sleep with us? You need to go find a hollow tree or something."

"Oh, there's a reason those are called widow makers. No, thanks. I'll make a rough shelter out here. Any chance you have some food to spare?"

"Sorry, man," Carl said. "We only brought enough for the week. Didn't count on visitors."

Erickson stood up and doffed his cap. "No worries. By the way, I'm chasing a murder suspect who's preying on campers. Have a good evening. Be safe." He moved into the dark. In the next lightning flash, he was gone.

"Carl, I'm scared. There's a murderer out here. For all we know, it's that so-called ranger." Miranda joined in the ruse.

Carl nodded. "Something's up for sure. Gonna be a long night. We should take shifts sleeping."

Miranda took the first watch, but the day of paddling and earlier rush of adrenaline had left her exhausted. Within half an hour, she was sleeping like the dead.

Eight hours later, Miranda half-woke to the smell of coffee brewing on a campfire and gave a sleepy smile. Then she realized Carl was snoring next to her.

She poked him hard in the ribs. He stretched out and smelled the coffee. "Mmmm. I'm glad you figured out how to make campfire coffee."

"I didn't."

They stared at each other. Carl unzipped the tent flap, and they scrambled out. Erickson was tossing their food pack into their canoe.

"Morning, folks," he called with a friendly wave. "Hope you don't mind, but I was hungry and I helped myself. I left you a day's rations and some fresh coffee. Don't worry. I'll send help for you. Moving on with my manhunt."

Whatever he was up to, she'd play along. "He's no ranger, Carl," Miranda whispered. "He's the killer."

"Okay, let's stay calm. Wait by the tent. I'll handle it."

Carl strode to the shore while Miranda watched from a copse of pines. He spun Erickson away from the canoe. There were words. Carl took a failed swing. Erickson picked up a rock and smacked it right into Carl's temple. He crumpled and lay still.

Miranda ran down to the lake. "Dennis! You did it!"

He turned to her and smiled. "I told you to leave it to me. Looks like he tripped over a root, doesn't it? C'mon, let's get out of here."

Miranda grabbed her gear; Dennis lashed it to the thwart. They hopped in, and Dennis paddled silently with firm, strong strokes toward the middle of Disappointment Lake. He didn't even ask Miranda to help. She began to feel like the Goddess of the Lake after all.

"I was afraid you weren't coming. How did you even find us? Anyway, you're here and everything is going to be okay now. Don't you think? Don't you? We'll be rich and free. Oh, boy, would I love to see Pepper's face when she finds out her gravy train finally ran off the tracks. Hah!"

When they reached dead center of the lake, Dennis stopped paddling. Miranda half-turned to face him. "What's up? Why did you stop?"

She followed his gaze to the shore. There stood Carl, smiling and giving the OK sign. Dennis gave a thumbs up.

"Wait. What? What's going on?" Miranda demanded.

Dennis leaned forward, forearms on his knees. "Miranda, shut up. Just shut up. I have had it with you and your scheming."

"But it's Carl . . . he's not dead." She pointed.

"Of course he's not dead. I didn't kill him. I didn't even hit him."

Miranda spun full in the canoe seat to face Dennis. The wind and waves were increasing, rocking their boat. She held tight to the cold metal gunwales, wishing she'd remembered a life jacket. "What are you talking about?"

"It turns out you were right that Carl wanted to dump you for Pepper. He hired a private investigator to see if you were cheating on him. Figured he could use that against you. He came into the shop last week to show me the photos the PI took of us—including one of a Glock under my front seat. That's a probation violation. I'd go straight back to prison for that. Carl knew he had me. We talked. Turns out he's quite a persuasive salesman."

"What are you saying?"

"He pointed out that I was in a very—what did he call it?—vulnerable spot. He could send me back to prison, or I could work with him to build a brighter future for him and me. He offered me $100,000 up front to—how did he say it?—secure his freedom. The man can turn a phrase."

"You'd *kill* me?" Miranda sputtered. "For *money*? I told you we'd get married. You'd have half of everything."

"Yeah, I don't think I'd get a dime from you, Miranda. You're not a halfsies kind of girl. You said it yourself. Carl agrees."

"What do you mean?"

"I sorta told him about your plan to kill him after you and I talked on Friday. Let's say he wasn't pleased. Upped his offer to $250,000. Cash. How could I say no?"

Miranda covered her gaping mouth with quivering hands.

"And there's one other thing. I don't love you anymore. You're good in the sack, but I'm going places once I own the garage. Might even build a chain. Carl's right; you're dead weight for a guy moving up."

Color drained from Miranda's cheeks. Her heart beat faster.

She turned toward the shore and shot an anxious glance at Carl. Desperate, she stood up in the canoe and signaled frantically. The boat rocked.

Dennis laughed. Carl waved.

Miranda stood frozen in the canoe. "What's happening here?" She barely squeaked the words out of her tightening throat.

Dennis surveyed the lake. There wasn't another soul in sight. He hunkered low, then without warning sharply rocked the canoe to one side and deftly snapped it back. Miranda pitched into the deep, cold water.

"The biggest Disappointment of your life, Miranda."

END

MARCIA ADAIR spent her childhood reading mysteries by flashlight under the covers. By the time adulthood rolled around, she had earned a master's degree in journalism and launched her career as a professional writer and editor. Her short stories appear in anthologies, including *Dark Side of the Loon* (2018) from the Twin Cities Chapter of Sisters in Crime; *Malice Domestic 14: Mystery Most Edible* (2019); and *Restaurant in Peace* (2020). She received the 2018 Dorothy Cannell Scholarship. She is a member of Sisters in Crime. https://www.facebook.com/MarciaAdairAuthor/

THE FIRST DAY

By Douglas Dorow

With her right hand raised she gave the oath: "I, Angela Rancone, do solemnly swear or affirm that I will support the Constitution of the United States and the Constitution of the State of Minnesota, and that I will discharge faithfully the duties of the office of Sheriff in the County of Otter Tail, the State of Minnesota, to the best of my judgment and ability."

The judge, county commissioners, mayor, deputies, and others in the room applauded.

Angela smiled, lowered her hand, and mouthed the word "thanks" to the judge who swore her in. A sense of relief swept over her. She closed her eyes briefly. It had been a wild ride since Labor Day when she'd worked with the FBI to bust the local drug ring and corrupt sheriff deputies. After losing confidence in the sheriff's department, a couple of county leaders asked her to consider leaving her chief of police position to run for sheriff. The campaigning, interviews, public speeches, and the campaigning from Labor Day to early November kept her busy. Now, here she was, starting the new year as the Sheriff of Otter Tail County. She'd continue to live in Pelican Rapids, but now her law enforcement duties expanded to cover the entire county.

Hiding her emotions, she walked among the people in the room, shaking hands.

"Sheriff, congratulations."

Angela turned to find Commissioner Anderson smiling at her. "Thank you."

"How does the uniform feel?"

Tugging on one sleeve and then the other to settle the uniform in place after the swearing in, Angela answered, "Feels about the same as the last one. I have to get used to wearing brown instead of blue."

Commissioner Anderson winked at her. "Some bigger shoes to fill with this job."

"Yes, some bigger challenges with the county versus being a small-town police chief: a bigger staff, a bigger territory to cover, but I'm looking forward to it and I've heard great things about the team we have."

"Once we got rid of a couple of bad apples."

"They're gone," Angela said. "We're looking forward not back."

Commissioner Anderson nodded in agreement. "Joining us for lunch?"

"Of course." Angela spied a deputy entering the room. He was dressed for the weather: coat, boots, gloves in his hand. His cheeks were red. What was his name? Started with a B. Too many new names. She hadn't learned them all yet. When he caught her eye, he raised his hand and flicked his head for her to join him. "Excuse me," she said to Commissioner Anderson. "Looks like a deputy needs to talk to me."

Angela joined the deputy by the door. "What's up?"

The deputy turned his head away from the room and spoke quietly. "I thought I should let you know. We got a call from The Minnow Bucket."

While he spoke, Angela glanced at the name badge pinned above his pocket. J. Barrett. She thought back through the roster she'd been studying. James? No, John. It was John. John Barrett.

"The bar out on the ice on Otter Tail Lake. Not sure what happened out there. Something about a big fight. The Battle Lake police chief is on the way. They're the closest. Deputy Jorgenson was out that way. He's heading over."

Angela turned and scanned the room. She returned her gaze to the deputy and looked up at him. "You going?"

Deputy Barrett nodded.

"I'll join you. It'll get me out of here." She looked out over the room of people again. "I'll let them know that I'm leaving, grab my winter gear, and meet you out in the parking lot."

"Okay," the deputy said. He walked down the hall toward the exit.

The five county commissioners stood in a circle, talking. Angela interrupted their conversation. "I'm sorry, but I'm going to have to skip our lunch. We've got a call I need to attend to. A busy first day." She gave them a quick wave and stepped away to her office.

In her office, Angela slipped on her winter coat and gloves, grabbed her hat and boots, and headed for the parking lot door. As she exited the station, the cold attacked her, biting at her exposed skin. She felt the freezing air on her tongue, in her throat, and in her nostrils. The packed snow on the sidewalk squeaked under her shoes as she walked to the idling truck in the driveway.

She climbed into the passenger seat of the Suburban and buckled her seat belt. The defroster was on high, battling to keep the windshield clear. She hit the button to warm her seat and said, "Let's go."

Deputy Barrett drove out of the parking lot and accelerated down the street. He turned on the lights and siren, and they sped off to Otter Tail Lake. Angela grabbed the radio and told dispatch they were on their way. She kicked off her shoes and struggled in the front seat to pull on her Sorel boots. "What's the temp?" she asked.

The deputy glanced at the dash. "It's ten below."

"Ooof," Angela groaned. "Thirty minutes to get there?"

He shook his head and smirked. "Twenty."

"Nice," Angela said. She grabbed the radio to call Deputy Jorgenson to update him on their ETA and to ask for updates.

❈

Deputy Barrett slowed the Suburban as they approached the public landing where the ice fishermen and snowmobilers accessed the lake. The entrance from the highway to the lake had been plowed, and they followed the path down a concrete apron and drove onto the frozen lake.

Through the windshield, Angela saw the snow-covered lake dotted with ice fishing houses, trucks, ATVs, and snowmobiles. A couple of hundred yards out from shore was a larger wooden building. Smoke floated out of a circular silver chimney. The police and sheriff vehicles with their lights flashing, trucks, and snowmobiles were parked around the building.

"How thick's the ice now?" Angela asked.

"With this cold snap? Maybe two feet or more," Barrett answered.

They bumped across the frozen surface, following the path flattened by vehicles in this well-traveled drive to The Minnow Bucket. Three snowmobiles drove away from the bar.

Barrett parked the truck in an open space close to the door. On the radio they heard a call that everything was under control.

"Let's go check it out while we're here," Angela said. She stepped down out of the truck and the cold attacked her again. She was better prepared this time, dressed in her boots, her long brown winter coat, gloves, and a hat with ear flaps hanging down on the sides of her head. She had a vision of Marge Gunderson from the movie *Fargo*.

Barrett held the door open and Angela entered the bar. She felt the warmth on her face and smelled the wood fire burning in the stove in the corner. Country music filled the air.

A group of men was to Angela's right. A sheriff's deputy, Jorgenson, was talking to three men in flannel shirts and Carhartt bibs sitting at a table. Henry Wolff, the Battle Lake Police Chief, stood behind the deputy.

Behind the bar was the bartender. A woman in her forties, her hair pulled back in a ponytail.

By the wood stove in the corner there was a group of four, twenty-something women, laughing and drinking.

Angela took off her hat and gloves and walked over to join the other officers. Deputy Barrett stayed by the door. "Hey, Henry."

"Angela, hi. Congrats on the election."

"Thanks."

"Sorry you had to drive all the way out here. It's all over."

"It's my first day. Nice to get out," Angela said. "We saw some snowmobiles driving away when we arrived."

"Yeah, we had a couple of groups of alcohol-fueled ice fishermen fighting over fishing spots. We let the first group go. These guys are next. Wanted to give them some space and time to cool down."

"Thanks for taking care of it," Angela said. "Can I buy you some lunch while you're here?"

"Nah. You guys got this. I should get back to town."

"Okay. I'm sure we'll see you around," Angela said. She shook hands with Henry. Turning to Jorgenson she asked, "Can I get you some lunch, deputy?"

He nodded, "Sure."

She called across the room, "Deputy Barrett, you want some lunch?"

He flashed her a thumbs up.

Angela crossed the room to the bar. One of the girls from the group beat her there. Angela leaned on the bar and waited for the girl to order and studied the chalkboard on the wall behind the bartender to see what The Minnow Bucket offered for lunch.

The girl ordered, "I'll take six minnow shots: three vodka, three Jaeger, and a Sprite, please."

Angela smiled and said to the girl, "Wow, minnow shots. You're all going to drink those?"

The girl nervously shook her head, "Not me. I'm the designated driver. The Sprite is mine."

"You could probably get a minnow in your Sprite."

"Yuck. No thanks," the girl answered and scrunched up her face.

"Bachelorette party?" Angela asked.

The girl nodded, "Yep."

They both watched as the bartender placed a tray on the bar, then a plastic cup of Sprite and six empty cups. Then she filled the cups: three with vodka and three with Jaeger. Next, she placed a minnow into each cup. "There you go," she said. "I'll add it to your tab."

"They aren't alive?" the girl asked.

The bartender laughed. "We used to serve them alive, but the state says we need to get frozen ones now. Enjoy."

"Yeah, enjoy," Angela chuckled.

"Thanks," the girl said. She picked up the tray and carefully carried it over to the table where her friends were sitting.

Angela returned her attention to the bartender. "Could I get six sloppy joes, three bags of chips, and three coffees?"

"You're the new sheriff, right?" the bartender asked.

"Right," Angela answered. She reached her hand across the bar. "Angela Rancone."

The bartender grabbed her hand in both of hers and held it.

"Congratulations. I voted for you. It's so nice to see a woman heading up the sheriff's department. And thank you for what you did with the drug problem last fall. You're kind of a hero around here."

"Thanks for your vote. I hope I can live up to your expectations," Angela said. She gently extracted her hand from the bartender's grasp. "I'll just be over here with the deputies."

"I'll let you know when the food's ready."

A shriek filled the air. It wasn't the sound of joy or happiness. It was the sound of fear and panic. Angela turned and scanned the room.

A woman in the corner called out, "Help!" Three women were on the floor and the other one, the designated driver, knelt over them.

Angela pushed a chair out of the way and rushed toward the women.

"Hey, boss, what should I do with these guys?" Deputy Jorgenson yelled behind her.

"If they're sober, let them go," she yelled back over her shoulder. "Deputy Barrett, over here."

One of the women was throwing up. Two were on the floor, not moving. The woman who screamed was shaking one of them. "Leanne, wake up," she said.

Angela knelt on the floor next to the other woman. She didn't appear to be breathing. Angela placed two fingers on her neck to feel for a pulse. It was rapid and irregular. Deputy Barrett joined her.

"What do you need?" he asked.

"Call an ambulance." Angela reached over and grabbed the arm of the woman shaking her friend on the floor. "Miss, go help her." Angela pointed to the other woman on the floor. "Turn her on her side so she doesn't choke on her vomit."

Angela pulled back the eyelid of the woman she was attending to. The pupil was very small. She stepped over the woman to check the other, who was experiencing similar symptoms: shallow breathing, constricted pupils. "Jorgenson!" she yelled across the bar. "Any Narcan in your vehicle?"

"Yes," he responded.

"Go get it," she yelled. "Miss," she said to the woman helping her friend. "What are their names?" Angela pointed to the two women lying flat on the floor.

"Are they OK?"

"What are their names?" Angela repeated.

"This one's Leanne," she said pointing at the woman she'd been struggling to revive. Leanne had brown hair and wore a fluffy white fleece jacket.

"And this one?" Angela asked. The second woman had shorter blonde hair, a silver stud in a nostril, and large pink T-shirt over a sweatshirt. It had printing on it, "I'm not married . . . yet."

The woman choked back a sob, "Her name is Tracy."

"What'd they take?" Angela asked.

"Take?" She had a confused look on her face. "They didn't take anything. They just did some minnow shots."

Angela turned to Deputy Barrett. "Help the one getting sick and sit this woman at a table. Calm her down. See what info you can get."

Barrett nodded. "Fifteen or twenty minutes for the ambulance," he said.

Angela refocused her attention on the two passed out women. She patted Tracy on the cheek and said her name. Then she shifted to Leanne and did the same thing. She glanced at the door. "Come on Jorgenson," she mumbled.

Barrett had the other two women sitting at a table. The sick one's head was on the table. The other woman, the designated driver, was crying.

Angela felt a cold blast of air sweep across the floor and heard the door to The Minnow Bucket slam shut. Jorgenson quickly walked over, stomping the snow from his boots, and handed her a cellophane packet. "I'll take this one," Angela said nodding at Tracy in her pink shirt. "The other one is Leanne."

Angela and Deputy Jorgenson each knelt next to one of the women, pulled on a pair of latex gloves, ripped open the cellophane from the package, and removed the Narcan nasal applicator. With the increase in opioid overdoses the last year, she'd used Narcan on a regular basis. She placed the nozzle in one of Tracy's nostrils and depressed the plunger. Then she ran a knuckle over Tracy's sternum to get a reaction while she said her name. "Tracy, come on, wake up. Wake up, Tracy." Angela pinched Tracy's earlobe between two of her fingernails. "Come on, Tracy."

"How's Leanne doing?" Angela asked.

"She's coming around," Jorgenson answered.

"Tracy," Angela said. "Come on, Tracy." She patted her cheek. No response. She grabbed her hand and noticed Tracy's fingertips were turning blue. "I'm giving her another dose," she said to Jorgenson. She inserted the applicator in the other nostril and depressed the plunger. Then she rolled Tracy onto her side. "Hey, Tracy. Wake up," Angela said into her ear. She pounded on her back.

Jorgenson had Leanne sitting up and talking.

"Where's the ambulance?" Angela asked.

"Ten minutes ETA," Jorgenson answered.

Angela pinched Tracy's cheek. "Come on," she said.

Tracy sucked in a breath.

"There she is," Angela said. "Tracy, you OK?" she asked.

Tracy mumbled a response.

Angela didn't understand her, but she was relieved she was trying to communicate. "I'm Sheriff Rancone. You just relax here." Angela placed a hand on Tracy's arm to comfort her and to keep her in position. She looked at Jorgenson and mouthed, "That was close."

Jorgenson nodded a response.

"You watch these two," Angela said. "I'm going to join Barrett and talk to the other two women and see if we can figure out what's going on."

Angela pushed herself up from the floor, stretched, and stepped over to the table to join Deputy Barrett and the other two women. She sat in the chair next to Barrett. Across from her sat the woman who had gotten sick and the woman who'd screamed.

"Ladies, I'm Sheriff Angela Rancone. Your friends are going to be OK."

"Oh thank God," said the woman who helped.

The sick woman lifted her head from the table and grumbled, "That's great. I feel better too."

"What are your names?" Angela asked.

The sick woman mumbled something and put her head back down on the table.

Angela shot a questioning look at the other woman.

"She's Kim and I'm Lori."

"OK," Angela said. "There were four of you, right? Tracy and Leanne and you two."

"Right," Lori answered.

"And you're here for Tracy's bachelorette party?"

"Right."

"Just the four of you."

"There were a few more last night," Lori said. "But, the four of us stayed at the hotel in Fergus Falls. We got up and had some breakfast at the Viking Café and then drove out here to play some games and drink a little bit. Someone last night told us about this place and their minnow shots and we decided to check it out."

Angela studied Lori's face. She seemed sincere. She turned to Deputy Barrett.

"Checks with what I got," he said.

"Kim, can you sit up and join us?" Angela asked. "Can we get you something?" She turned to Deputy Barrett. "Why don't you see if the bartender has some Sprite or Ginger Ale and some crackers or something."

Kim lifted her head from the table. "Some chips?"

"And some chips," Angela said. "Kim, did you hear what Lori told me?"

Kim nodded.

"She miss anything?"

"No," Kim whispered.

"Well, nobody has said anything about the drugs," Angela said.

"We were just drinking," Kim said.

"They didn't do any drugs," Lori said. "They were just drinking. A mixture of wine, beer, and shots last night. Bloody Marys and then the minnow shots and then they all got sick."

"How about you?" Angela asked. "You seem OK."

"I'm pregnant, that's why I'm drinking the Sprite."

"Congratulations," Angela said. She studied Lori: the only one not drinking, not doing minnow shots, the only one not sick.

Barrett returned with some crackers, chips, and a couple glasses of Sprite.

"Thanks," Angela said. "We sure the booze is good? It's not some home brewed hooch?"

"I'll check again," Deputy Barrett said.

"And make her show you the minnows too," Angela said. She refocused on Kim and Lori, the two women sitting across from her. "You say your friends didn't do drugs, but they showed signs of opioid overdose and Narcan saved them. That also demonstrates that they OD'd on opioids."

Lori started to say something, but Angela held up her hand to stop her.

"If they didn't take the drugs on purpose, then it appears someone gave them the drugs. And though you got sick," she said to Kim, "you're not showing signs of taking drugs like they are."

Kim sipped her soft drink. "Maybe somebody slipped them something last night?"

Angela shook her head. "That's too long ago. It was ingested shortly before they passed out."

Barrett returned to the table. "New bottles of booze from the distributor and the same minnows they've always used."

Angela closed her eyes and digested the situation and the facts she knew. The door opened, followed by a new blast of cold air. Angela turned to see a couple of paramedics enter the bar. "I'll be right back," she said to Deputy Barrett.

She met the paramedics by the two women still sitting on the floor. "We found these two women on the floor, showing signs of opioid overdose," she told them. "Deputy Jorgenson and I administered Narcan. I gave two doses to this woman, Tracy, and the other, Leanne, got one. It seemed to take effect right away."

"OK," the first paramedic replied. "We'll check them out." The two paramedics each took one of the women, checking their blood pressure, pulses, etc.

Angela knelt on the floor by Leanne. "Tell me again what you had at the bar here this morning."

"We had Bloody Marys, and the minnow shots."

"How many shots?" Angela asked.

"Two each."

"You swallowed the minnows?"

Leanne shook her head. "No. Just the first one."

"What happened to the second one?"

Leanne made a face. "The first one was so gross, with the second shot I kind of pursed my lips to suck the alcohol out of the glass and then I threw the cup under the table."

"Thank you, Leanne." Angela said. "You're going to be okay. These paramedics and Deputy Jorgenson will take care of you and get you to the hospital to get checked out."

Jorgenson nodded.

Angela pulled out her cell phone, turned on the flashlight feature, and looked under the table where the girls had been sitting. She saw a plastic cup reflecting the light from the cell phone lying on its side near the middle of the table. Angela reached under the table and pulled the cup out. A minnow was in the bottom of the cup.

"Okay, girls." Angela sat at the table across from Kim and Lori. She set the cup with the minnow in it on the table. "How did you all become friends?"

The two girls stared at the cup. Lori said, "We were sorority sisters at NDSU. We've known each other for years."

Angela kept her eyes on Lori. "Who is Tracy marrying?"

"Todd? He couldn't have done this." Lori said.

Angela waited for her to continue.

"We all hung out together in college." Lori paused and looked over her shoulder at the table they'd been partying at.

"What is it?" Angela asked.

"Kim and Todd dated for a while."

"Lori. What are you doing?" Kim asked.

"They were pretty serious. Then something changed. I don't know the details, but Todd and Tracy ended up dating, and that got serious over time and now they're engaged." Lori glanced at Kim.

Kim closed her eyes and slowly shook her head.

Lori continued, "She seemed okay with it. You know, college love, things change." She returned her focus to Angela. "Tracy and Todd are in love and we're all so happy they're getting married."

Angela smiled at Lori and reached over and placed her hand on her forearm. "Everybody's going to be okay," she said.

Lori smiled and nodded. A tear formed at the corner of her eye and slipped down her cheek.

"Deputy, do you have a pocketknife?" Angela asked.

"Yes, ma'am," Deputy Barrett responded. He dug in his pocket, pulled out a pocketknife, and pulled the blade out to lock it in place. He held it out for Angela.

Angela unfolded a couple of napkins and spread them out on the table in front of her. She scooped the minnow from the plastic cup and placed it on the napkin. Then she carefully grabbed the knife from the deputy. "Let's see what we have here." Angela gently ran the knife blade along the minnow's stomach. Then she peeled the skin back to reveal the insides. She used the point of the knife to pull out a white gel capsule. Then she carefully pulled the gel capsule apart and dumped a white powder onto the napkin. She folded the napkin to save the contents.

Kim moaned.

"Deputy, will you search Kim's pockets?" Angela asked.

Deputy Barrett checked Kim's coat pockets and pulled out a plastic bag. He placed it on the table. The bag held a few minnows.

"Kim, did you bring your own minnows spiked with drugs and swap them for those in the shots?" Angela asked.

"Kim?" Lori asked.

"It should've been me with Todd," Kim cried and put her head on the table.

Angela nodded at Barrett. "Kim, you're under arrest."

❈

"You okay to drive?" Angela asked Lori.

Lori nodded.

"Follow me back to the station in Fergus Falls. I'll be driving Deputy Jorgenson's truck."

Deputy Barrett joined them after helping Kim into the back seat of his vehicle. "Ready to go?" he asked.

"Drive carefully," Angela said.

"It's been a heck of a first day, boss."

Angela laughed. "Thanks for introducing me to The Minnow Bucket."

END

DOUGLAS DOROW is a Minneapolis crime thriller author. A graduate of the Minneapolis FBI Citizens Academy, he is writing two FBI Crime thriller series: the FBI thriller series with Special Agent Jack Miller pursuing cases in Minneapolis, outstate Minnesota, and North Dakota and the Critical Incident FBI Hostage Rescue Team novella series. Learn more at www.douglasdorow.com.

IT NEVER ENDS WELL
By Thekla Fagerlie-Madsen

September 1876—Hanska Slough—Southern Minnesota

Hans scrunched his eleven-year-old body as far down in the slimy mud as possible, wishing he could just disappear. The September rains that had soaked southern Minnesota the last two weeks filled every depression with water, including the rut where he lay hidden. He raised a hand and inched a branch aside, revealing four men whose faces he'd recently seen on a wanted poster—outlaws—resting around an old cottonwood tree. If they found him, he'd surely be killed.

Hans slowly let the branch fall, concealing what was left of the James-Younger gang that had attempted a daring daylight robbery of the Northfield First National Bank just days before. If he could catch up with the posse, he could tell them where the robbers were. Maybe then Pa would overlook the fact he had disobeyed him.

Two days ago, old Mister Johnson had ridden into the yard and told Pa about the Northfield Bank robbery. "They got in the bank but didn't get much," he'd reported. "But they killed a teller. Shot him in cold blood." Mister Johnson had showed Pa the wanted poster and Hans had peered over Pa's arm, right into the grim faces that seemed to stare right at him from the crinkled page.

Any able-bodied man with a gun and a horse was being recruited to join a posse. Mister Johnson was joining the Mankato posse and said Pa should get his gun and horse and come along. While Pa saddled his horse, Hans begged to go too but Pa said no. Hans had to stay home and protect Ma.

Well, he was going anyway.

While Ma made dinner, Hans saddled up Baldy, the big, white plow horse. He put a couple sticks of dried jerky and three apples in a burlap sack, filled a canteen with water, and tied both to Baldy's saddle. The shotgun Pa had given him for his birthday was tied to the other side. Hans put his boot in the stirrup and swung his leg over the saddle. The boy guided the old gelding down the lane behind the barn—so Ma couldn't see him—then urged Baldy into a slow lope in the direction he had seen Pa and Mister Johnson ride.

Hans traveled over thirty miles in two days, which was about twenty-five miles more than old Baldy had ever gone for such a stretch. The jerky and the apples were gone. Hans's stomach grumbled but he kept going, eyes focused on the road, following the print of a horseshoe angled to the inside right; the signature print of his father's pigeon-toed horse. He was on the right track.

It was early afternoon of the second day that Baldy's ears pricked forward and his pace quickened from a slow plod to a jog step. *Probably just a deer up ahead.* Hans jerked Baldy to a stop when his eyes finally saw what the horse's keen senses had already detected. *Men! Not deer.* Hans slid out of the saddle, led Baldy into a thicket of trees, and tied the reins to a branch. Using the brush for cover, he moved closer to where four saddled horses grazed, their riders huddled nearby. *Couldn't be the posse. Not enough riders.* He sunk to the ground and crawled elbow to knee, ending up here in the mud, just yards away from Charlie Pitts and brothers Cole, Jim, and Bob Younger.

The boy thrust his head down into the muddy ground as one of the men he recognized as Charlie Pitts got up and headed in his direction. He came so close Hans thought the man was going to step on him when the outlaw veered off toward an old apple tree, out of the gang's line of sight. Hans slowly raised his head and watched as Pitts knelt down in the mud, picked up a nearby rock, and started digging at the base of the tree.

The outlaw reached inside his long duster jacket and came out grasping a leather pouch. He drew the pouch strings apart, looked inside, and then jerked his head back, as if surprised, Hans thought. The man looked into the pouch again, then cinched it closed, dropped it into the hole, and covered it with mud. He marked the spot with the rock, then walked back to the where the gang was now readying their horses to leave.

Hans watched the men get on their horses and ride away down the slough. He looked back at the apple tree. *What was in the pouch?*

Hans rose up out of the mud and was wiping his hands off in the damp grass when he heard the outlaws meet their fate.

Gunshots.

Shouting.

Silence.

The Battle of Hanska Slough was over as quickly as it had begun for the remaining members of the James-Younger Gang that rainy day in southern Minnesota.

Hans ran over to the apple tree and, using the same rock Pitts had used, dug up the pouch. Without even looking inside, he put the pouch in his jacket pocket, ran back for Baldy, then rode in the direction he'd heard the gunfire. He'd find Pa and face whatever whupping he had coming to him.

Hans never noticed how low the corner of his coat hung or the heaviness of the pouch. All he could think of was how much that whupping was going to hurt.

Present Day in August—Hazel Run, Minnesota

"This is it?" Dolan Miller stood at the side of the rutted gravel road; his gaze centered on the grove of trees surrounding an old farmstead. An old barn was the only structure still standing in the grove's shadowed embrace. On the east side of the circle gravel driveway was the faint outline of a foundation where a small farmhouse once stood. A clump of lilac bushes hovered over the outline, unaware its fragrant blooms were no longer being clipped for pretty table centerpieces. That time had long passed.

"Yup," Conrad Felstrom confirmed. "This is where my great-grand-father, John Felstrom, lived. What kinda story did you say you're work-ing on?"

"History of Minnesota pioneers," the *St. Paul Pioneer Press* reporter answered, his brown eyes not meeting Felstrom's blue Norwegian gaze but rather searching along the tree line looking for . . .

"You should talk to the Lynstads," Conrad said. "Their family was the first to settle in these parts. George Lynstad was even Lieutenant Governor. I can give you Mary Jo Leindecker's number. Her last name's Leindecker but she's a Lynstad. Knows everything about the family."

Dolan turned to the farmer who had brought him out to 840th Street and wondered about the numbering system. How could there be 840 streets in this county? "The Lynstad's history is pretty well documented," he said. "We want to dig into the stories of the everyday folks that settled and lived out here. Where they came from, how they made a living, things like that."

"It's a pretty common story," Conrad stuck his hands in the pockets of his overalls, looked down at the ground for a few minutes, then back at Dolan. "My ancestors came from Norway in 1866, then lived in a few different places before settling here. They were mostly farmers. There's not really anything special about them."

"Were any of your family involved in any unusual events that you can think of?" Dolan prompted. "Blizzards? Flu epidemics? Or maybe victims of bandits or robbers? After all, the late 1800s was still considered the wild west out here."

Conrad looked at Dolan, then stamped a booted foot, splattering gravel in a small explosion. "Well, there were always tornadoes in the summer and blizzards in the winter, but that was normal and something to get through. No one ever made much of a fuss back then. Not like today when you get an inch of snow and people act like it's the end of the world." Conrad paused. "I remember my parents talking about something but I never really payed that much attention."

"Yes?" Dolan asked hopefully, holding his breath.

"My great-grandfather—the one who lived here—his sister died mysteriously on the trip over. There was another boy who survived, but just barely. He died later."

"That was pretty common," Dolan said. "Those sea crossings were rough back then. Not like the luxury cruise ships today. And with all those people traveling together, diseases were easily transmitted. Is the brother buried in the cemetery I passed on Highway 67?"

"No, he was buried somewhere else, where the family first settled."

"Where would that have been?" Dolan asked.

"Somewhere south."

Dolan's eyes narrowed slightly as he thought about Conrad's answer that wasn't an answer. His research had the Felstroms settling in the southern area of the state all right, specifically in Mankato. *Wouldn't Conrad have known that?*

"How'd the family get here?" Dolan asked. "To Hazel Run, I mean."

"Well, my great-grandfather came here when he was about twenty years old. He started with a quarter section of land around here under the Tree Claim Act. My brother Julian still farms the land."

"What's the Tree Claim Act?"

"It's responsible for all the groves of trees you see in this part of Minnesota."

Dolan had noticed that the further west you traveled away from the Cities, the flatter the land became, which of course was ideal for farming. Every section or so a clump of trees appeared, like punctuation marks sprinkled over the blank pages of the landscape. And usually those clumps of trees clustered around a farmhouse, much like the remnant of what he was looking at now.

"There didn't used to be a lot of trees out here. This was all prairie," Conrad explained. "The state would give 160 acres of additional land to settlers if they set aside forty acres to grow trees and could prove they lived on the land at least five years. They needed the wood to build houses. The trees also provided shelter from the elements. You may have noticed it gets pretty windy around these parts."

Dolan didn't doubt that. As he continued to stare at the grove of trees, there courtesy of an act of Congress and a settler's hope, a wind gust blew some low hanging branches aside.

There! Something gray—concrete? Could be.

Two years ago, while researching another story at the Minnesota Historical Society archives, Dolan had come across the diary of Johannes Felstrom. Something unusual had happened to the writer as a young boy, something that could make Dolan rich. He became obsessed with the Felstroms. The writer had mentioned a well. If that was *the* well . . . Dolan coughed to conceal his excitement.

Conrad pounded the middle of Dolan's back. "You okay?"

"Yeah," Dolan said. "Swallowed some dust."

"I don't think there's really anything else I can show you," Conrad said. "The barn was cleared out years ago. There's really nothing left from that time. You should try the Clarkfield City Hall. They have more information about the history of this area."

"I'll do that," Dolan said. "Thanks for bringing me out here. Oh, one last thing. How old was your great-grandad when he died?"

"I'm not sure," Conrad replied. "Maybe early fifties."

"That seems young," Dolan commented.

"Yeah, it does now. Well, if there's nothing else . . ."

"No, nothing else I can think of. I'll call if I have any more questions." Conrad nodded; end of conversation. Dolan took a last look at where he'd seen the branches part, then walked over to his car. He pretended to look for something in the glove box, hoping the farmer would leave so he could explore the area by the barn. But no, Conrad got into his dusty blue pickup truck, tugged the brim of his Clarkfield Elevator Co-op hat down snug on his forehead, and waited.

Giving up, Dolan started the car and pulled around the truck. With a wave in Conrad's direction, he headed west toward Clarkfield. After a couple turns on the rough gravel roads, Dolan reached the intersection of Highway 67. But rather than turning left to go to Clarkfield, he turned right and headed back to Granite Falls and his hotel, some twelve miles away. He'd get dinner, sleep a couple hours, then head back to Hazel Run to search for a well.

Wonder if he knows, Dolan thought. Probably not. Otherwise he wouldn't be living out here in the cornfields, driving that old dump of a truck.

✼

Dolan was prepared for the cool September Sunday evening. The "city" clothes he'd worn for his meeting with Conrad (light blue denim shirt, khaki pants, and tasseled loafers) were swapped for hiking boots, wool socks, insulated jeans, flannel shirt, a dark jacket with corresponding dark gloves, and a knitted cap. He set his gym bag on the hotel bed's rust-flowered bedspread, zipped it open, and took stock of the contents.

Flashlight, rope, grappling hook, pocket shovel.

He brought out a sheaf of papers; photocopies from the diary of Johannes Felstrom, and read the words again.

Pa gave me a whupping like I've never had in my life, but it was worth it! When I finally opened up that pouch, I couldn't believe my eyes. It was a bar of gold! I figured I'd get another whupping if I showed it to Pa so I hid it in the barn. Later, when I left home and moved to Yellow Medicine County, I brought it along. By then I was in my twenties and felt guilty—I should have turned it in but I didn't. I've read every account of the North-field robbery I could get my hands on but there was never any mention of gold. Thinking about it now, I realize Charlie Pitts must have planned to come back for it. He probably didn't want to share it with the gang. I'm 52 now and getting old, but I'm going to wait a few more years before I do something with it. But for now, I'm burying it in the well at the . . .

The last few words of the diary had been obliterated by water damage. Dolan considered the name of the man who first homesteaded this property; *John, not Hans.* But it was Johannes Felstrom's diary. *John* was probably the Americanized name for *Johannes*, and correspondingly *Hans* could be a nickname. Using old maps and property records, as well as the more modern Google Earth, Dolan had poured over land deeds and plat books across the state, leading him to the Hazel Run farm where Johannes had once lived.

When he saw the flash of gray earlier that day, he figured it could be an old well—and his best guess for where Hans, *or Johannes*, had hidden the bar of gold. A bar that no one else knew about. *It could be his.* He could quit his job at the newspaper and retire in style. Move to Florida or maybe Mexico. He smiled at the thought.

Dolan considered the legend of the Younger brothers. They had survived the Hanska Slough battle, but Charlie Pitts had been killed. It was rather ironic, Dolan thought, that while the Younger brothers all went on to serve life sentences in Stillwater Prison, Cole Younger was responsible for starting the oldest, continually published prison newspaper in the U.S., *The Prison Mirror*. And here Dolan was, a newspaper reporter about to unearth the biggest scoop of his career. One that would never be reported. *What a shame.*

Dolan zipped the bag closed and headed out the hotel door, locking it behind him. He looked around before going to his car, but at this time of the evening everyone was either at home or at Tolley's Bar & Grill watching a Twins baseball game.

He left the motel parking lot, headed west down Highway 212, then picked up Highway 67 that would take him back to Hazel Run. It was almost dark. Deer would be on the move this time of the evening.

Dolan found 840th Street and the old farmstead's driveway. He shut off the car and rolled down the window. It was so dark out in the country. No streetlights, not even a pair of headlights in the distance to break the blackness. A breeze rustled through the trees and the crickets were obnoxious with their chirping. They were louder out here than in the Cities, Dolan thought. *Kind of creepy.*

Dolan got out of the car and using the flashlight, made his way to the side of the barn. He parted the brush with a gloved hand, his flashlight easily finding what he had glimpsed earlier, the rounded form of a concrete well.

It was about three feet high with a few cracks running down the sides. A thick, wooden lid covered the opening. Dolan set his bag down and with both hands, lifted the heavy cover off the top of the well and eased it to the ground.

"Shit!" Dolan gagged. He backed away from the well and caught his breath as the smell of rotting earth poured into the night like an invisible stream let loose from its earthen spring.

He waited a minute, then approached the well, leaned over and pointed his flashlight straight down into the yawning darkness. He estimated it was about twenty feet deep. All he saw was mud, leaves, and rocks. But what did he expect? A glinting bar of gold? That would be too easy. He was going to have to go down.

Dolan removed the pocket shovel from the gym bag and attached it to his belt with a carabiner clip. Next, he removed the rope, unwound it, and tied one end to the grappling hook, giving it a hard tug to test the knot. Satisfied it would hold, he attached the hook to the side of the well. He gave the rope two more hard tugs to see if the well wall would crumble, but it held firm. After securing the flashlight in his pocket, with the light pointed up so he could at least see something, Dolan threw one leg over to the side, got a grip on the rope, brought his other leg in, and slowly crab-walked his way down to the bottom. He still had a hold on the rope just in case the ground wasn't stable, but it seemed to be hardpacked and solid. He let go of the rope.

Dolan took a moment to get his bearings. Despite the dampness of the well, he was sweating. He removed the flashlight from his pocket, squatted down and started sweeping debris away with his bare hand. Something slimy slid across his fingers. *String.* There was probably a lot of debris that had been dumped in here over the years.

He unhooked the pocket shovel and started to dig. More string, then something solid. He turned the flashlight on the object now partially visible. It was hard. White. With string attached. He dug around the object until he was able to release it from the earth's hold.

Not string . . . hair! And the hair was attached to a skull.

"What the . . ." Dolan stammered.

"Hey, Dolan," Conrad's voice bellowed down the well. "Whatcha' doin' down there?"

What was Conrad doing here? Dolan's mind strained to come up with a plausible answer, but too late, his brain registered the whispery slither of the rope being pulled up the wall. His flashlight played frantically over the sides of the well and then locked on Conrad's face looking down at him, the farmer's earlier friendly features now a macabre mask in the flashlight's beam.

"Wait!" Dolan yelled, finding his voice. "I can explain. I'm looking for gold! Your great-grandad had robber's gold from the James-Younger gang. He found it at the Hanska Slough when he was tailing the posse that went after the gang. I found his diary at the Historical Society. Look, I'll split it with you," he pleaded. "Fifty-fifty."

No sound from above.

"Okay. Sixty-forty. You get the sixty."

Still no sound.

"Okay, okay! A seventy-thirty split. You get the seventy! After all, I'm the one that found it. You'd never know about it if I hadn't come here. Just throw down the rope. Let me dig a little more—I know it's here."

"Yes, it's here," Conrad agreed. "And here it will stay."

"You knew?"

"Of course, I knew. Just like I knew that you came looking for gold, not a story. Well, now you're part of the story. Our story."

"Waaaaiiiittttt!" Dolan wailed.

No answer, just a scraping from above. Maybe this was just a big joke to teach him a lesson, Dolan thought, his mind struggling with an unacceptable truth.

But the scraping Dolan so fervently hoped meant salvation was Conrad dragging the wooden cover back over the opening. Dolan's screams rose in rage, then plunged to despair, but his cries were absorbed in the heaviness of the earth.

❈

Conrad shook his head and stared at the well. There was no one to hear Dolan out here. Soon, the screams would stop and the crickets would resume their night melodies. He sighed. The September anniversary of the Northfield Bank Robbery inspired history buffs and conspiracy theorists to dig into news archives and personal accounts. And sometimes they found the diary.

Folks from the city come out here thinking they can take what they want.

There was no shortage of trespassing strangers chasing after robbers' gold.

Dolan wasn't the first.

He wouldn't be the last.

END

THEKLA FAGERLIE-MADSEN has fond memories of visiting her uncle's farm in Clarkfield, Minnesota, where this story is set. She is also co-author of the Detective Nicholas Silvano crime thrillers. *Bad JuJu in Cleveland* involves drugs, murder, and voodoo and is loosely based on a real case investigated by co-author and retired Cleveland police detective Karl Bort. Their second book, *Angry Nurse,* is set on a psych ward of a big city hospital. The pair are at work on the third book in the series. Thekla and her husband live on their 150-year-old family farm in Western Wisconsin.

MARY, MERRY, MARRY
By Barbara DaCosta

Hey, Thea! It's Mary. I'm coming to the Twin Cities for a linguistics conference next week and—"

I grabbed the phone before the answering machine cut her off. "Well, if isn't my favorite roommate," I said. Mary Gaudio and I had lived together for a year during grad school. Luckily, our friendship had survived. "You'll stay here, of course."

"Naturally."

"Pack your long johns. We're having a cold snap. Hey, we can go together to see the Holiday Train Saturday night!"

"Holiday Train?"

"You know, a spruced-up, decorated train, Santa in a down jacket, music and fun. It's free. All we have to bring is a donation for the food shelf."

"Outdoor music in a cold snap? Not like here in Florida!"

"Come on, it's only ten below zero. You do remember winter, don't you?"

"Brrr! How could I forget? See you Thursday night!"

❖

"Mary, merry, marry," we crowed, spotting each other at the airport on Thursday. Those three words had been our running joke ever since we met decades ago in Professor Taylor's introductory linguistics class at the University of Minnesota. He had chosen us for a demonstration in front of our classmates, almost all of whom were from the Upper Midwest, and the majority of whom appeared to be of Scandinavian or German descent. Like me, Mary was of Italian extraction, but unlike me—a local—Mary was a real, live New Yorker, a rarity here.

"Language is all about context, ladies and gentlemen. Listen carefully," Professor Taylor had said. "I want you to identify the differences in pronunciation of these three words." He wrote on the blackboard: *Mary*—the name, *merry*—as in Christmas, and *marry*—as in wedlock. "Miss Franco," he gestured for me to begin.

I gave my rendition: *Mary, merry, marry.* The three words were homophones.

"Can you hear the differences?" Professor Taylor asked. No one responded. "Well, then, let's try candidate number two, Miss Gaudio."

Mary jumped to her feet. "New York City, here ya go!" Her accent sounded like she'd just come from rehearsals for *West Side Story.* She theatrically pounced on each word, hand gestures accompanying: "Mary" came out pretty familiar, minus the sharp turn of the "r" that marked us Minnesotans. Then, "merry" came out as an oddly shaped, quick bouncing of syllables that elicited a few titters. But when Mary got to "marry," the room erupted in laughter and cheers at the nasal, long-as-a-foghorn sound.

Mary and I became inseparable friends and study partners. We spent that quarter strolling around campus with clipboards in hand, buttonholing people into taking our linguistics survey: did they have a sofa, couch, or a davenport; did they drink pop, soda, or soda pop; how did they pronounce shibboleths of roof, orange, car, poem, hoarse, or carrell, and was it okay to interrupt others in normal conversation. The next year, we got an apartment together in a rickety old building a few blocks from campus.

Mary became captivated by linguistics and went on for a PhD. Now she was teaching at the University of Southwestern Florida, where, close to forty, she was an anxious assistant professor still without tenure. Myself, I'd gotten a PhD in the incredibly small field of Turko-Mongolian studies, a field that had an opening at most once every twenty years. I couldn't find work beyond as an underpaid adjunct "gypsy scholar" teaching world history in small colleges around the Midwest.

"Here's the latest winter fashions." I handed Mary my spare ski jacket, wool hat, scarf, and mittens. "So, what's your topic for this conference?"

"The sub-glossial remnants of ü-vowel shifts in statistically significant textual samples in northern Czech white-collar, post-Communist-era Prague," she said, zipping up the jacket.

"You'll explain that to me later, I hope." We began hiking to the parking ramp where my rustbucket waited.

"Thea, I'm worried sick over this conference." Mary got in the car and huddled down in the seat, chin tucked into scarf.

"Why, what's up?" I turned the car heat up high in consideration of my southern guest.

"My future, that's what's up. Last gasp. This conference is going to make or break my career. Every single person who's anyone in my field—"

"This sub-glossial-whatever is a whole field?"

"You should talk. You're the one who's in a narrow field. Turko-Mongolian studies, hah!"

"I'm not in it anymore, double-hah! Besides, I never really had a chance to work in my field. I was too busy teaching world history all day to hundreds of freshmen."

"Okay, okay! Anyway, here's my situation: I'm on a panel tomorrow morning and give my paper on Sunday. If these don't go perfectly, Thea, I'm not going to get tenure, end of career, end of story. Then I'll be sleeping on your couch again for real. You remember how *that* went, right?"

As roommates, we'd been opposites in the worst of ways: messy versus neat, noisy versus quiet, plus one really ugly confrontation involving pork chops and tofu.

"The panel is going to be especially tough. The chair is my biggest nemesis, Alexander Rodsky. He's president of the association and editor of the field's leading journal; is married to a high-profile federal prosecutor. He's bullied the association for years, hates my former advisor and her research, and, by extension, hates me and my research. Unfortunately, he's one of the outside reviewers for my tenure application. If that weren't enough, there's also Idaho and Ellesara."

"Idaho? For real?" I navigated out of airport parking and through the maze of exit roads and across the long bridge over the confluence of the Mississippi and Minnesota Rivers. Mary was so preoccupied she didn't even notice the idyllic nature scene.

"Yes, Idaho, for real. Child of hippies, brother of Oregon and Montana. Believe it or not, teaches in Wyoming. Fancies himself the cutting-edge theoretician, but he's actually a radical outsider. For being raised on peace and love, he's got the personality of someone who had a miserable Oliver Twist childhood."

"Who's Ellesara?"

"Hmmph! Yes, Miss Prima Donna Feminist, is wedded—no, cemented—to political correctness. She's hated me for years. But that's another story. Most importantly, there's Cintia Flaubert, from my department at Florida—brains and boobs, a wicked combination. A vindictive manipulator. Because of budget cuts, we've ended up both competing for the same associate professorship. And unfortunately for me, Cintia's married to the dean. So you can see, the cards are totally stacked against me."

I glanced down at Mary's hands. She'd slipped off her mittens to examine her bitten-down nails.

"If this conference doesn't go perfectly, Thea, I'm done for, *finito*," she said. "I kid you not."

✦

"Northern Pines" was a narrow, stuffy, overheated hotel meeting room filled with narrow tables and uncomfortable chairs, and the scent of stale institutional coffee. I stifled a yawn as I listened to the panelists bicker over linguistics minutia. Unpleasant memories resurfaced. The brain-breaking labor of getting a degree, the uncertainties of one's future in a finite job market, the fear of getting stuck in a fifth-tier college or with colleagues you didn't like; the striving, hope, and neuroticism that lurked beneath the surface of too many people you met.

And it brought back memories of the karate lessons I'd taken in Omaha, Nebraska. I had a one-year gig at a small college. I felt pushed to the edge by colleagues and students alike. By the end of each skirmish-filled week I was desperate for an outlet for my aggression.

So I signed up for karate class, where I got to sweat, kick, punch, yell, and fight for real. Well, at least it gave the *illusion* of fighting for real. After all, in karate, you and your opponent both knew you were pretend-fighting. There were clear rules of engagement, elaborate rituals and etiquette. If you transgressed, you were disqualified. You competed in pursuit of excellence, self-discipline, and the possibility of winning a trophy.

Academics was the opposite. People were *truly* fighting, but pretending they weren't. They were competing for high stakes: job tenure, book contracts, stature in the here-and-now, and elevation to the pantheon of great thinkers in the hereafter. Competitiveness, back-biting, and professional jealousies were all couched in a false veneer of politeness, rituals, and etiquette that masked maneuvering infused with egos and politics. Their thrusts and parries were done with weapons of words and ideas.

The room's fluorescent lights blanched the faces and clothes of the panelists. Mary, seated in the center, did her best to defend herself. From where I was seated, I could see everyone's reactions to her ideas: Alexander's furrowed brow, Ellasara's false smile, Idaho's outright frown, and Cintia's pressed lips. Whenever Mary would finish a sentence, the others, like verbal tag-team wrestlers, would jump on and tear apart whatever she'd just said.

At noon, the exhausting exercise was over. The attendees clustered around the panelists, continuing to argue.

Mary tore herself away as soon as she could.

"Thea," she rushed over, panic in her voice. She grabbed my arm and pulled me out into the hallway. "My laptop is gone! Someone stole it! I put it down for two minutes during the break, and when I turned around, it was gone!"

"Gone?"

"I can't do my talk without it!"

"You had it backed up, didn't you?" I asked with a sinking feeling. Mary shook her head and bit at her knuckles.

"You don't have a paper copy?"

"No."

"When's your presentation?"

"Sunday morning. Oh, Thea! My world is falling apart!"

"There's plenty of time to pull something together. Don't worry."

"Time?" she wailed. "Thea, you don't understand. This is years of work! Everything is on my laptop. My data, my notes, my Powerpoint slides, my whole presentation. What am I going to do?"

After reporting her loss to the hotel front desk, it was all I could do to drag Mary to dinner. She sat slumped in her chair, picking at a plate of pad thai. "Maybe I can reconstruct the major themes, but there's so much data, maps—"

"You didn't see anyone near your things?"

"There was such a crush of people. Alexander's sycophants. Idaho's revolutionaries. Ellesara's politico-feminists. Cintia's grubbing grad students." Mary suddenly sat up straight. "Wait a minute! Cintia's grad students—maybe it was one of them!"

"You don't think they'd risk expulsion, do you?"

"Do I think three easily intimidated, insecure kids would get sucked into Cintia's orbit? You don't know how manipulative she is. She's got them totally twisted around her little finger." Mary grabbed a pen and began writing down names on her napkin. "Lana Filipovna, Avi Omar Lindstrom, Hiroki Pantages."

"Come on, really—"

"Shh! Let me think." She jotted down a few notes and muttered to herself.

✿

My computer was out being fixed, so Saturday morning we headed to the public library near my place.

Mary quickly set to work at one of the public access computers. I busied myself with a jigsaw puzzle on a nearby table; every week a new one was put out.

I was deep into a challenging section of sky and clouds when I heard loud voices.

"Ma'am, please. Your hour's up," the library clerk said firmly, pointing at the schedule on the clipboard.

"But I need to—" Mary pled.

"You can sign up for another hour later on."

"I've got a paper to present tomorrow morn—"

"Ma'am, Saturdays are always our busiest days. You'll simply have to wait your turn."

Mary gnashed her teeth. Three boys pushed and shoved past her to crowd around the computer. In seconds, they had a video game running. At the next computer, a middle-aged man scanned the used-car want-ads; at the next one, a teenage couple scrunched together on a single chair and updated their Facebook pages.

"My whole career is hinging on this and they're just playing silly games—"

"Come on, Mary, use this time to calm down and relax. Hand me those sky blue pieces over there, please."

"What?" she sputtered, "Thea, you don't get the gravity of this. If I don't get rave reviews with this presentation, my committee will trounce me. They already say my research is outdated, flawed, and irrelevant. I'll lose my job and end up . . . ."

"Teaching in Nebraska like I did? Mary, I do understand, but there's no sense wasting your energy fretting. You'll get done what you get done. Look, work till closing, then we'll grab a bite and go see the Holiday Train. We'll be back home by eight, and you'll still have plenty of time to work. I'll proofread what you write. And then, we can both get a good night's sleep."

"I can't possibly take time off, Thea, I need to work on—"

"Mary, Mary, Mary," I said, shaking my finger at her. "You are already totally in command of your material. You need to rest your mind or you'll flame out before you go on stage."

Mary wasn't paying any attention to me. She was staring at the teenagers' Facebook page.

Fifty minutes later came Mary's next turn at the computer.

"Come," she commanded, dragging me and an extra chair from the puzzle table. She surprised me by opening a web search page instead of the online document she'd created for her presentation.

"Linguistics, Filipovna, Lindstrom, Pantages," she typed, and then rapidly scrolled down through the search results, and clicked on a link that took her to Facebook. "Hmm, mmm . . . Look, Thea!"

Hiroki Pantages had neglected to keep his Facebook wall private. A string of exchanges yesterday between the three students were short and cryptic—unless one knew the context.

❋

Mary managed to log a total of five hours work at the library by hopping from computer to computer. At closing time, she printed out her notes, and some Facebook evidence. We went back to the restaurant for more Thai food. She ran through her observations as we ate.

"These three are all Cintia's advisees. Filipovna is the pinnacle of self-absorbed. She'd do anything to promote herself. Lindstrom is a pleaser. However, I can't see him sticking his neck out like this. Underneath it all, he's a coward. Pantages, on the other hand, is impulsive and careless, as we've already discovered."

"Maybe it's the three of them together; they'd behave differently as a group," I suggested.

"Interesting proposition." Mary paused, serving spoon in hand. "You know, I think you're right—a gang, a conspiracy. Individually, they a) aren't motivated enough, b) aren't politically savvy enough, and c) aren't mentally mature enough. However, if it was any one of them—or the group of them—they would have had to have been manipulated in some way."

"Manipulated, how? By Cintia?"

"Thea, you've forgotten. They're toadying for fellowships, recommendations, grants, post-doc positions, you name it. Their futures are completely dependent on Cintia and members of their thesis committees."

"But what about your colleagues? There seemed to be plenty of pettiness and animosity running around in that meeting room."

"But how could it be a colleague? Who'd want to risk a career in progress?" she mused.

"I don't know. People get caught up in their emotions and stop using their brains. What about Idaho?"

She turned as red as the hot pepper sauce in the condiment rack.

"No, Mary, you didn't—"

"Yes," she said, shaking her head and covering her eyes. "He and I had a torrid affair three years ago. Didn't end well."

"Well, how about Ellesara?"

At that, Mary put her head down on the table and mumbled into her arms.

"Mary, I can't hear you," I said.

She reluctantly lifted her head. "Idaho and Ellesara were living together when we had the affair. Oh, Thea," she moaned. "They all hate me."

I looked at my watch. "Well, you'll have to get over it pretty fast. It's time for the Holiday Train."

"I don't want to go. I want to go back to the apartment and work on my paper."

"Come on, just for an hour. It'll cheer you up."

"Thea, I really don't want to go!"

In the end, Mary had no choice, since I had the car keys and the car. Mary sulked.

"Come on," I coaxed, remembering that petulant face from years ago.

"Okay," she growled. "But just for an hour."

❈

The Holiday Train event was in a corner of an industrial area that abutted a huge railyard. When we turned the corner around a warehouse, we found a cheery oasis of bright lights, decorations, bluegrass musicians, with a great, big freight train that dwarfed everything else. Excited children ran about. The smells of pine boughs, fresh-baked cookies, cider, and diesel exhaust mixed with the crisp arctic air. The bluegrass band, dressed in ski jackets and outfitted with gloves without fingertips, played a blend of seasonal songs.

"Thea, come on, I really need to get back. I have to—I really want to—" The furrows in Mary's brow began to soften.

A country-western band took the stage. The mandolin started to play.

"Thea—look!" Mary's grip on my arm was so tight I could feel each of her fingers through the thick padding of my parka sleeve.

"What?"

"It's Alexander!"

"Who?"

"You know, Alexander Rodsky, the president of the linguistics association. The one who's the external reviewer for my tenure application."

"Where is he?"

"In the dark brown ski jacket, with that ridiculous Indiana Jones fedora—oh, my God—he's with Cintia! Why are those two together?"

"Tourists coming to enjoy the show?"

"Oh my God, if they're friends, I bet he's going to slam me in his review. What am I going to do?"

"First find out if they're friends. Don't jump to conclusions."

"Thea, they don't know you—go eavesdrop."

❈

I reluctantly squeezed through the crowd until I was right behind Alexander and Cintia, within range of his musky aftershave and her sweet perfume.

Cintia bobbed her head in time with the music. Over her deep navy wool coat she wore a shimmering leaf-green scarf. On her head was a fur-trimmed hat. Her carefully plucked eyebrows arched over makeup worthy of a fashion model.

She turned toward Alexander. Her lips turned into a sly half-smile, then opened slightly as if she were about to say something, but instead, she elbowed him.

Colleagues?

Alexander smiled back at her.

Cintia said loudly over the music, "You did great today."

"Ah, it's nothing," he answered. "Whatever I can do to help."

Then he reached his arm back around her shoulders, accidently brushing against me as he did so. "'Scuse me," he said over his shoulder to me.

"No problem," I answered, my brain rapidly measuring, calculating, and interpreting the meaning of their closeness and their gestures.

Friends?

Alexander pulled Cintia close. "This spring, we'll celebrate in Hawaii. I promise." He nuzzled her cheek, and she turned to kiss him full on the lips.

Lovers.

❖

Livid didn't begin to describe the look on Mary's face.

She smacked the car dashboard angrily. "Cheating on their spouses, cheating the university, cheating on the system, and cheating me! This is outrageous!"

It was a good thing I was driving.

Mary's eyes narrowed. "Hah! I know what I'm going to do."

As soon as we got back to the apartment, she grabbed her sheaf of computer printouts and took out a red felt-tip pen. "Linguistics has context, remember?"

She began making notes in the margins.

❖

Sunday morning, another day in this narrow meeting room, filled with the few people interested in Mary's narrow topic. She had stayed up until 2 a.m. perfecting her presentation. I couldn't wait to hear the result of her labor.

Alexander wore a smug smile on his face. Idaho's eyes were sharp as knives. Ellesara's arms were tightly folded in front of her. Cintia's graduate students obsequiously buzzed about her.

Mary stood at the lectern, sans slides or Powerpoint or computer. She was armed only with a few notes and the Facebook printouts. At 9 a.m. sharp, she began to authoritatively deliver her talk about the sub-glossial remnants of ü-vowel shifts in post-Communist-era Prague . . . .

Two-thirds of the way through her allotted time, Mary put down her notes. Her voice changed from international scholar to New York street orator. People's ears pricked up.

"We scholars easily get caught up in our individualistic research and our academic status. We lose sight of what's really important about life: people, family, friends. Honesty and ethics." Mary's finger jabbed the air for emphasis.

"Academia can help save the world, but misused, it can devolve into dishonesty, deceit, and deviousness." I could see a muscle twitching in Alexander's clenched jaw.

"Cheating, immorality, and robbery," Mary spat out.

Cintia's red-lacquered nails nervously touched at her hairdo.

"It's quite easy, in fact, to see who's at fault—" Here, Mary paused and let her eyes rove the room, her gaze touching on each of her audience members. Then Mary grabbed the sheaf of Facebook printouts and thrust it up high for all to see.

Avi sat bolt upright and blanched. Lana covered her mouth with her hand, her face beet-red. Hiroki curled over, looking green.

"It is our *responsibility*," Mary thundered, fist pounding the lectern. "to maintain academia in TRUTH and to actively root out transgressors."

There was dead silence in the room when she finished.

I'd never seen a room empty so quickly. The audience stumbled over each other in their haste to escape Mary's accusing finger.

"Brava," I gave her a hug. "I knew you could pull it off."

Mary heaved a sigh of relief. "It remains to be seen whether or not it has any effect." She glanced at her watch. "Omigosh! Gotta go! Frontal vocalic concantation of fricatives session. I told my colleague Janie I'd be there for moral support. Then the wrap-up, then we're done. I'll get the shuttle to the airport. Thea, you've been a doll." She hugged me. "Thanks for putting me up."

Mary strode off, but then stopped. She came back and gave me another hug. "And thanks for putting *up* with me!"

❖

The phone rang just as I finished washing the dishes.

"Thea, it's Mary. I can't talk long—my plane's about to board, but you won't believe what happened. After the closing session, Alexander comes up to me and, after much hemming and hawing, says I'd raised some provocative ideas to which he'd be giving careful thought. No eye contact. Three minutes later, Cintia slinks up and says almost exactly the same thing. After that, each of the grad students, like they'd rehearsed it, mumbling their appreciation, how they'd never met a professor as insightful as I am."

"So we must have been right! The devils! What about your computer? Did it ever turn up?"

"Funny thing—when I was checking out, the concierge told me that a laptop computer had just been turned in."

"Yours?"

"Yes!"

"Intact?"

"Fortunately. Anyway, whoever took it didn't have the password, so they couldn't have gotten into it."

"Mary, I keep telling you—you've absolutely got to start making regular backups! What if they had guessed your password?"

"Oh, Thea, come on. I might not be great at backing up my computer, but a password? Please, I'm a linguist!" Mary gave a sly laugh. "As a matter of fact, *you're* probably the only person in the world who could ever guess my password."

"How's that?"

"Let's just say whoever took my computer didn't know how to spell 'Mary.'"

END

BARBARA DaCOSTA delights in finding the quirky things in life to write about. Her stories have appeared in *Resort to Murder* and *Why Did Santa Leave a Body*. Her children's picture books, illustrated by Caldecott Medalist Ed Young, include *Nighttime Ninja* (Little, Brown 2012; Children's Choice Award and ALA Notable), *Mighty Moby* (Little, Brown 2017; Minnesota Book Award finalist), and *Night Shadows* (Triangle Square, 2020).

COUGAR CROSSING
By Barbara Merritt Deese

At first, all I saw was a pair of shoes, stiletto-heeled mules designed for a life-sized Hooker Barbie. Peering through the crack in our bedroom door, I let my eyes travel up the shapely legs to the stranger sitting on the side of the bed. She wore her hair in a shoulder-length bob that looked suspiciously like the wig I wore on bad hair days. The hand mirror she held, the one that usually lay on my dresser, blocked her face. My mouth went dry.

Oblivious to my presence, the woman stood, and in that brief, heart-stopping moment, I recognized the wearer of my wig as my husband Daniel. He was not actually in the buff, as I'd first thought, but sported a shell pink bra and panties—my shell pink bra and panties, to be exact. I must have gasped, because he swung his head up so fast he lost his balance and fell onto the bed. "I'm sorry. I'm sorry," he moaned as he hastily gathered the bedspread around him.

In the days of tearful conversations that followed, Daniel admitted that even as a kid, he'd been uncomfortable in his boy's body. I had not seen that coming, not once in our almost five decades of marriage. He tried to make me understand the pain of keeping a secret like that, growing up as he did in a small farming town in southern Minnesota, and I wish I could have been more sympathetic, but I was reeling from my own pain. I picked through the life we'd shared, wondering if it had all been built on lies.

The divorce was remarkably civil. Daniel moved to the other side of Saint Paul, and I bought a condo in Minneapolis, where I could be close to my dearest friends, who kept me from completely falling apart. A few months passed. Taking stock of myself in the mirror, I could see I wore my seventy years well. But my self-esteem had taken a major hit, and every time I tried to imagine dating again, the image rose up of my ex-husband looking better in my lingerie than I ever had.

In other words, I was ripe for the picking.

Chuck found me at the exact moment I was sick enough of my single life to throw caution to the winds. He was nicely built, not overly handsome, but aggressively manly. We shared a love of the outdoors, and spent our days biking around the Chain of Lakes in Minneapolis or hiking along the network of trails in and around the Twin Cities. I did my best to hide my labored breathing and keep up with his energy so he wouldn't regret dating someone twelve years older.

One day we biked past a mansion on Lake of the Isles with a *For Sale* sign in the yard, and he explained his ex-wife was living there until it sold. Meanwhile, he said, he was staying on his boat on Lake Minnetonka. "How romantic," I said.

His boat was nothing like the high-end yachts I'd seen there. Like Chuck, the *No Regrets* was charming, but had seen better days, and needed even more loving than I did. We took it out on the lake, anchoring in a quiet bay, where I dove in and cavorted in the water. Refusing to join me, he sat in the cockpit, throwing back a couple of rum and cokes. That night, with the boat gently rocking, we lay in each other's arms in the forward berth. In the weeks that followed, it became our rhythm to sleep at my place once a week, and on the boat a night or two. Chuck never did swim with me, and finally admitted he never set foot in water where he couldn't touch the bottom. Why, I wondered, would someone afraid of water want to live in the Land of 10,000 Lakes, much less, own a boat?

I should have been suspicious too when, only a month into our relationship, he said he wanted to get married—just as soon as the house sold. When the leaves turned and the *No Regrets* had to go into storage, Chuck moved into my condo. This would have been the ideal time for him to have the boat overhauled, he said, but it would have to wait until he had the cash. Like a dope, I offered to loan him the money. Reluctantly, but gratefully, he accepted and had an informal agreement drawn up.

I like to think that if my reading glasses hadn't gone missing that morning, I would have read the fine print, which, as it turned out, granted him access to my main bank account. By the time I discovered he'd withdrawn over a hundred thousand dollars, he was gone.

As crazy as it sounds, I missed Chuck, at least the person I'd thought he was. Mortified and mistrusting my own judgment, I avoided everyone, but after spending the winter holed up in my condo, I called my three closest friends. Over brunch, I told them everything.

Sheila took a sip of her Bloody Mary. "He's a grifter. Trust me, you're not the first and you won't be the last. Your boy toy hit on Kim too, you know."

I swung to face Kim, who shrugged and made no attempt to deny it. "Luckily, I saw right through him."

I looked around the table, unable to hold back my tears. "And you never said one word to me? Why didn't you warn me?"

Kim glanced at Sheila and they both looked away. Bonnie sucked in her breath and said, "We didn't think you'd believe us." Her sad head-shake made me feel more pathetic than ever. "The girls and I talked and talked about it, and we decided it was none of our business. We just figured when a woman takes up with a much younger man, she knows she's paying for, well, you know."

I rose with all the dignity I could muster and said, "In other words, you spent months talking *about* me, but not one of you took the trouble to talk *to* me." Before I turned to leave, I swiped my arm across the table and sent their Bloody Marys flying—not one of my finer moments. So much for Minnesota Nice.

I was single again, and apparently friendless. Days passed and not one of my alleged friends reached out to me, not even to send a cleaning bill for their drink-stained clothes. After weeping for two full weeks, I did the only thing I could think of. I called my ex-husband and poured out the whole sordid tale.

In the silence that followed, I braced for some kind of scathing comment, but all he said was, "I can assure you, humiliation is not fatal."

His kindness toward me was a stark contrast to the harsh way I'd judged him.

"Do you want to press charges? I can talk to some people." His offer was a gentleness I did not deserve.

I was devastated a few days later when Daniel called to report that since I'd signed a legal document, suing Chuck was not a viable option. Burning from shame, I was about to hang up when he said, "Wait. I have an idea."

❈

It had been months since I'd last seen Daniel. The transformation was striking. He'd always been fit. Now he looked years younger and, I realized with a pang, genuinely happy. I also realized how much I'd missed him. Despite the changes in his appearance, Daniel's new-found confidence put me at ease and we settled in for the afternoon. We spent the afternoon together, and after a few beers, he said, "Don't flip out, but Chuck's been married three times to older women. The second one died. You should also know that mansion on Lake of the Isles never belonged to him. Neither did the boat. They belong to a widow he was seeing the same time he was with you."

I wanted to throw up. "How'd you find out?"

"I've been checking up on him for a while." He looked abashed. "I'm not proud of it."

"Really!" I burst out laughing for the first time in this sordid mess. "That's so sweet! You care about me after all!"

His eyes got shiny. "I'll always care about you." After an awkward pause, he said, "Yesterday I followed him to a grief sup—"

"What was he doing at a grief support group?"

Daniel splayed his hands and shrugged. "It's what Chuck does. He was there chatting up, you know, the kind of woman he preys on."

"You mean *old*," I said.

"*Our* age," he corrected me. "Chuck picked up his next mark, and they went straight to a bar. You can bet she paid the tab."

I felt cold all over.

He reached for my hand. "Are you angry?"

"Just at myself."

Daniel handed me a piece of paper with two names—Fay and Ursula—along with phone numbers. "You might want to call these ladies. Chuck bilked them too."

The three of us met the next day. Ursula reeked of old money, and like me, she'd helped finance the boat's "overhaul." Fay wore gold jewelry, lots of it, and must have spent a small fortune on plastic surgery. After sharing our stories, it was clear we all wanted justice to be served.

❈

Within days, my ex tipped me off that Chuck was seeing a new wom-an. I rushed to the address he gave me, a bar near Daniel's place. From my corner table, I watched the two of them with morbid fascination. Chuck appeared to have met his match when it came to seduction. As soon as he headed toward the men's room, I bustled over to his latest quarry, a fetching woman who introduced herself as Benita. Her move-ments were sinuous, her eyes full of mischief. She didn't flinch when I told her Chuck was a rat.

Two days later, Chuck and Benita met again at the bar, where he entwined his fingers through hers as they flirted. When he tipped her chin and planted a long kiss on her mouth, I had to look away. They laughed and talked some more before he looked at his watch. As soon as he left through the front door, I slipped in next to Benita, who said Chuck had just invited her to go on a cruise.

"Wow, that was quick."

Benita sighed. "It's all a bit awkward. See, he wants me to put the trip on my card. But not to worry. He'll pay me back when the check from the sale of his house clears the bank." She flipped open a compact mirror and reapplied her lipstick. "The man can't keep his hands off me." She winked at me.

"He does know how to make a woman feel desirable." I looked into her eyes. "Benita, you can't go through with this."

She arched an eyebrow.

"I think it's time you met my friends." Until I said the words, I hadn't realized how much I cared about Ursula and Fay.

When I called them and told them about Benita, they came right over. Benita fit right in. We all agreed Chuck must be desperate for cash to be working so fast. I told them the plan Daniel had cooked up.

❈

Mid-afternoon on the appointed day, Fay, Ursula, and I drove north to the address Benita had given us. The house, owned by friends of hers, was situated on a spit of land jutting into Mille Lacs Lake. Its heavily wooded lot made it seem more secluded than it actually was.

Benita met us at the door, wearing a shimmery gray dress with a side slit.

"You look s-stunning," I stammered.

"This is way more than just a summer cabin!" Ursula said.

Benita grinned. "I told Chuck how much I hate this place sitting empty ten months of the year. I let it slip that if I were to find just the right person, I'd let them stay here for next to nothing,"

I looked at Benita with new respect. "You're kind of amazing."

We wandered down to the lake where I looked out at the seemingly endless expanse of water. I'd forgotten how huge Mille Lacs was. Clouds scudded across the sky, and the waves built to whitecaps. Not a good day to be on the water.

Back inside, we gathered near the massive stone fireplace and went over our plan one more time. After a long silence, Ursula threw her arms out, her face radiant. "I feel empowered, don't you?"

"More than you know." Benita's voice was husky with emotion.

Ursula's mouth formed a hard line. "After what that creep did, I was so ashamed, I was a complete recluse."

Fay said, "As soon as my friends found out Chuck's age, they dumped me."

"Then they weren't real friends." Benita spoke as much to me as she did to Fay.

It was time to take our places. Benita slid open the glass door, staying inside while Fay, Ursula, and I walked across the grass to where three beach chairs sat, hidden from view by a boat garage. We spoke in hushed tones until we heard the car pull up the drive.

A door slammed. We waited. After several minutes, Fay poked her head around the garage and reported that Benita and Chuck were sitting on bar stools in the kitchen, drinking.

Darker clouds loomed in the distance. The sun went down and still the lovebirds hadn't come out. After checking my phone for Benita's signal, I couldn't stand the suspense any longer. Keeping myself in shadow, I tiptoed over and looked through the window. A nearly empty bottle of rum stood on the coffee table, and Benita and Chuck were in a lip-locked embrace on the sectional. I turned away before finding out just how far Benita was going to take this charade. I skulked back to join my friends.

"Do you really think it'll make any difference?" Ursula asked. "I mean, even if we scare Chuck into giving back our money, do you really think he'll change?"

I'd had the same thought. "At least we can run him out of town."

Ursula snorted. "And then what? He'll just move to another town and bamboozle some other unsuspecting cougars."

I hated that term for women who dated younger men, but I had to admit what she'd said was the most likely outcome.

Just then, the sliding door opened. Chuck backed out and stumbled a few steps. He was stark naked and yelling something incoherent.

Benita, still wearing her gorgeous dress, strode after him. "C'mon, Baby," she coaxed, "It's too cold for skinny dipping."

"Get away from me!" he screamed. He swayed in the strong wind.

Benita laughed. Kicking off her heels, she grabbed Chuck by the hands, and pulled him waist-deep into the water.

"What is she doing?" Ursula hissed.

"I'm not sure, but we've got this." Fay and Ursula followed me toward the water's edge.

When he caught sight of our little tribunal, Chuck's jaw literally dropped. His mouth stayed open as he looked at each of us in turn.

Fay took a couple steps toward him. "We're onto you, Chucky."

Chuck struggled to stay upright.

Ursula chuckled. "Here's what's going to happen, you pathetic worm. We're gonna follow you wherever you go, and warn any woman you so much as talk to."

I crossed my arms. "We'll post your face all over social media."

He sneered. "How many old ladies even know what social media is? Good luck with that!"

I think I might have growled.

For all Chuck's bravado, his eyes darted about, and though he was clearly inebriated, he managed to stagger by inches toward dry land.

Until Benita gave his arm a jerk and he went under. "Don't even think of driving away," she said when he came up, spluttering. "You're stuck here until you agree to repay every penny you stole from these amazing, trusting women."

Chuck threw his head back as he laughed. "Joke's on you. I don't have it."

I'd been afraid of that.

"You really thought I found you cows attractive? That I actually enjoyed it?" This time when Benita grabbed his arm, he shook her off. His eyes landed on the little dock where a skiff was tethered, and he began moving toward it, crablike.

"Stop him," I said through clenched teeth.

"Let him go," Benita snarled as she waded to shore, shivering in her wet dress that clung to every curve and bulge.

Lightning fast, Chuck dove down. His head popped up yards away and, grasping the boat's gunnel, he threw a leg over and clambered in.

"Stop!" Ursula commanded.

"Let him go," Benita said again. This time I noticed her enigmatic smile.

As soon as he'd untied the skiff, Chuck dropped the outboard. "Freak!" he shrieked just before the engine started. He pointed the little boat out to the middle of the lake, where it bounced and rolled in the waves.

Confused and outraged, I turned to Benita. "You're just gonna let him go?"

Benita chuckled. "That boat's seriously damaged. Even if the engine mount doesn't break away, there's a hole in the hull the size of my fist, and with the engine down and running, that hole's well under the water line."

Fay let out a whoop. Ursula did a fist pump.

I was horrified. I looked directly into Benita's eyes. "But Chuck can't swim. He'll drown out there."

"Then, he shouldn't have stolen the boat."

"But murder? That wasn't our plan, Daniel." I was shivering now.

"Benita," she reminded me. "I'm Benita now. And it's not murder if the damn fool did it to himself." She bent to pick up her size thirteen stiletto heels from the grass. "Think you can live with that?"

Tears coursed down my face. Finally, I nodded. "I know you're right, Da—Benita." I looked into her eyes. "Sorry, it's going to take a while to get used to the new you." We broke into grins at the same time. Then I threw my arms around my ex-husband and planted a big kiss on her cheek.

END

BARBARA MERRITT DEESE writes the No Ordinary Women mystery series, set in Minnesota and featuring five book club women who keep finding themselves up to their bifocals in real-life mysteries to solve. She lives in Bloomington, Minnesota.

A TRIP TO THE FAIR

By Karen Engstrom Anderson

Henri was only ten when he decided he wanted to be a police-man. It was 1898, and his parents decided to take the family to the Minnesota State Fair. He and his sister, Ahni, who was six, had never been out of Hibbing, Minnesota, since they settled there five years before. The Pittellas were among the first families to move into the planned community that Mr. Hibbing had built for the men who worked in his iron mine. Hardworking men like Henri's father, Toivo Pittella, and their families deserved good pay, good schools, and a good life—that was Mr. Hibbing's philosophy and one which brought him success.

The Pitellas planned to take the train from Hibbing to the Twin Cities 175 miles to the south. Siiri, Henri and Ahni's mother, packed a carpetbag for each family member and another with some food for the train ride. She was very excited by the upcoming trip to the big city and the new things they would see. Her enthusiasm was contagious, and the family could hardly get to sleep the night before their departure.

Early that Wednesday morning in late August, Toivo hustled his family onto the streetcar that stopped near their house. The paved streets and streetcar lines, along with large schools, a public library, hospital, and community theater were all part of the planned commu-nity courtesy of Mr. Hibbing. The Pittellas got off at the train station and waited patiently for the daily steam-driven passenger train from

Fargo, North Dakota. It would stop in Duluth and a few other towns and arrive at the Midway Station between Minneapolis and Saint Paul early that evening.

They settled in at a bank of seats facing each other with a table between and spent the day pleasantly playing cards, snacking on the food Siiri had packed, and watching the scenery fly by. The ride took them through miles and miles of peat bogs, a few old stands of huge pines, vast areas of lighter green deciduous trees where the big timber had been cut years before, and endless lakes. At Midway Station, they gathered their belongings and stepped out into the hustle of the big city. They hailed one of the covered horse-drawn cabs waiting by the station's exit. The cabbie jumped down from the small front seat after securing the reins. While Toivo was discussing the fare to the hotel, the family climbed aboard.

"Here, here. Let me help you with that," exclaimed the cabbie with a charming smile as he ran to take Mrs. Pittella's carpetbag and help her into the cab. He swooped Ahni up and set her on the seat next to her mother while Toivo got in from the other side.

"Young man, why don't you sit up front with me," he said to Henri. He stepped up onto the dickey box and turned to his passengers. "My name is Giuseppe. You folks look like you've yet to see our wonderful city. Would you like a tour? For only a twenty-five cents more, I'd be happy to show you the sights on the way to your hotel."

Toivo looked at Siiri, who shrugged and nodded. "All right, then," Giuseppe hooted. For the next hour, the cabbie drove them around St. Paul, keeping up a constant chatter full of information and commentary. First, to Capitol Hill where construction was well underway on the new State Capitol building. He drove them up and down the streets of Crocus Hill. Grand homes set back from the broad boulevards appeared enchanted, their sparkling chandeliers shining through large beveled windows. Heading south toward the river, then down the steep hill, Giuseppe described the area called "Little Italy," also known as the Upper Levee. The area right next to the Mississippi River, which flooded every spring, was filled with squatters' shacks and small houses with unkempt yards. Giuseppe showed them where he lived and described the neighborhood in happy terms—home to hardworking immigrants who loved their children and hoped they would be able to move up the hill someday. He showed them the majestic cliffs of the Mississippi

River from below and the undersides of the high bridges that crossed the wide expanse of water. Finally, he made his way to Lower Town further up the river, then up the hill to downtown. When Giuseppe dropped them at their destination, the Saint Paul Hotel where they were to stay, Toivo arranged for the friendly cabbie to take them back and forth to the fair every day.

The first day at the Fair was so exciting for the children. They pulled at their parents to hurry from place to place. So much to see. The colorful sights and smells. Masses of people moving along the streets and boulevards of the fairgrounds created a noise unlike anything they had ever heard. The Pittellas stood out in the crowd, even among all the Scandinavian Minnesotans. They were tall people with exceptionally light hair and features, handsome with the solid look of mythical Norsemen. Ahni, pigtails flying, and Henri, eyes wide with wonder, held hands as they had been instructed and ran ahead, beckoning for their parents to come see the next display, then the next.

In the midway, barkers hailed them from left and right. They tried their luck at the games and watched magicians on small stages perform amazing sleights of hand. They rode the Merry-Go-Round and the Carousel and finally worked up their courage to ride the sixty-foot-tall Ferris Wheel which had just been built the year before.

They lingered over the amazing new technologies, like Tesla's radio-signal remote control which turned an electric motor on and off from across the room, marveled at how the newly invented muffler quieted the internal combustion engine, and how an invention called a "dimmer" could make electric lights brighten or fade.

They saw the very first butter sculptures, sampled all kinds of food, and tried the new sensation everyone was talking about—cotton candy. They went to the Grandstand and were happy to sit for a while watching the tight-rope walker risk his life to make the crowd ooh and ahh. The Daylight Fireworks display made Ahni cover her ears, but the spectacle delighted everyone else, never having seen pyrotechnics before.

As they left the arena, they bought paper cups of lemonade from a boy with a large glass dispenser strapped to his shoulder. Sticky, tired, and a little sunburned, they met Giuseppe at the appointed time and place, thankful they didn't have to negotiate the long ride on an electric trolley with the crowd of exhausted people.

At breakfast the next morning, they decided to spend the day in the agriculture and farm area of the fair. They had heard about the prize-winning animals from several people they talked to the day before. Bulls as big as a shed. Pigs as large as a davenport. Roosters with feathers on their legs. Horses as shiny as gold. So much to see. The children couldn't wait.

The sun was halfway up the sky as they hopped out of Giuseppe's cab and entered the fairgrounds at the main gate on Snelling Avenue. It was a long walk to the far end, where lay many huge barn structures filled with all sorts of farm animals. They were amazed by the sounds and smells, so foreign to residents of a mining town. The first building they entered was the Pig and Sheep Barn. They were immediately blinded by the change from bright sunshine to the cool darkness of the high-roofed open space lit only by light entering through the large horizontal spaces between walls and roof. As their eyes adjusted, they saw they were in a maze of stalls with aisles between them. Some of the stalls were made of wooden slats, some were just wire fencing, and some were a combination of both. The children giggled and held their noses. Lots of people were milling about, leisurely moving from one stall to the next, talking about the magnificent animal specimens. The Pittellas held hands as they walked up and down the aisles, trying to stay together in the crush of the crowd. They stopped at one of the stalls, the children peering between the boards to look at a pale pink sow lying on her side with twelve piglets nursing, pushing at each other to find an open teat. Henri found it fascinating and embarrassing at the same time. When the embarrassment became too strong, he dropped his mother's hand and continued to the next stall, pulling Ahni along with him.

The left eye of the biggest pig Henri could ever have imagined was staring directly at him through the wire fencing of its pen. The huge animal was standing with its side against the cage. To Henri, it seemed as big as the Pittellas' kitchen table and when he started walking along the fence, he couldn't help but reach out to see what the pig felt like. He dropped Ahni's hand to touch it through the wire. The hairs here and there on its skin were as thick as shoelaces. When he looked across the pen to the next aisle, he saw Ahni petting a lamb that someone was holding in their arms. The person was leaning over so she could reach the soft white fleece of the lamb with ease. Ahni had a big grin on her face and was nodding, answering some unheard question. The person, head tilted to the side listening to Ahni, had unkempt brown hair almost shoulder length and wore a dirty light blue shirt and dirty denim overalls. Henri noted all this without thinking, and even though he couldn't see the person's face, he knew it was a young man. Without knowing why, he suddenly filled with dread.

He had to get to Ahni. He should have held onto her hand. His heart was beating faster as he turned to go to her. Just then the pig began rubbing against the cage, and Henri's hand was caught between the wire and the pig. He cried out in pain. His skin was torn as the pig moved back and forth scratching itself. He screamed as his hand was twisted and smashed by the massive body. A few people near him worked together to push the pig's bulk away from the fencing and managed to free the boy as his parents rushed to him. Henri's hand was bleeding badly, and Siiri drew him tight against her to comfort him. Through his tears of pain, he cried, "Ahni!" and pulled away, trying to get to where he had last seen his sister and the strange man. She was nowhere to be seen.

It was only a matter of minutes before a uniformed officer in a wide-brimmed hat and shiny black shoes appeared. He introduced himself as Officer Timothy Dolan and asked the hysterical parents what had happened, but their crying and speaking Finnish made it difficult for him to understand them. Henri, despite his injury and tears, spoke clearly and explained that his sister, Ahni, was missing. Another policeman appeared, and Dolan asked him to go for help to search for a missing child.

Once everyone calmed down, Toivo and Siiri described their daughter, and Henri told them about Ahni petting the lamb held by the stranger, describing as much as he could remember about him. Dolan put his hand on Henri's shoulder and looked into his eyes for a minute. "Your description is very clear, son. Are you certain of what you saw?"

"Yes, sir," nodded Henri, cradling his wounded hand.

Dolan accompanied the family to the building's office by the main entrance. As he left to join the search, he said to Siiri, "We will find her, ma'am, don't worry."

Many different people came into the office to talk to them during the day. A representative from the fair spouted cheery words about little girls wandering off all the time to pet the baby animals. Not to worry. A detective and other police officers came and went asking questions but offering no words of hope. Newspaper reporters were turned away at the door by an officer who stood guard there.

By the time a nurse arrived, Henri's hand had stopped bleeding. She was concerned that there were broken bones, but he put on a brave face and told her it didn't hurt too badly. Siiri refused to let Henri leave her side and told the nurse she couldn't take him to the hospital.

As the day wore on, Siiri grew rigid and sat staring into space. Toivo went out to search with the others. When Officer Dolan returned to check on them late in the afternoon, Henri stopped him.

"I remember the man had dirt on his pants, red dirt like a miner's. You know, down the front of his pant legs like he had wiped his hands on them a lot," Henri told the officer.

Dolan nodded and patted Henri on the back, "Good job," he said, "every little detail matters."

At dinner time, the detective came to tell Mrs. Pittella that she and Henri should go back to their hotel, but she refused. Someone from the fair brought them food which they barely touched. The hours seemed endless and when it turned dark outside, the search continued with lanterns. The nurse came back and brought blankets. Siiri and Henri huddled together on the settee and dozed off and on.

At midnight, the detective and Toivo came in together talking. Toivo was upset, saying they had to keep searching, but the detective was adamant that they stop and resume early in the morning with a larger group of searchers. Toivo was angry and started to berate the detective when Officer Dolan stepped up next to him.

"Mr. Pittella, may I speak to you a moment?" he asked.

As Toivo turned to Officer Dolan, the detective quickly left the room, eager to take his leave of the desperate father.

"What is it?" said Toivo, irritated.

"I have an idea and I need your help." Dolan proceeded to lay out a plan to observe a certain area of the grounds where he had a hunch Ahni might be hidden.

"Why didn't you tell the detective this?"

"I did, earlier. Unfortunately, I am a first-year officer and was told I had overstepped my bounds. Are you with me?"

"Yes, of course. Let's go!"

Henri had heard the two men talking and jumped to his feet.

"I want to go with you," he cried.

Dolan turned back from the door and approached the boy. He held the boy's shoulder as he met his eye, "You have a solemn duty to support your mother. She needs you. Be strong and stand guard here."

Henri's eyes were wide with comprehension and anxiety. He looked at his father who nodded and held his arms open. Henri buried his tears in his father's chest for a moment. He went back to his mother's side as the men left.

As they walked past the barns, Dolan explained, "I have been walking the beat at this end of the fairgrounds now for a week. I have seen a young man several times working around the sheep who fits the description your son gave us. Actually, he is more like a large boy. He is a simpleton, if you know what I mean. He seems to be a sweet boy, but very slow in the head. I haven't seen him since early this morning, and I don't know where he sleeps. But I figure a big kid like that will be plenty hungry in the morning before he must start doing chores. If we can keep watch over the area from above, I'll bet we'll spot him at first light. Are you up for that?"

"Of course."

Together they climbed the wooden lookout tower at the southwest corner of the fairground. The tower was manned during the day but stood empty at night. They took turns keeping watch, one standing in the tiny, dark observation deck, the other sitting with his back against the half wall. There was just enough light to follow a few people appearing and disappearing in and out of the shadows. A drunk staggered to find some place to lie down. A couple with arms locked around each other looked as if they had the same goal. Noises that farm animals make at night mingled with the more distant sounds of the midway cleanup crew. Dolan was still napping as the sky began to lighten ever so slightly. Toivo, whose turn it was to keep lookout, began to make out shapes in the dim light. Many rows of carriages and wagons—some closed vans, some open carts, some large animal transports—spread out below the tower. At the far end of the rows stood the long stable buildings that housed the livery horses and their tack. Early risers were moving about, starting their morning chores or heading for the laborers' mess tent.

"There!" Toivo cried out. "There he is."

Dolan roused from his sleep, stood. "Where? How do you know it's him?"

"The rust on his overalls. Look!"

Sure enough, the husky young farm boy walking in their direction had streaks of rusty red color down the thighs of his faded overalls. They took stock of the boy's direction and descended the tower ladder as quickly as they could. When they got to the bottom, Dolan grabbed Toivo's arm. "You must restrain yourself, you know. Can you do that?"

Toivo stiffened. "I understand we must not jeopardize Ahni's safety. If he has her hidden, we must follow him. I won't risk scaring him away. I am a patient man but once I have her back safely, I cannot guarantee my actions will be as tempered."

"Good. Just follow my lead."

The young man, almost as tall as Toivo, and larger around by half, walked toward the mess tent. Dolan and Toivo hurried after him and hid in the shadow of the Horse Barn across from the entrance. When he came out a few minutes later, he had some paper-wrapped food in one hand and a glass bottle of milk in the other. Dolan and Toivo followed him as he walked back toward the carriages and wagons. Dolan had opened his shirt collar and removed his policeman's jacket. He carried it slung over his shoulder. With his other hand on Toivo's shoulder, he talked to him as if they were good friends returning from a long night of drinking. The boy paid them no mind as they followed him down one row, then another. Finally, the boy stopped at the back of a wagon with a tall wooden box built on the back. He set the food down and used both hands to pry up the large rusty latch. He wiped his hands on his pants, opened the door part way, set the food inside and climbed in, pulling the door after himself. The rusty hinges kept the door from closing all the way and Dolan and Toivo approached the cracked door quietly, listening and hoping.

"I brought you some milk and bread," they heard the boy say in a sweet high-pitched voice. "Are you hungry?"

Dolan pressed his hand on Toivo's chest, making it clear he needed to stay calm. Then he slowly opened the door enough to see inside. The thin sunlight shone on the boy with his back to the door. He was kneeling, offering Ahni the milk bottle and some bread. Some bales of hay were stacked against the back wall. Ahni was sitting cross-legged facing the door, holding her hand out for the food. She looked puzzled at the stranger in the door, but then she saw her father behind Dolan. She jumped up and pushed past the boy, who made no attempt to stop her. Toivo hugged his little girl to him and took off for the Pig Barn.

"Don't you want some milk?" the boy called after Ahni.

Dolan talked to him, coaching him to come out and take a walk. He had put his jacket back on and identified himself as a policeman. The boy smiled and said he liked policemen. Dolan held him gently by the arm and talked to him calmly as they walked back to the mess tent together. Once inside, Dolan led him to a bench in the corner and called someone over and told them to go find some help.

When Dolan got back to the Pig Barn office, the Pittellas were sitting cramped together on the small settee, arms around each other, Ahni on her mother's lap. Dolan pulled up a desk chair and sat facing the four of them. He told them about the boy who had taken Ahni. He lived with his parents on a farm outside Alexandria, Minnesota. The boy had told Dolan that his little sister had died a few months before and that his mother was very sad all the time. She hadn't come to the fair because she was too sad. Only the boy and his father had come to show their prize sheep. When Ahni came to pet the lamb he was holding, he had asked her if she wanted to come see all the little lambs back on his farm and Ahni had said yes. So, the boy had put her in the back of their wagon and hoped to take her home to his mother to make her happy again.

Siiri held onto Ahni tightly as Dolan recounted the boy's story. Dolan sat in silence for a time, staring at the floor. Finally, he looked up and said, "He is being held now at the fair's main office. We will take the boy to the home for the mentally ill. Kidnapping is a serious offense and he really isn't fit to stand trial as an adult." He paused, "Or we can have his father take him home. It is up to you."

Siiri and Toivo shared a long look, then shook their heads.

"We cannot cause that poor mother any more grief. But please make them promise they will keep him at home." It was Toivo who answered. He stood and shook hands with Dolan.

The officer stopped at the door and turned back to Henri. "Young man, I am impressed with your composure through all this. And you were more observant than most adults. I hope you put your talents to good use when you grow up. You should become a policeman."

And so he did.

END

KAREN ENGSTROM ANDERSON, although she never worked in the field, claims her degree in Cultural Anthropology has given her a most interesting lens through which she views the world. She grew up barefoot in rural Florida, lived on the northside of Chicago, but spent every summer on Lake Vermilion, Minnesota. She moved to Minneapolis in 1984. "A Trip to the Fair" is her first published short story. She has written a soon-to-be-published mystery, *The Fox*, set in northern Minnesota, and a second novel is ready for editing. She recently had an article featured in the *Star Tribune*.

THE NEWSROOM
By Colin T. Nelson

I'm in my car spying on his condo in downtown Minneapolis. I've come here for several nights, studying his movements. I watch the women who flock to him and leave early in the morning, trying to walk on last night's high heels. It was a woman, after all, that caused me to be here, to plot the unthinkable: I am going to kill him.

While I wait for the bastard, I may as well tell you what forced me to this point. Looking at me, you'd be shocked. As I am when I honestly think about it. Mid-thirties, slender, starting to bald. I don't look like a killer. My personality wouldn't pass the job interview. After all, I have done nothing more sinister than catch a second speeding ticket.

It started at the TV station. WMNN, broadcasting news to the upper Midwest. An old, staid company that traces its founding back to when licenses were first granted by the federal government. A guy like me, I fit in there. Conservative and dedicated to the journalistic craft since my dreams in high school.

Ben Christy, the manager of the station, recruited me three years ago from a sister station.

"I like people from Iowa. Honest. Maybe it's the corn you eat?" He laughed while pumping my hand.

The first years were wonderful. Ben coached me, gave me meaty stories to work on, and, equally important, raised my salary. To be an effective reporter, sometimes you've got to be an asshole to get the story. I did it gladly.

I never dated much and I liked to think it was because I am pretty ordinary. Come across like a brother. Probably, there was more to it than that, but it's hard to be honest with yourself sometimes. In any event, I met a woman at the station. One of the sports reporters, Stephanie introduced herself at the company coffee kiosk.

"Hey, Jim, I like what you're putting out there," she said. "You must have to be tough to cover those gang shootings."

"Yeah and thanks."

She wasn't the prettiest woman at the station and I hesitated to date someone I worked with, but I was lonely. She combined an exuberant personality with a reputation as a tremendous athlete. Within a month we were dating and within a year engaged. Because of the company's anti-nepotism rules, we kept it a secret.

My life was wonderful in all aspects. What could go wrong?

Scott Simpson.

One of the station's owners brought in Simpson from the Columbia School of Journalism. No one knew him, but I remember the impact Simpson had when he stepped through the door into the newsroom.

A tall guy with thick blond hair that fell into his face all the time, a grin that turned-up one side of his face, and energy that came off him like heat off a racing car engine. Usually careful women and the uber-feminists, who pretended to ignore men, flocked around him without embarrassment.

I admit to some envy on my part, but the real test would be how good a reporter he was going to be.

For the next five months, I didn't see Simpson much, even though he was also on the crime beat. I worked hard, broke tough stories, and planned the wedding with Stephanie. The price tag climbed, but luckily Steph was a conservative person. She tried to save where we could.

I ran into Simpson in the newsroom one morning.

"Hey, Smoke. How does a guy get ahead around here?" he asked while slouching with his hip cocked to one side.

"The name's Jim. All the usual ways: work hard, be aggressive out on the street, and develop your sources. Didn't you go to J-school?" It felt good to insult him.

"Top of the class." When he grinned briefly, it was infectious, I admit. But I could also sense something brutal underneath the frat boy insouciance. A Stanley Kowalski attraction that could explain the effect he had on women. "Okay, Smoke. Don't let your meat loaf."

I thought he was too lazy to become much of a reporter. I was wrong.

A month later, I was in the newsroom chatting with my editor. Simpson called in, out of breath, and actually yelled, "Stop the presses!" Most of us laughed with self-righteous experience.

Turned out, he'd broken a murder story. A big one. Simpson was on the scene, calling in the story. He demanded a camera crew as soon as possible. A lone woman had been attacked after leaving a bus transit station on her way into the Southdale shopping center. She'd been bludgeoned in the head. "Cops just got here. No witnesses, but I can scoop this one."

It became a two-day story, running on print and TV, and Simpson was in the middle of everything. When he came into the newsroom, both the women and the men poured water out for him to walk on.

Even Stephanie was impressed. "How'd he get that one? You better watch out, Jim. Scott might knock you off your pedestal." She joked with me.

In a week things settled down. Thanks to a source in the Bureau of Prisons, I broke a story about the head of the state prisons allowing an inmate to use her state-paid cell phone for personal calls. Not much of a scandal, I know, but this is Minnesota where politics is squeaky clean. Steph and I met with her parents. A big question loomed among us: how much would they contribute to the cost of the wedding?

Surprisingly, Simpson congratulated me about the story. "Home run, Smoke. A born reporter." He gave me a soft punch that glanced off my shoulder. "You can pick up the slack when I'm gone."

"Where are you going?"

"Mt. Rainier. I'm climbing with a select group. We got our tickets punched, so we gotta grab it now."

Good riddance, I thought.

Then, it happened again. As Simpson was leaving the office, he strolled through the skyway to the parking ramp. On his way, a mugger grabbed a woman's purse. Simpson grabbed the thug and threw him to the ground until security could catch up. And, of course, the victim was the proverbial "little old lady." This time the notoriety only lasted a day, but Simpson's reputation soared.

I was impressed also. Not only did Simpson break up the robbery, he tackled the perp and subdued him until security arrived. A gutsy move that proved his physical chops.

Ben Christy suggested nominating Simpson for an OTO TV Reporter award. I was disgusted. What about me, Ben? Years of hard work for you and the station?

That night at home, Steph calmed me. "Sure, he's got a streak going. But you've been in the business long enough to know that luck doesn't last. Besides, this competition you have with Scott is childish. Let go of it." She wrapped warm arms around my neck and pulled my face close to hers. I looked at her eyes, the shape of her nose which I thought looked "noble," and her full lips. She kissed me for a long time.

When we separated, she said, "Of course, he is cute."

"Don't trust that guy."

Stephanie dismissed my concerns with a flip of her wrist. "Come on, we're meeting Mom and Dad at Antonio's for pasta. Another boring night of talking money."

Simpson "came down from the mountain" two weeks later. His face tanned, he smiled broadly at everyone as if they were best friends. Energy popped off him and he almost smelled of fresh air. "Back on the streets," he promised. "I'm after another big one. Somebody else can cover the 'parking tickets.'" He laughed and skipped out of the newsroom.

Ben called me into his office. Directed me to sit down. Something unusual. "Can you believe Scott? Beginner's luck?" he asked.

"Probably."

"I've never seen a reporter find stories so fast. Rumor has it he's banging a female cop who works homicide and gives him all his tips."

I shrugged.

"Listen, Jim, I want to talk about him. And you. I've always supported you, but all the board talks about is Scott. Meanwhile, they're digitizing everything around here, and they reminded me labor is our biggest drag on overhead." He wouldn't look at me.

"So, you're saying I'm a 'drag on overhead'?"

"No, no, I never said that. But, uh, the auditors are coming next month. They're going to dig into our budget like they're fracking."

"So, I may be fired?"

"Not necessarily. But, Jim, I need something to demonstrate your value proposition to the organization."

My face started to get hot. When I jumped up, the plastic chair clattered onto the floor behind me. I slammed the door when I left. Childish, I know, but it sure felt good.

Steph and I met again with her parents. The endless maneuvering about money tired me out.

Then, lightning struck again for Scott Simpson.

He broke another murder story. He was in Uptown and stumbled on a dead body outside of Carl's Crab Shack. A young black man who had gang signs spray-painted in yellow across his back. Head crushed in. The cops got there just before Simpson. Which sounded suspicious to me. Maybe Ben's idea of Simpson's affair with a cop was true. How else could he scoop everyone else again?

Since Uptown crawled with tourists from the suburbs, the murder scared lots of people. So, beyond the tragic death of a young man, the murder generated collateral issues. All covered by the media and led by Scott Simpson.

I'm sure that story caused Ben to call me into his office two days later. "We need more production out of you."

"Dammit, Ben. I've done nothing but great reporting for you and this station. What's wrong with that?"

"Nothing, but Scott Simpson has raised the bar now. You know that." One of the only people in the station to wear a necktie, Ben loosened it and sighed deeply. "I've got an idea to save your career. There's a journalists' conference in Philadelphia next week. You know, the basics all over again. I want you to attend."

"I don't want to."

Ben pushed his palm toward me. "You *need* to attend."

I sat there for a long time without speaking. Finally, I got up and walked to the door. "Okay." I closed it softly.

Ben was correct about one thing: I needed a break. A fresh perspective. When I had free time, I saw the historic sights of the city and missed Stephanie. Trying to reduce our dependence on electronics, we texted just enough to keep in touch. The weather in Philadelphia was warm with clear skies. I cleared my head and realized that I had to let go of my envy of Simpson. As for my career, I'd hate to leave WMNN, but I talked to a few editors at the conference. I could get another gig.

My reunion with Steph was passionate and she wanted to know

everything I'd learned at the conference. Afterward, in that satisfied feeling, she put on her robe and moved into the living room. I followed.

"Jim, I've been thinking about us. I mean, all the problems with money and the wedding. My parents being such a pain in the ass." She turned her head away from me.

"Yeah?"

"Well, I was thinking, uh, maybe we should postpone the wedding. Save our own money."

That surprised me. Six months earlier, she'd been pushing to move the date forward. "I suppose we could talk about it. What changed your mind?"

She stood and walked into the kitchen. I followed. "I had time to think while you were gone. I just don't know if I'm really ready."

Something unspoken grew between us. I couldn't describe it but could certainly feel it.

Next morning at the station, Ben asked how things went in Philadelphia. "I hope this will save you, Jim."

"What do you mean?"

"Auditors told the board we can only afford one reporter on the crime beat." He didn't look at me.

"And?"

"I'll advocate for you, but Scott's the star now. Just being honest with you."

Later in the newsroom, I ran into Simpson. He asked, "How'd the retraining go, Smoke? Ready to kick some ass now?"

I scowled at him. "Did I miss anything here?"

He shrugged. "Quiet week." Then, his eyes opened wide. "Quiet for news, that is. But getting laid, well, I scored a new one. Might even share her with you." He leaned closer to me and grunted, "There's a hot one in sports. Don't know why I didn't get some of that earlier. Stephanie. You know her?"

I staggered and grabbed for the edge of the desk, trying not to let Simpson catch on. The air in front of me blurred.

"You okay, Smoke?"

"Yeah." I staggered outside to try and breathe again. I walked east, into the late afternoon shadows, and found myself at Elliott Park. I stood in the middle of adjoining soccer fields. Peaceful green grass surrounded me while I stood still.

It surprised me that, somehow, I didn't blame Steph. Clearly, she had agreed to it. I just felt numb to her. That night I confronted her. She admitted quickly and with lots of crying. But Steph never said it was a mistake. Afterward, she stood up from the couch and left, walking out into the night.

I was also surprised at how quickly another idea built in me and finally took over: I would kill Scott Simpson.

Over the next few days I plotted how to do it. A gun seemed like the easiest. I wouldn't have to get any closer than about twenty feet. No blood on me, no struggle with him. As a crime reporter, I knew the clues the police would look for and I could eliminate all of them.

I felt like I lived outside my body while I focused on killing him. What drove this strange man hovering around my body? In my mind I could see flesh colors tangled across lavender sheets, hear the groans, smell the sweat, and see Stephanie, naked, jerking underneath Scott Simpson.

Beyond the plan, the next step was to get a weapon. In Richfield I walked into a pawn shop. On the back wall, from side to side, hung hundreds of handguns. An American flag draped across the upper right corner of the wall. A guy in a basketball T-shirt and a ponytail slid along the counter. "Help ya?"

I bought a Ruger SR9C automatic. The salesman told me this one would fit my hand better and packed a "shit load of bang for a little bitch. You hit it with this mother, and they're down for good." Using his tongue, he shifted a toothpick to the left side of his mouth.

On Fridays, Ben Christy always held an office-wide meeting to pull together the week. People were usually in that Friday afternoon mood, knowing they'd soon be in bars within walking distance of the station.

Ben quieted everyone. "Our rookie's making us all look like monkeys. How does he do it? To find out, I've asked Scott to tell us his secrets." Ben stretched out his arm to find Simpson.

He pretended to hesitate, dropped his head an inch. Then, looked-up and hurried to the center. "Hey, thanks, dudes." He grinned. "What I was taught back at Columbia was to work hard. You can't out-source that. Develop your sources and don't abuse 'em." A few people applauded. "Tough part is, you gotta be willing to poke your nose in every rat hole in the city." He left the circle in a swirl of clapping.

Ben sat us down for a final recap. Thank God, Simpson was several chairs away from me. Since I had decided to kill him, I couldn't even look at him.

Meeting over, the room cleared quickly. I stood slowly. A blue flash drive resting in the bowl of a plastic chair seat caught my eye. Simpson's seat. Must have fallen from his pocket. I grabbed it.

Two days later, I was so nervous I worked like a demon to keep my mind occupied because this was the day I would kill Simpson. I had studied his patterns. He always entered the condo through the front door which was flanked by two tall Arborvitae bushes. They created a short canyon from the sidewalk to the door. That's where I'd wait. Off to the side, hidden behind the bush. The impact of the bullet would probably throw his body across the sidewalk to fall behind the opposite Arborvitae.

That night, I drove to Simpson's condo a full hour before I expected him home. I shut off my car and peered through the shadows cast by the distant street light. The gun jammed into my lower back.

The faint sound of someone's TV couldn't mask the crackling of crickets along the edge of the bushes. I remembered the flash drive in my pocket. Looked at my watch. Plenty of time. I lifted my laptop off the front seat and inserted the drive. It opened quickly and, oddly, there were no passwords required. I scrolled through photos of women and found a file labeled, "Night Work." I opened it.

In a few minutes I came to a page of notes, like a reporter would record. The upper corner of the page was dated three months ago.

5' 4" blonde heavy build
maroon jacket with hood
walks transit station at Southdale to fitness club
5:17 bus
4th cement column no light.
drags heels—hear coming

My chest tightened. I scrolled further. This was the first murder story Simpson claimed to have "scooped." Here were all the details of the killing. Recorded *before* the murder actually occurred. I managed to get the page moving until I came to notes about a man at Carl's Crab Shack. There was a note reminding Simpson to pick up a can of yellow spray paint before the murder.

My fingers shook as I scrambled to the end. I found the latest notes, dated from one month earlier.

The notes identified a woman who left work at 9:46 each night to walk one block to a parking ramp at 6th Street and Chicago in Minneapolis. She carried pepper spray in her right hand and wore high heels that made her unsteady. At the corner, she'd enter a tunnel of scaffolding above the sidewalk. Cardboard ads covered the side. I found the date the woman would be killed—tonight at 9:52.

My watch read 9:07.

❖

The story ran later in the last news spot. I scooped all the other media. The anchors, speaking in the studio, threw it to me while I stood before two lights and a camera, darkness enveloping me from behind.

"A tragic loss for everyone at WMNN. Scott Simpson was a star reporter and loved by all. Apparently, he walked under some scaffolding and was attacked. Police have given me a preliminary cause of death. He was shot once in the head from behind. WMNN is the first to interview a witness who was going to her car when she heard a loud bang. She spun around to see Scott fall about thirty feet away from her. Unfortunately, she didn't see his killer."

After I signed off, Ben Christy called me. "Great work, Jim. Too bad about Scott. Can't believe it. Why are there so many murders all of a sudden?" Ben sniffed and remained silent for a long time until his voice cracked, "Well, guess it's you on top again."

"Yeah, hate to say it. But I'm determined to follow in Scott's footsteps. I promise you I'll scoop the next serious crime story just like he did."

End

COLIN T. NELSON became hooked on mystery stories at ten when his grandmother gave him a copy of *The Hound of the Baskervilles*. A lawyer, he worked as a prosecutor and a Public Defender, providing much of his story ideas. Eight of his books have been published including the Pete Chandler series which are set in exotic locations around the globe. Colin is married and has two adult children. He also plays the saxophone in a jazz group and a Bob Dylan tribute rock band.

THE A TO Z SOLUTION
By Brian Lutterman

Abby Lockhart finishes applying her makeup. Her friend Zoe would be completing her own preparations in her own mirror right about now; what would she be thinking about?

She would be thinking about Abby's husband.

"Ready to go?" Rick yells up the stairs.

"Just a minute," she calls back, wondering if she can endure another dinner with the Reiters. And wondering if she can endure Rick.

She finishes the rouge, grabs her purse, starts for the door. Then she stops, goes back to the dresser, and opens the drawer containing Rick's clothing. Rummaging through the stacks of T-shirts and underwear, she finds the pistol. She knows it's loaded. She stashes it in her purse.

Rick is waiting in the pickup, engine running and blasting out heat. The truck, an aging heavy-duty GMC Sierra, is equipped with a snow-plow blade for Rick's plowing business. They need the income brought in from plowing snow, since Rick's primary business as a landscaping contractor is seasonal. There hasn't been much snow this winter, so Rick has spent a lot of time fishing and doing nothing. Abby, for reasons she can't articulate, hates the snowplow.

She scurries out of the house through the single-digit cold and gets into the truck. "You're looking nice," he says, giving her a compliment as rare as it is unenthusiastic.

And Zoe will look nicer, she thinks. About fifty pounds lighter, without the wrinkles and worry lines.

Rick pulls out of the driveway and onto the road for the three-mile trip into Pine Lake. The parking lot is filling up at Mort's, the supper club on the edge of town. Rick, as always, backs into his parking space. She has never figured out why he does that, except that he can. Abby opens the door and slides down from the cab into the piercing cold, and she looks at her husband, all six-foot-four of him. He's recently cut his hair short, to hide the creeping baldness. He has also dropped a few pounds, occasionally declining dessert and even cutting back on the beer. He is her age, forty-six, still looks good, and knows it.

Zoe and Larry Reiter are seated at the bar when they walk in, chatting with another couple. When they stand up, Abby studies Zoe, with her glossy, shoulder-length dirty blonde hair, snug-fitting pants and sweater clinging to her petite, yet curvy frame. Zoe has not endured the trials of raising two kids. She doesn't spend twelve-hour nursing shifts on her feet at the local hospital, dealing with pain and blood and vomit and a tyrannical boss. *Yes, Zoe looks terrific.*

Abby fingers her purse, thinks about the gun.

"Hey, guys!" Rick, expansive as always, gives Zoe a peck on the cheek and shakes hands with Larry, an agreeable guy of medium height, average looks, brown hair, and brown eyes. An Everyman.

Rick and Zoe, the two extroverts, engage immediately, exchanging enthusiastic, extravagant banter as the two couples are shown to their table. Mort's is the nicest restaurant in town, as good as could be expected in a place with five thousand inhabitants. The interior is decorated in a North Woods motif, the walls covered with knotty pine, the tables and chairs made of dark, heavy wood. Abby and Rick order beers from the thin young waitress. Larry and Zoe have brought their drinks to the table.

"So," Rick says, "you guys enjoying a real Up North winter?"

"Cold down in the Cities, too," Larry replies. It has been more of a typical Minnesota winter. Last year was so warm, with only short, unpredictable bursts of cold, that Rick didn't even take his beloved fish house out onto Pine Lake. He settled instead for a portable folding shelter, brought onto the ice with a snowmobile instead of the pickup. And the year before that, slightly less warm, Rick, after towing the fish house onto the lake, didn't drive on the ice again, using the snowmobile for the trek to the fish house.

Rick grins. "Did you know what you were getting into, Larry?"

"Oh, sure. Remember, I came up here fishing in the winter all the time. I'm used to it." After his previous employer in the Twin Cities downsized him last year, Larry and Zoe moved to Pine Lake, Zoe's hometown. Larry, who has a college degree, took a job as a quality control manager at a factory that makes equipment for dairy farms. Zoe opened her own nail salon, and by all accounts, business is good.

The Lockharts' beers arrive. Rick hoists his glass. "Here's to the ladies. We love them, from A to Z."

Abby and Zoe exchange a glance, rolling their eyes as they drink. As best friends in school, they were known as A and Z. Loudmouths in the boys' locker room would boast of going through the school's girls "from A to Z." But most of the boys, as far as Abby could tell, skipped directly to Z.

Abby and Zoe became inseparable friends in middle school. As they reached their high school years, they remained best friends, at least officially. But their differences became more apparent, as the exuberant Zoe continued to collect friends and boyfriends. The quieter Abby was still part of Zoe's group, but increasingly hung back, dubious of the newer members of her friend's wider circle. After high school, they largely lost touch.

The quartet orders dinner. Rick takes healthy gulps from his beer and soon orders another. Zoe does likewise, and the show is on. Rick and Zoe do most of the talking, the volume gradually increasing along with the beer consumption. Zoe touches Rick's arm as they share a good laugh. Larry, Zoe's second husband, smiles politely and contributes an occasional comment. Abby does likewise.

The arrival of their meals does little to slow the boisterous conversation. In between laughs, Zoe's face assumes its trademark expression, the one that looks as though she's holding in a secret. A mock-serious look that seems always ready to burst into laughter and frequently does. In high school, the guys found it irresistible. They still do.

She touches his arm again.

Abby's fingers tighten around the buckle of her purse as she thinks about the heavy object inside it.

As the group enjoys coffee and dessert, during a lull in the conversation, Zoe looks over at Abby, as if just noticing her presence. "So, how are the kids?"

"They're fine."

"Both in college. One at Duluth, right?"

Abby nods.

"And the other at . . . North Dakota?"

"North Dakota State."

"Right. Smart kids. And how are things at the hospital?"

"Just peachy. They've cut back on staffing again. We're running ourselves ragged."

"Well, *that* sucks." Zoe sips from her coffee. After a pause, she smiles. "I'm so glad we moved back here. I told Larry, this is the right move. It will be fun—the people in Pine Lake are great."

Larry lifts his coffee cup. "Here's to great people."

Abby fingers her purse buckle again, exerting a huge amount of willpower to avoid opening it.

On the way home, Rick says, "You were quiet tonight."

"Just tired. It's been a long week."

They pull up at the house. Abby remains seated.

"Something wrong?" Rick asks.

Abby glances at her purse again. Hesitates. "No, everything's fine." She opens the pickup door and slides out, going inside ahead of him to replace the gun. Afterward, she sits on the bed, pondering her next move.

Abby accepts that her husband is a jackass. A fool, shallow and self-centered. She accepts these failings but doesn't like them. She wonders, not for the first time in their twenty-two-year marriage, if he is also unfaithful. That, she would never accept. Never.

❖

Abby goes through the motions of life for several endless days, not sure what will happen, but knowing this situation will not stand. She tries to distract herself with work, avoiding thoughts of Rick and Zoe, of the years she's given Rick, of the grinding life she's lived, sacrificing, putting up with Rick and his bullshit and his coldness in bed. She knows that some night this week Rick will go fishing, at his comfortably heated fish house, equipped with satellite TV. And a bed.

It happens on Thursday. After supper, Rick announces he's going out to the lake. He grabs a six pack of Leinenkugel, bundles up, and heads for the truck. Abby waits half an hour. Then she begins her own bundling-up process. And after completing that, she pulls the gun from the drawer, shoving it into the pocket of her snowmobile suit. She's tired of being made a fool of. This situation will be resolved, tonight.

The temperature is twelve degrees when Abby fires up the Arctic Cat and eases it down the driveway. Reaching the road, she glances both ways. No neighbors in sight, which isn't surprising; the nearest ones live nearly half a mile away. She looks back at her own house. Plain, worn, modestly sized. Rick talked idly over the years about building a new house out on the lake, but with two kids in college it would never happen. She thinks about Larry and Zoe's house in town, a newer two-story with sharply angled roof lines and tricked-out kitchens and bathrooms. It's one of the nicest houses in Pine Lake.

She turns toward the lake and guns the sled for the mile and a half trip, reaching the public landing in a few minutes. In the thin moonlight she can see the outlines of dozens of fish houses, most of them clustered in an area about a mile off to the right. An informal road through the snow, formed by repeated traffic and occasional plowing, leads to the cluster. A few lights shine from fish houses that are occupied and have windows. Off in the distance, she can see the twin lights of a vehicle making its way among the structures. She eases her machine onto the lake and heads down the road.

She proceeds slowly toward the cluster. The road hasn't needed much plowing this year; the ice formed early, and there has been little snow. As she approaches the first few structures along the road, she begins looking off to the left. Rick's fish house is not hard to spot; it's off by itself, about a quarter mile from the main ice road. Rick told her that this year, he'd give himself a little distance from the crowd. He's always thought prospects might be better to the southeast of the cluster, and he was tired of fighting everybody else for the dwindling number of walleye in Pine Lake. Rick never expressed such sentiments before this year. Before the Reiters.

Abby swings in a wide arc to the southeast, toward the far side of Rick's fish house. There isn't much wind tonight and it would be quiet, but the sound of snowmobiles on the lake was common, and she wouldn't alert Rick. She slows down, and as she nears her destination, feels a slight give in the ice. She slows down some more. More give. Her heart rate, already elevated, ticks up a notch. She's heard there are underwater springs out in this area of the lake that might compromise the safety of the ice. Ice is a living thing, she knows—always shifting, expanding, contracting. And sometimes thinning.

She guns the sled, and feels a little more give. She guns it some more, moving away from the thin spot until the ice feels solid. Then she slows down again, finally stopping and shutting down the snowmobile. She climbs off. It's quiet. She's still some distance from the fish house, and she begins walking across bare ice and crunchy snow. She has a partial view of a pickup that's parked on the other side of the house. As she gets closer, circling carefully, she sees it's Rick's truck.

But there's a second vehicle, parked on the far side of Rick's pickup. She widens the arc of her path so she can see the second vehicle without getting too close to the fish house. And there it is: A shiny, late model Ford 250 pickup. Larry and Zoe's. Her heartbeat accelerates again. She pats the outside of her snowmobile suit, feeling for the gun.

She trudges slowly toward the fish house, toward an uncertain future, toward a situation that will not stand. She walks up to the door, listens, hears the sounds of a hockey game from the TV. Rick's idea of romantic, she supposes. She tries the door—locked. *The lock is designed to deter thieves and vandals; why would you need it when you're inside?*

Abby removes her chopper mitten, unzips the small pocket on her suit, takes out the spare key. She found it in a box in the closet, inside a plastic bag containing the warranty, manual, and paperwork for the fish house. She inserts the key, fumbling with it in the cold, and quietly turns it in the lock. Then she unzips her other pocket, takes out the gun.

She pulls the door open a crack, peers inside. Rick, predictably, is not fishing. He's not watching the hockey game. He's on the bed, half-clothed, making out passionately.

With Larry.

She drops the gun, closes the door, and staggers away, out onto the ice. Leans over and vomits. Continues, blindly, away from the shack. Between the sound of the hockey game and his . . . preoccupation, Rick never heard her. Nothing new there.

She walks farther away, not really hearing the noise until it's very close. She looks up. It's a snowmobile. No, an ATV. It circles around the fish house, toward her.

The ATV slows down, continues to approach her. She watches as it leans over slightly. Then it tilts even more, down into a crack its weight has created. It's the same area where Abby rode across thin ice. The machine stops, perhaps thirty feet away. Abby holds her breath. The rider slowly leans away from the crack, reverses direction, backs carefully out of the fissure. The rider kills the engine, gets off, walks toward Abby. She can't tell who it is; the figure is bundled up with a hat and face mask.

Abby gulps, stands her ground. The rider strides up to her, stares at her. Then screams and shoves her. Abby reels backward and slips, landing hard on the ice. And then the figure is on top of her, screaming in her face. It's Zoe.

"I *knew* it was you! I knew he was going out here to see you!"

"Zoe, it's not—"

"How long have you been doing this? Do you think I'm an idiot?"

They roll on the ground, clutching and hitting at each other. Abby finally manages to hold her still. Then she gets into her face and says, *"Listen to me. I'm not screwing your husband. I'm not."*

This gets Zoe's attention. "Then what are you doing here?" she demands. "Why is Larry here?"

Abby tells her.

Zoe pauses. "That is the biggest crock I've ever heard." But her statement lacks conviction, and Abby can see she isn't truly surprised.

"Go check for yourself," Abby says.

Zoe slowly shakes her head. "No. No, I don't want to see it." Abby is relieved.

They slowly get to their feet, and Abby can see the tears in her friend's eyes. Meanwhile, Abby's shock, and her own tears, have given way to anger. The *bastard.*

"I should have known," Zoe says. "Maybe at some level I did know what he was. But he married me anyway. He's been married before—he knows being married won't change things." She's starting to get angry, too.

Zoe starts toward the fish house.

"Where are you going?" Abby asks.

Zoe stops and turns back. "Where do you *think* I'm going? I'm putting an end to this."

"And then what? We all just go on like nothing happened? Cheating is cheating, Z." She realizes she has used her friend's high school nickname.

"Well, what do *you* think we should do?" Zoe demands.

"I think—I think we should . . ." She pauses, reevaluating, reviewing the lie that was her entire married life. All her husband's unexplained absences. All his coldness toward her. All his chummy, slightly uncomfortable friendships with other men. She chokes back her anger and tears. Then she remembers a whole lot of other things about her husband, things that have nothing to do with his sexuality. His indolence. His indifference toward the children, and toward her. His willingness to let her work herself to the bone to support the family. And his loud, embarrassing bullshit—the nonstop, inane patter that drives her up the wall.

She walks over, retrieves the gun, lingers in front of the door, rage building. Her hand reaches for the door handle. She takes deep breaths, snuffling through her tears in the frigid air. Then she carefully relocks the door and returns the key to her pocket. Her hand is numb. *She* is numb. She shuffles back to Zoe.

Zoe's eyes widen when she sees the gun. "You're going to shoot him?"

Abby looks down at the pistol in her hand, then up at her friend. Rick has destroyed her life. If she shoots him—goes to jail—the remainder of it will be destroyed, too. She pockets the gun and puts her chopper mitten back on. "I've got a better idea, Z. We need a girls' night out."

❈

Five nights later, Abby and Zoe sit in the Reiters' truck, engine running, lights out, on the shore of Pine Lake, with a clear view of the fish house in the moonlight. "How did you get the truck?" Abby asks.

Zoe shrugs. "I just told him I needed it tonight. I grabbed the key off the hook and walked out."

"The direct approach," Abby says. "Couldn't Larry take the ATV?"

"It won't start. I made sure of that."

Rick told Abby he's coming out here tonight. Zoe has made sure Larry won't be joining him.

They sit in silence. Then Zoe says, "Larry really is a sweet guy. He's really fond of me. He just . . . is how he is. We'll both have to move on."

Abby asks, "What will you do?"

"After I leave Larry?" She shrugs. "I'm going to stay here. I'll rent a cheap, crappy apartment somewhere in town. I'll keep doing nails. And eventually I'll latch onto some other man. Maybe a loser, maybe better. That's what I do."

"It shouldn't have to be that way."

Zoe doesn't respond. After a while, she says, "What about you? What will happen after—this?" She gestures toward the lake.

"I'm thinking about moving."

"Where?"

"The Cities are too big for me. Maybe Duluth."

"Don't," Zoe says. "Stay. Keep me company."

A faint smile crosses Abby's face. "We'll see." It might be interesting, she thinks. Living in this town could be a different experience without Rick. She might be able to look people in the eye instead of dying of embarrassment. The kids might not mind coming home once in a while.

But, whether she stayed or left, this situation would not stand. She would not put up with it for a single day longer. Rick would not be hanging around to torment her, mooch off her, humiliate her, keep destroying her life. Or destroy anybody else's life.

Their girls' night out, two evenings ago, took place not at a bar or restaurant, but here at the lake. It was past eleven when Abby told Rick the hospital called her into work. Then, after throwing some tools into the truck, she drove to the lake, where she met Zoe. With her friend's help, she pried the fish house loose from the ice. It wasn't hard; there hasn't been any thawing or refreezing. Some chipping, some prying with a crowbar, and some careful pushing with the truck, and they had it loose in less than half an hour. Then they extended the wheels on the house—thanks to a YouTube instructional video from the manufacturer, Abby knew how to do it. After that, they hooked the structure up to the truck and towed it two hundred feet to the south and east.

After retracting the wheels, they drove in a wide, careful circle around the house, stopped, and examined their handiwork. The new location is roughly the same distance from the ice road, but at a slightly different angle. Out by itself on a large lake, with no nearby houses or other landmarks, Rick wouldn't notice the change.

Now they sit in silence. Then Zoe says, "You sure about this?"

"More than anything in my life."

They watch the ice road. A vehicle drives out onto the lake from shore. They watch the headlights move slowly along the ice road—and past Rick's fish house. A few minutes later, a snowmobile zooms by about a quarter-mile away.

They wait.

Twenty minutes later, another set of headlights begins to make its way across the ice. They can now make out the outline of the vehicle; it's a pickup. She can't make out any details of the truck, but somehow, she knows it's his. Abby's breathing becomes shallow as her husband proceeds to the turnoff from the ice road. And then he turns.

He makes directly for the fish house. He doesn't slow down. He doesn't have a clue.

It happens suddenly. The headlights drop to the ice. Then below it. Then, after shifting and rocking, bobbing and churning, the rest of the truck goes in. Goes under.

Zoe grabs Abby's hand. But Abby is calm. Dry-eyed. She's made the decision, and she's at peace with it. Moving the fish house behind the area with the thin ice seemed a more logical option than shooting Rick, and it still does. And, of course, it seems a fitting way to go.

They watch the darkened area on the ice where the truck went through. It's quiet now. Nothing happening. They wait another twenty minutes.

Zoe says, "Time to go home, Abs."

For the first time in twenty-two years, that's a suggestion that sounds good to Abby.

END

BRIAN LUTTERMAN is the author of *Downfall*, which launched the Pen Wilkinson series and is described by *Mystery Gazette* as ". . . an exhilarating action-packed financial thriller . . ." His other books include *Windfall*, *Freefall*, and *Nightfall*, the highly praised sequels to *Downfall*, and *Bound to Die*, a Minnesota Book Award runner-up. Lutterman, a former trial and corporate attorney, writes cutting-edge corporate thrillers, bringing to life the genre's outsized conflicts and characters with breathtaking action and suspense. He lives with his family in the Twin Cities. Visit his website at: www.brianlutterman.com.

PRANK
By T.S. Owen

"G et down! Get down!" Jack grabbed Blair, pulling her down behind one of the overgrown evergreens lining the path to Nopeming Sanatorium. Thundering footsteps approached them as two bodies flew past, running as if the devil himself was behind them.

"Run, dude! Run! Keep going! We'll be able to get a signal back at the car!" shouted one of the boys. Their voices faded into the darkness of the late summer night as the two disappeared around a curve in the trail.

Blair jumped up, weaving a bit. "Chickens!" she yelled after them. She drained her beer and tossed the empty bottle at the retreating figures. It shattered a good way down the path. "Jeez! Kids these days. Scared of a few ghosts! Hand me my backpack, Jack." She laughed out loud. "Back. Pack. Jack. I'm a poet and don't I know it!" she sang.

"Come on, Blair. We should leave. I don't think this is such a good idea." Jack swatted at the legions of mosquitoes that swarmed around them. He got to his feet, handing Blair her backpack while reaching for her arm, hoping to lead her in the direction the boys had taken.

"Nope, nope, nope. Nopeming awaits." She danced just out of his reach as she dug into her backpack and pulled out a bottle of Bent Paddle Black Ale. Twisting off the cap, she drained half the bottle in one long pull, releasing a loud belch that echoed into the night.

"Nice, Blair. I'm sure they heard that over in Wisconsin." Jack grimaced, shaking his head.

Blair stumbled forward, arm outstretched, her finger pointing the way. "Follow me, baby cakes."

They rounded another turn in the path and there stood the imposing remains of the legendary Nopeming Sanatorium. Once a thriving hospital, the forty-acre complex of century-old brick and stone buildings was now abandoned, a dare for every first-year frat boy at UMD and the dream location of every paranormal investigator in the upper Midwest.

"Crap, that's frickin' huge!"

"Yep! Come on, Jackie Boy, we're headed for that roof top." Blair pointed to the top of the tallest building. "Just wait till you see the view. I bet you can see all the way across the lake to Canada from up there."

"You'd lose that bet, Blair. We shouldn't even be here. We passed at least a hundred 'No Trespassing' signs on the way up here."

"Sixty-seven actually. Sixty. Seven. I counted." Blair drained her beer and tossed the empty across the cracked cement sidewalk. She pulled out another and shoved her backpack into Jack's hands. "Come on, college boy. We'll take the fire escape on the far side of the main building."

Jack shook his head. He reached into the pack and grabbed a bottle of Black Ale for himself. His first. Someone had to keep a clear head.

"This is gonna be a long ass night," he mumbled.

"Heard that!" drifted back to him as Blair disappeared around the corner of the building.

�֎

"Well? Is this the view I promised you?" Blair spread her arms wide and spun in an unsteady circle before collapsing on the tarpaper rooftop with a giggle. She waved her hands around her head. "Except for the mosquitoes. Blood thirsty buggers."

Dark wooded hills stretched out in all directions. The lights of Duluth were visible to the northwest, but the vast blackness of Lake Superior dominated the horizon. Freighters anchored offshore sparkled like stars in the night sky. Jack had to admit, it was breathtaking.

"Once in a while, when the wind shifts, you can hear music from the Blues Fest in the Park. It's pretty cool if you like the blues." She pushed herself up to her feet, swaying back and forth. "Come on, Jackie Boy. Dance with me."

"No thanks." He shook his head, pulling his cell phone from his back pocket.

"Put the damn phone away, Jack. She's not gonna call you or text you. Dude, she broke up with you. Move on."

He raised his arm, watching the lit screen. "Damn it. There's no signal up here either."

Jack slipped the phone back in his pocket and sat down, dangling his feet over the edge. "She texted me, Blair. A damn text. Who breaks up with you by text message? I've been trying to call her for two days. What the hell?" He finished off his beer and tossed it over his shoulder into a pile of bottles near a vent hood. The odor of stale beer drifted back, making him wonder how many times Blair had been on this rooftop.

Off in the distance, a police siren broke the still night air. It was going to be another busy night for the boys in blue, he thought.

She dropped down beside him, laying her head on his shoulder. "Jackie. My Jackie Boy. She's not worth it. Let her go." She wrapped her arms around him, snuggling as close as she could. "You asked a girl to marry you by text. That's so uncool. What did you expect?"

Jack jerked his head around to stare down at her. "I never asked her to marry me. I said I had something important to ask her . . . and how do you even know about that?"

"I was with her when you sent it. She freaked out, man. Said she wasn't ready to get married." Blair rubbed her face along Jack's arm, purring like a kitten . . . a drunk kitten. "I'll take your mind off her. Promise. I'm a much more fun date than boring ol' Amanda."

"You know, I always thought you two were best friends, but it's just been a competition for you. Right? When did it start? High school?"

"God, yes! High school sucked! All I ever heard was 'perfect Amanda, pretty Amanda, sweet Amanda.'" Blair spat the words out like poison. Her dark eyes glittered in the moonlight. "Everybody loved her. Teacher's pet. Everyone's favorite cheerleader. Made me sick."

"It was you, wasn't it?" Jack tried to pull away from her, his eyes wide. "You were the one who moved the 'thin ice' signs on Fish Lake. The night her snowmobile broke through? She nearly died that night!" Blair grinned and nodded her head. "And you put the hair remover in her hair conditioner before the Dairy Queen competition. You did it."

She threw her head back and laughed. "Hell yeah! Funny, right?

That was my crown and I did what I had to." Blair closed her eyes, a malicious smile spreading across her face. "My crown. My sash. Princess Kay of the Milky Way. I'm royalty, Jackie Boy. Come on," she cooed, snuggling closer. "Let's have an adventure."

Jack unwound himself from Blair and stood. His face was unreadable.

Blair jumped to her feet, rocking unsteadily toward the edge of the roof. He grabbed her shoulders, pulling her back.

"Careful, Princess. It's a long way down."

"My hero!" She batted her eyes at Jack in a failed attempt to be seductive.

"Yeah, right. So, where are these ghosts that you keep talking about?" He slapped the back of his neck. "Please say somewhere deep inside this building because these mosquitoes are eating me alive."

❖

They accessed the main building through a broken window midway down the fire escape. Blair took the lead using a flashlight she'd pulled from her backpack. She seemed to know her way through the maze of hallways and staircases.

"This way," she whispered. "Be really careful. There's crap all over the floor." She turned and placed the flashlight under her chin. "Some say it's the bones of the lost souls who never made it out of here alive. Bahahaha!"

"Yeah. Not. More likely the bones of dead rodents. Can you smell that? What is that?" Jack covered his mouth, gagging. "We should've brought face masks."

They stumbled deeper into the building led only by the unsteady beam of Blair's flashlight. The constant drip of water and the occasional squeaks of four-legged critters were the only sounds they could hear deep in the old building. That and the persistent crunching underfoot.

Not bones, Jack repeated to himself. Not bones.

"How much farther?"

"Just up ahead. Shhhh . . . hear that? Hear that wailing sound?" Blair paused for effect. "They say it's the ghost of a nurse who hung herself because her one true love abandoned her for another woman. Isn't that sad?"

Jack stopped for a moment, listening intently. He could hear a faint voice. "Sounds more like someone calling for help." He yanked the flashlight from Blair's hand and ran down the hallway, following the sounds of the voice.

"Wait up, Jackie. Don't leave me all alone." Blair jogged after him, laughing.

Jack burst through a doorway and skidded to a halt. "What the hell?"

The handles of two massive cast iron doors were wrapped with bike chains and padlocked shut. Faint pounding came from inside the massive boiler followed by a weak voice. "Help me. Please. Someone. Help me!"

"Amanda? Amanda! Is that you, baby girl?"

"Jack? Jack! Get me out of here. She tricked me. She trapped me in here and locked me in."

Jack spun around to face Blair. "You did what? Are you crazy? You could've killed her! Where's the key to the padlock, Blair? Where's the damn key?"

"Aw, come on, Jackie Boy. It was just a prank. Just having a laugh." Blair stumbled backwards under Jack's glare and the harsh beam of the flashlight. "Just a prank. No harm done."

"The. Key. Where is it?"

Blair's face went blank. She gave him no answer, only stared back at him.

In disgust, he turned and began to scour the floor, looking for something to free Amanda. He dropped the flashlight, grabbed a large rock in both hands, and began to beat on the padlock.

"Freeze! Don't move!"

Jack spun around. Two St. Louis County deputies stood in the doorway, weapons drawn and pointed directly at Blair. Their flashlight beams reflected off a length of rebar held high over Blair's head.

"Drop it. Drop it now!" shouted Deputy "Trunk" Miller.

The rebar clattered to the floor.

"You okay, son?" Deputy Miller asked without taking his eyes off Blair.

"What the hell, Blair? What the hell?" Jack shook his head in disbelief. "Yeah. Yes, sir. I'm okay but my girlfriend, she's trapped in the boiler here." He dropped the rock and pointed at the chained doors.

Blair let out a wail and ran blindly for the door. She bounced off the brick wall that was Deputy TC Leville. Arms flailing, she fell back and hit the floor raising a cloud of dust.

"Let me help you up." Deputy Leville holstered his weapon and offered a hand to Blair.

She slapped it away, struggling to her feet. Strings of profanity laced the air. "Don't touch me. Don't you touch me. Do you know who I am? Do you?"

"You best restrain her, TC. Search her backpack, too."

Blair began to cry as the deputy brought her arms behind her back and slipped a pair of cuffs on her. He pulled on a pair of latex gloves and lifted her backpack. "Ma'am, is there anything in here that's gonna poke me or hurt me?"

"Of course not," she replied indignantly. "Wouldn't tell you if there was, you idiot. Would serve you right," she said under her breath.

"You know I can hear you, right?" TC said as he began to search the bag.

Deputy Miller holstered his own weapon and stepped back into the hallway. He returned with a pair of large bolt cutters. "You don't know just how lucky you are. A couple of boys called 911 a bit ago. Claimed they were down here and heard some woman trapped in the old boiler. She was screaming for help. They said she was chained in." He maneuvered the bolt cutters in place. After a couple of tries, he was able to cut the lock and began unwinding the chains. "We thought at first it was a prank but figured we best check it out."

As the ancient doors creaked slowly open, Amanda's tear-stained face appeared. She was covered in dust, her long blond hair matted and tangled with debris. "There you go, miss. Be careful now." Deputy Miller offered his hand to Amanda, helping her through the rusted opening of the boiler.

She ran into Jack's open arms.

"It's okay, Amanda. You're safe now." Jack held her close.

"Blair tricked me. She said 'Get in and I'll take a picture. We'll send it to Jack.'" Amanda sobbed and pointed to Blair. "She took my phone and left me here to die."

"Liar!" Blair screamed. "It was just a prank!"

"Well, what have we here?" TC pulled two cell phones out of Blair's backpack.

"That's mine!" Amanda shouted. "The one with the pink case? It's mine."

All eyes turned to Blair.

"It was just a freakin' prank, you guys. Can't you take a joke? A prank. A prank!"

"Well, this is no joke, Blair. Listen carefully," Deputy Lavelle said as he took Blair by the arm and led her away. "You have the right to remain silent. Anything you say can and will be used against you in a court of law. You have the right to an attorney . . ." His voice faded away as they moved farther down the corridor.

Blair could be heard screaming: "I'm Princess Kay! I'm royalty. My head was carved in butter! In freakin' butter!"

"Deputy, could you give us a minute alone please? We'll be right up, if that's okay?" Jack asked, holding Amanda close.

"Sure thing. We have EMTs en route to check her out. See you up there. Don't be long." He handed his flashlight to Jack, pulling another from his duty belt, and left the boiler room.

Jack held Amanda at arm's length and looked her over closely. "You okay? I bet you're starving."

"I am. My food ran out last night. Water ran out this morning." She smiled up at him. "You were right. I should've packed more, but I didn't want Blair to get suspicious."

Jack shook his head. "You are either the craziest woman I've ever known or the bravest. Don't you realize she could've killed you?"

Amanda smiled weakly. "I've known her forever and I know all too well how that twisted little mind of hers works." She shuddered, recalling the events leading up to Blair's latest prank. "I knew if I planted the idea in her head, she'd run with it."

Amanda reached back into the boiler to grab her backpack. "We were watching one of those paranormal investigator shows. You know, the one with the guy who always takes his shirt off? Anyway, as soon as they showed this boiler room, the idea just came to me and I said 'Wouldn't it be an awful way to die? Trapped in that rusty old tomb?' I could practically hear the wheels start to turn. She was all over it."

"It was so risky, Amanda. I don't know what I would've done if she'd"—he hesitated to even say the words—"if she'd killed you."

"She'd never kill me outright. She'd rather imagine me suffering a long slow death, trapped in that monstrosity," she said pointing back at the boiler. "And thinking you were ready to propose to me, well that just set her off. I knew it would."

"She never suspected a thing and now she's going away for a very long time. She won't be able to hurt you anymore." Jack pulled her close and kissed the top of her head. They walked out of the boiler room, hand in hand.

"No more pranks?" she asked softly.

"No more pranks."

END

After kicking around the corporate nonprofit world for over twenty years, **T.S. OWEN** escaped to the exciting life of broadcast sports production and cat herding. She began writing mysteries shortly after and co-edited the *Dark Side of the Loon* anthology (published 2018). Ms. Owen is the immediate past president of the Twin Cities Chapter of Sisters in Crime and serves as Advisor to the Board. She moderates author panels across the upper Midwest, and manages TCSinC's social media presence. She resides in Woodbury, Minnesota.

CHOICES

By Carol Huss

September 1984

Three miles after Karen turned onto County 11, her Crown Vic's high beams flashed over a figure trudging along on the gravel shoulder. The man wore a filthy camouflage coat and a knit beanie pulled down tight on his head. He carried a rifle straight up behind his right shoulder.

She slowed and the engine pinged. He turned at the sound, sticking out his thumb.

The light glanced across his face. He looked young, seventeen or eighteen. He squinted when he saw the roof lights and "sheriff" written across the side panel, turned his back and kept walking, shrugging his rifle higher on his shoulder. There was something familiar about the defiant lift of his chin.

She let the car crawl along beside him and rolled down the passenger window.

"Where're you headed?" She kept her voice neutral.

He hunched his shoulders and kept walking.

"I'm going to Enid," she said. "Happy to give you a ride."

He kept walking.

Stubborn piece of—and just like that, she remembered his name.

"Sean Thorvaald." She stopped the car with a jolt. "Get in."

Sean took two more steps, then stopped, staring straight ahead. The morning mist clouded the windshield and she flicked on the wipers while he weighed his options. After a long moment he unslung his rifle. Her right hand instinctively moved toward her sidearm as he opened the door. He wasn't looking at her though; he settled into the passenger seat, holding the rifle like a shield in front of his chest. He stared out at the pink-orange horizon above the half-harvested cornfield. Karen stepped on the gas and continued toward town.

The radio squawked with chatter between county deputies and the state patrol. She turned the volume down.

"Karen Swanson," she said, holding out her hand. "You and my son went to the same grade school."

He ignored her hand. "I know who you are."

Neither of them spoke for several miles.

"Ever notice that towns around here have grandma names?" she asked as they passed the green 'Enid—Population 304' sign. "Florence, Ruth, Luverne, Enid . . .'"

She glanced sideways. No reaction.

"You gonna do some hunting?"

No answer.

She abandoned small talk. "I'm sorry about your dad, Sean." She kept her voice even. "I didn't get a chance to tell you at the funeral." Because Sean hadn't gone to the funeral.

His shoulders hunched higher. She reduced speed as she reached Enid's main street.

"Have you had breakfast?"

A slight shake of his head. "Gonna get my dad's truck from Yancey's." His voice tightened, the words forced out.

"They won't be open yet. My treat."

She backed into a space next to Ada's Café. As she opened the café door, a rush of deep fryer-scented air ruffled her hair and the jukebox's bleating "Karma Chameleon" offended her ears. Alice Gruber, the café owner, waved a hand from behind the counter. There was no "Ada" at Ada's Café and as far as Karen knew, there never had been.

"Deputy Karen," Alice called. "I've got your eggs started."

"Make it two." Karen nodded toward Sean.

Karen filled two mugs of coffee and sat elbow-to-elbow with Sean at the counter.

"Staying with your mom?" Karen asked.

A small shake of his head. "My dad's place."

She raised her eyebrows.

He shook his head. "Not the farm. He was renting ten acres near Florence."

Alice's curious gaze, like a lighthouse beam, swung across the griddle and then back around to her only customers.

"What're you going to do now?" Karen asked. It was none of her business, but he was just a few years older than her son.

He shrugged. "He had a dozen dairy cows; I'll keep going with them."

Karen sipped her coffee.

"I know how to farm," he said, as if she argued with him. "All I need is an operating loan to feed my cows, then sell the milk. Tomorrow I'll go see the banker."

She merely nodded. Alice set two plates in front of them. Sean gripped his fork tight, shoveling in the eggs and hash browns as if he hadn't eaten in a while. Likely he hadn't.

Karen figured his chances of getting a loan were less than the odds of winning the rib-eye steak at the Legion's Wednesday night meat raffle.

❈

Enid High School closed two years ago, another casualty of the population decline, so Karen's son Mark bussed to Pipestone Senior High. Today, he'd stayed late for wrestling practice and she had to pick him up. She welcomed the trip, though. The seventeen-mile drive fostered conversation with the teenager; Mark just couldn't keep quiet the whole way home.

Mark bounced out of the gym doors, swinging his Class of '86 jacket and running backwards while talking to a very cute girl. Karen knew better than to mention this when he got in the car; instead she asked about something that had been on her mind all day.

"Mark, do you know Sean Thorvaald?"

"The kid whose dad offed himself?" He tossed an M&M into the air and let it plop into his mouth. He caught her look. "What? That's what happened."

"You don't have to be so—" she shook her head. "Yes. His father committed suicide after he lost his farm."

"Seen him around. Don't really know him." He tossed another M&M. "Why?"

"I picked him up this morning, hitchhiking into town."

Mark shrugged. "Well, I know he's a military fanatic. He dresses like a commando. Always carries his rifle. Good shot, too."

"Does he have any friends?"

"He never hangs out with anyone I know." He turned in his seat. "Is this how it's gonna be, Mom? Asking me 'bout people you're arresting?"

"I didn't say I was arresting him."

"Do you expect me to rat people out?"

"Mark—"

"Your job sucks, Mom, you know that?"

She tightened her lips against a reply.

"Sorry," Mark said. "I know you grew up around here. You probably didn't have many choices for work."

She sighed. "We used to have three groceries and five restaurants in Enid. Today there's one of each, and neither is doing too well."

"With the town shrinking and all the farmers are selling out, why do we stay?"

"I ask myself that every day."

"What do you answer yourself?"

"I still—" but she ended her thought with a shrug.

Mark turned his head away. "I don't understand why you do anything. Like why you and Dad are divorced."

Bam! It struck like a lightning bolt on a sunny day.

She swallowed. "What did your dad say?"

"He said it was between you and him and none of my business. But that you would always be my parents."

Mark's mock sweet voice didn't detract from the sensibility of that statement. She felt her eyes fill. Sometimes Tom could be—

"And he said it was all your fault."

—such a jerk.

✳

The next morning, Karen parked the squad outside the Enid Community Bank. Harv Anderson, the bank's owner, needed an escort to serve a farmer some papers. As she stepped out of her car, Sean Thorvaald stomped out the bank's front door.

One of Harv's sons—eight-year-old Jimmy, she thought—skipped around the corner and reached for the door.

Sean stopped and looked at the little boy. "Hey, kid. That banker your daddy?"

Jimmy nodded, backing up a little.

Sean aimed his index finger at the boy. "Bang," Sean said. "Dead before you hit the ground."

"Sean!" Karen stepped between Sean and the little boy, pushing Jimmy toward the building. The boy turned and ran around to the side door of the bank.

"Oh hell, lady, what?" He raised his chin. He was four inches taller than her and his short-cropped blond hair made his head look round and bare.

"Was that necessary? He's just a kid!"

Sean flung up his middle finger, jumped into a rusty two-toned pickup, and gunned the engine. Its damaged muffler roared like a badly tuned tractor as he drove away.

Harv Anderson stepped out, buttoning his topcoat.

"Harv." She nodded.

"Deputy. Sean Thorvaald just scared the crap out of my boy Jimmy."

"I saw. Was he looking for a loan?"

Harv raised his eyebrows. "Let's just say I wasn't able to help him."

She watched the receding truck. "Did he say where he was going?"

Harv shook his head. "He said he was leaving town, and I say good riddance. One less hot-head to deal with." Harv held up a large brown envelope. "Onto the next unpleasant task. Thanks for doing this."

"It's my job," she said.

"Yeah. And this is my job." Harv looked down at the envelope, nearly crushed in his grip. "You know what? Our jobs stink."

"Let's go," Karen said, pointing to the passenger door.

"Okay. The car and your uniform should head off any rash response to this notice."

"You expecting trouble?"

"Petersen, like most farmers, is an independent cuss and won't admit he needs help. Hate to say it but most of his problems are the result of poor farm management. Judy got a job in Marshall and that helped." He sighed. "Last time I went out there, I suggested he sell some land to meet the loan obligations."

"What did he say to that?"

"He ordered me off his property."

✳

The visit to Petersen's went as Harv predicted; her official presence kept the mood restrained. Harv delivered the papers and they left.

"Can we swing by the old Thorvaald place?" Harv asked.

"Sure." Karen turned onto County 11. "You think the Thorvaald kid will try something before he leaves town?"

"No. Power's off. Ronnie Thorvaald trashed the place. He even ripped out all the plumbing fixtures before he—well, there's nothing left to steal. But the bank owns it, so I'd like to check on it. You never know when a buyer might turn up."

✳

The white and green farmhouse looked solid from the road, but as she drove into the yard she could see the peeling paint and drooping gutters. She pulled up behind the shed and they walked toward the house. Knee-high grass nearly obscured the stone walkway. The shed door hung on one hinge.

"I hate to see it like this," Harv said. "Ronnie kept his place in order. He was one hell of a chore-man—a real hard worker. Never was much with numbers, though. He didn't know an asset from a liability."

Harv unlocked the back door. A gaping hole in the wall and pipes snaking nowhere showed where the kitchen sink used to be.

"Just like he left it. He even ripped out the bathtub." Harv shook his head. "Guess he figured to make it harder for the bank to sell. That was three years ago. He moved to that place near Florence, and did odd jobs. Sean went to his mother's. Last month, the neighbor, Mrs. Rubbelke, called me when she saw Ronnie's truck out here. I came right out; I was afraid he was gonna burn the place down. Instead, he went out to the barn and . . ." His voice trailed off.

They walked through the house, but Harv didn't see anything amiss. They headed back outside. Karen glanced into the shed; there was nothing inside but equipment parts scattered on the dirt floor. They moved to the barn and swung open the small service door.

The pole barn had a cement floor with milking bays in two rows down the center. Unlike the shed, it was clear of debris.

"Ronnie was over there," Harv pointed to a workbench in one corner. "Shotgun blast to the head."

Karen could see a dark stain on the cement floor.

"I'll wait by the car," Harv said.

Karen walked deeper into the dark space. The chilled air smelled of mold and machine oil. She ran her hand along the battered bench top. No dirt, just a faint oil residue. She looked around, then squatted down. Underneath the bench, nearly out of sight, was a tarp-covered crate. She dragged the crate out, pulled back the tarp and shined her flashlight inside. About a dozen silver boxes of Winchester .308 shells filled the crate. She stood, looked around the barn. Nothing else. She carried the crate out to the car.

"Hey Harv, pop the trunk for me," she called.

"What'd you find?" Harv asked

"Boxes of ammo. I don't suppose it belongs to the bank?"

Harv shook his head. "No ma'am."

"Looks like about two hundred rounds. I'm confiscating it. And I think I'd better find out more about the Thorvaalds."

❊

The sun hovered low in the southwest when she dropped Harv back at the bank. She sat for a moment, then picked up the radio.

"Pipestone County," Marjorie's voice crackled a little.

"This is 244."

"Hey, Karen."

"Can you pull the Ronnie Thorvaald file?"

"Sure thing. What do you need to know?"

"Who did the autopsy?"

"Anoka County's the closest Medical Examiner. Doc White."

"Can you read the findings?"

"One sec."

The sound of paper rustling. Marjorie always left the microphone cued.

"Here it is. Cause of death: shotgun blast to the head. Shotgun was next to the body."

"Can you get me the doc's phone number?"

She wrote it on her hand and went over to Ada's to use the phone.

❊

On Thursday morning, Karen stopped at Ada's on her way to Pipestone.

"Breakfast?" Alice called.

"Just coffee. Mark missed the bus, so I have to take him to school."

"In the county car?" Alice asked.

"Yeah. Maybe riding in the 'fuzz-mobile' will make him think twice about sleeping in."

Alice handed her a to-go cup. "Looks like Harv's finally got someone interested in the Thorvaald place. A guy wanted to meet him out there this morning."

Karen sipped the coffee. "Good for Harv," she said. "Selling that place might bring closure for everybody."

Harv had said it earlier: their jobs stunk. Bankers like Harv did what they could to keep their own businesses going but that meant serving papers and auctioning off equipment. Over the last three years, she'd had to evict neighbors from land they'd held for generations. Friends lashed back at her because of the star she wore. She used to think of herself as someone who settled problems, but seeing all sides during this farm crisis made settling them harder, not easier.

Mark's head nodded against the door as she eased the car onto County 23. The radio squawked.

"244—Lyon County deputy advises someone shot all the cattle and burned the trailer on a rental farm in Florence. Fire department just left. Property owner is pretty sure the tenant did it."

She knew the answer, but she asked anyway. "Who's the tenant?"

"Originally, Ronnie Thorvaald. His kid took over the lease. Sean, I think his name is."

"Damn it! I hoped he was leaving. Marjorie, call over to the bank and tell Harv Anderson to stay put. I'll head to the old Thorvaald place after I drop Mark."

"Calling now."

"Mom!" Mark leaned forward, wide awake. "That's the opposite direction. It'll take an hour to get back there from school."

She looked at his eager eyes. "You have any tests today?"

He shook his head. "Swear to God."

"Karen." Marjorie sounded worried, even through the radio static. "Harv already left to meet that buyer."

"Heading there now. Have Bill meet me out there."

She U-turned, stomped on the gas, and sped north.

❖

Mark leaned into his shoulder belt, as if he could push the car faster with his body weight.

"You think Sean Thorvaald would hurt Mr. Anderson?"

"I don't want to take any chances."

"Who's that?" Mark said, pointing down the hill.

A two-toned truck idled on a side road, about a half-mile ahead. She eased her foot off the gas. A figure in green camouflage stood next to the truck, holding a rifle in classic aiming stance.

"Down!" Karen pushed at Mark's head as she slammed on the brakes. Two spots of dust geysered ten feet to the left of her car. Karen reversed and backed as fast as the Crown Vic would go. The figure got into the truck and drove away, its muffler a loud growl in the distance. Karen braked, put her car in drive, and followed.

"Pipestone County, this is 244, the suspect for the Florence arson is headed north on County 23, a half mile north of Aetna Township Road. Shots fired. I repeat, shots fired. He may be headed toward the old Thorvaald place."

"Copy," came Marjorie's voice.

"Marjorie, have Bill call me on tac 2."

"Tac 2. Copy."

"He shot at us?" Mark asked, still crouched, head below the dashboard.

She nodded. "Twice."

"I didn't hear anything."

"Stay down."

Ahead, the truck topped a rise, its brake lights bright as it went over the hill and disappeared. Karen stomped the brakes and stopped the car, breathing hard.

"What?" Mark asked. "Aren't you going after him?"

Karen shook her head. "He hit his brakes as he went over the hill. He's waiting for us."

She switched the radio to tac 2. "Bill, what's your location?"

"Fifteen miles north of Florence."

"Sean Thorvaald just took two shots at my vehicle. I think he may be headed to his dad's old place."

"I'm headed there now. ETA 15 minutes."

"Have Marjorie alert the state patrol. We need back-up."

"Wait for back-up, Karen. Sounds like the kid's nuts."

"Can't. Harv Anderson is on his way out there to meet a potential buyer."

She rolled her window down and leaned her head out.

"What are you doing?" For some reason, Mark whispered.

She held up her hand. In the distance, she heard the growling muffler, growing fainter on the other side of the hill. She put the car in gear.

"Bill, I'm approaching the Thorvaald place from the east. There's a new driveway behind Rubbelke's that the kid may not know about. ETA 5 minutes."

"Copy 244."

She turned right, then left, pressing the accelerator hard. After three miles she pulled into a farm yard and jolted to a stop.

"Mark, out. Go to Rubbelke's and stay there."

For once, Mark didn't argue, but his eyes rounded as she released the strap on her handgun. After he slammed the door she drove across the yard to the back drive, then accelerated. She could see the green roof of the Thorvaald house. Harv's gold Impala sat next to it.

"Damn!" She stepped harder on the gas, crossing the unplowed pasture, swearing again as the car bottomed out in an unseen rut. She steered right and the car answered, groaning as it crossed a cattle guard. Harv, standing near the shed, looked up in surprise.

Over to her right, Sean Thorvaald's truck roared down the half-mile driveway.

❈

She picked up the mic and toggled the outside speaker: "Harv! Get down! Down!" and willed Harv to understand.

Harv jumped behind his car and hugged the ground as Thorvaald fish-tailed into the yard, braking in a big arc. The truck door flew open and he rolled out, rising to one knee to aim at the banker. She could see his mouth move, heard a shot. She steered right at him, then swung the wheel left and skidded sideways in the gravel.

Sean swung the rifle toward her.

Don't let Mark see this, she prayed, braking hard and opening the door. She slid out of the car, her service weapon in her hand. The windshield shattered and a bullet tore through the back of the headrest. A single siren wailed, then a second, but too far off. Her heart pounded. God! She was going to have to shoot this kid.

"Drop your weapon!" She shouted, bracing her forearms on the hood of her car. Sean fired again and she squeezed the trigger. Once. Twice. The boy dropped.

Harv poked his head around the front of his car.

"Stay put, Harv!" She stood slowly, watching the hand that clutched the rifle. The kid groaned and she ran, stepping on his arm and pulling the rifle away. She rolled him to his belly, pulled out her handcuffs, and cuffed him. She rolled him back, and saw that she'd shot his right arm and shoulder.

"God, Sean," she whispered. "What were you thinking?" As she ran back to the car to radio for an ambulance, another deputy sheriff and a state trooper raced into the yard.

⁕

Shootings generated more paperwork than foreclosures. Mark waited through the afternoon as she typed her reports. He stayed uncharacteristically quiet and she found she couldn't stand his silence.

"Regardless of the circumstances," she said, feeling her way, "this happened because of who Sean was."

Mark looked up. "But how did he get to be that way?"

She leaned back in her chair and looked into her son's troubled eyes. "I think it takes lots of choices, day after day, like drops of water filling a bucket. Sure, his family and experiences shape him. Nature plays a part, too. But he chooses for himself, thousands of times. No one makes him what he is—he makes himself."

"But what if he doesn't *have* a choice?" Mark asked.

"It might seem like there's no choice because he's blind to other possibilities. Refusing to see any other option *is* a choice."

Mark absorbed this, and as she expected, turned the conversation to the question he really wanted to ask.

"So what's your choice?" Mark's brows twitched a little. "Are we staying or going?"

She took a big swig from her soda. "I'd like to stay. Maybe I can help a few people with their choices." She watched his face. "You okay with that?"

Mark nodded. "Yeah. Your job still sucks, but you're really good at it. If it wasn't for you, Mr. Anderson . . ." He sighed. "I feel like I should hug you, but I'm all hugged out." After the shooting, Mark had run over from Rubbelke's and grabbed Karen hard, taking them both to the ground. It had taken him a long time to let her go.

He stood and tossed his soda can into the trash. "*I* choose to not think about this any more."

She laughed and tossed her can, too.

❊

She stopped by the hospital after taking Mark home.

"You gonna preach at me?' Sean sneered. "I already got prayed over by a professional, so don't waste your time."

She stood a foot inside the doorway. "Just wanted to see how you were."

"That banker had it coming," he said.

"You're still under arrest," she said. "Your words can be used against you."

Sean sank back into the pillows, his face turned away.

She watched him closely. "Your dad worked hard trying to keep his farm."

"Hard work don't matter when bankers want their money."

"Harv is not responsible for years of drought, rock-bottom milk prices, or sky-rocketing interest rates. Your dad had other choices. So did you."

Sean kept his gaze turned away.

She took a step closer to the bed. "I asked the Medical Examiner to take a second look at how your dad died. He did some new calculations and said that shotgun blast had to have come from several feet away. No way your dad fired that gun himself."

Sean sat up, his lips a feral snarl.

"My *dad!*" A drop of spittle flew onto his bedsheet. "Every choice he made turned to crap! Those leeches took our home, our cattle. 'Just bad luck,' he said. That's when I saw what a loser he was. He couldn't manage the farm. *I* had to get a job. He couldn't feed the cows—*I* had to steal corn from the neighbors. He couldn't do anything! I had to step in every time! And when it was time for him to go, I had to help him with that, too."

End

CAROL HUSS is a graduate of the University of Minnesota and has worked as a laboratory animal technician, a technical writer, and a trainer. She currently provides technical support for medical devices. Her short story, "Escape to Skunk Lake" appeared in the 2018 Twin Cities Sisters in Crime anthology, *Dark Side of the Loon*. She is currently working on a mystery novel.

THE BEST DECISION FOR ALL CONCERNED

By Steven G. Hoffmeyer

The early wisps of dawn were still only a faint possibility as Sheila Emerson followed her ever-eager Spaniel down the wooden stairs of the small, comfy West St. Paul two-story house. A house in a long stretch of originally identical homes. The neighborhood had vastly changed over the decades. But not the Emerson's. It had no fresh lawn or immaculately trimmed hedges, no crystal globes highlighting diverse flower beds or cascading multicolored water fountains. Nor large, obnoxious rocks turned into tiered landscaping. A one-time blacktop driveway beaten down to little puddles of pebbles led to the now dilapidated single car garage behind the house.

The stairs, creaking under even Sheila's slight weight, gave encouragement to the dog who was now by the back door, looking forward to the first backyard exploration of the day. Sheila paused at each step with her ear tilted back toward the darkened master bedroom and listened for sounds, any sound from Harvey, her husband of eons. There was nothing, of course.

Before today, Sheila had been comforted by the slow, raspy breaths eking out of the bedroom, knowing that, at least in these early morning moments, Harvey was finally at peace from his daily battle for life. Sheila wondered if her feelings of warmth at these times were in any way related to her having some peace, some time to herself after all their troubles. Maybe she was feeling some guilt in her enjoyment of Harvey's quietness.

Sheila heard the knocking at her front door. Quickly letting the dog into the backyard and automatically lifting the doorknob to get the door closed again, she padded across the blistered salmon-colored linoleum of the kitchen, through her worn living room to the front door as the knocking grew insistent. As she opened the front door Sheila took a deep breath and relaxed, knowing she was ready.

"Oh, hello, please come in. Let's go back to the kitchen. Let me get you a cup of coffee."

Without waiting for a response, Sheila turned and headed back to the kitchen. Her visitor paused for a moment in confusion before following her.

Sheila walked, glancing over her shoulder. "I was just thinking back to when Harvey and my, ah, our mistake became apparent. My father, bless his dearly departed soul"—she crossed herself—"told us marriage was the only thing we could do. This was back in the early fifties, mind you. We didn't have any choices about whether the baby was coming or not."

Sheila pulled down two coffee mugs from the battered, chipped cupboard next to the sink, one of the mugs a St. Paul Winter Carnival 1970 souvenir, the other a White Castle restaurant memento, and gave them a quick rinse. A morning ritual required by frequent and ample nocturnal bug activity. She toweled them dry, then placed them on the counter. Her visitor pulled out a chair by the battered kitchen table and sat down with a blank expression. Waiting.

"The baby was coming and that was that. Marriage would correct the mistake and life would go on. 'It was the best decision for all concerned,' my parents said.

"Oh, the suddenness of the engagement announcement, arranging the wedding hall, band, all of that was politely undiscussed by friends and family, at least in front of us. But they knew. We knew but we didn't care, we were so much in love. So much, then."

Sheila opened a lower cupboard, pulled out the worn but reliable coffee pot, set it down near the light oak Wonder Bread box and two-slice toaster, and began to make coffee. She was careful not to overload the grounds basket.

"We got a house near my parents. Figured Harvey could catch a ride with Dad to their jobs at the Whirlpool factory up in East St. Paul, which was changing from military weapons to household appliances. Being so close also let Mom help out in getting the baby's room ready."

Sheila sighed before she capped the coffee pot, plugged it in, wiped down the counter, then put the coffee grounds away.

"There were just so many tasks to do. Papering the room, making clothes. Harvey hoped for a boy. I didn't care. I just wanted a healthy baby. A baby I could hug, talk to, play with, nurse into a great person. Maybe someone who could make the world nicer, softer. I had such plans. Such unbelievably strong hopes for the baby's future.

"Harvey was working hard at the plant. His first real job. A lot of changes from bombs and bullets to washing machines and dryers. And Harvey and I were going through a lot of changes too. Sure, we were teenagers, but we had responsibilities now—a house, a job, and the baby on the way. It seemed more and more like we didn't have enough money to go see a show or even go down to the diner."

Sheila brought the coffee to the once shiny kitchen table, the dark green shamrocks faded at the two customary eating spots. Then with a slight smile she did a twirl to the fridge, pulled the handle of the door, and felt a pleasing chill as the fridge's coolness hit her. She retrieved some creamer from the refrigerator, returned to the table, and passed it and the Paul Bunyan and Babe the Blue Ox decorative sugar bowl to her guest. Two battered but still bright smiles beamed up from the bowl.

Sheila's visitor declined the creamer and sugar, did some texting on her phone, then put it back on the table and continued to listen patiently, looking uncertain if she should interrupt. Or perhaps she was she waiting for something.

"How I wanted to dance. Harvey thought it was foolish for a married woman with a belly sticking out to Green Bay to wanna be twirling around—shaking up the baby.

"These months were tough, especially the first few. My body was still changing, growing, developing from a teen to an adult and here I had a baby doing all that inside me also. At first it didn't seem fair to the baby to come into the world to parents who were so recently kids themselves. What did we know about being parents? But something happened after about the fourth or fifth month. I became oblivious to all of mine and Harvey's day-to-day problems. More Harvey's, his problems got worse for a little while there, almost lost his job over some safety problems, arguments with my dad. But I suddenly became aware of the fullness of being a mom, to be truly nurturing another inside me. I think I actually started to glow. Why I bet if I had gone outside at night the neighbors would have had to draw their shades, what with my motherly glowing slicing through their windows, disrupting their Canasta games and TV dinners."

Sheila could hear multiple sirens, loud and wailing out of sync from outside, quieting as they neared. Like the eye of a Minnesota tornado stalling overhead, a solitude of silence centered over this kitchen.

Sheila rinsed and diced some potatoes and a small onion, then put them in a crock pot with some oil. She covered the pot while turning it on low.

"A mother is never prepared for and never recovers from the loss of a baby. It was so sudden. Bright sunny day, about lunchtime. I was hanging bedsheets on the clothesline out back when something happened. I can't recall the exact sequence. But I remember laying on the ground, screaming and thrashing holding my belly. A young neighbor boy, Daniel, heard me and ran for Mom. Mom called the doctor from her house then raced over here. Before anyone arrived, I pleaded, 'Please, God, if I'm too young to have this baby, take good care of him and let him come see me before I die.'"

Sheila sat down at the kitchen table and sipped her coffee.

"Mom and Daniel tried to comfort me, but I knew, and I think Mom knew too that the baby wasn't going to make it. After the baby died inside me that spring day something died between Harvey and me also. The doctor said, with a lot of medical mumbo jumbo, that attempts to save the baby on my lawn had . . . had scarred me inside. Doctors, to be charitable, were less sophisticated in those days.

"Maybe it's wrong, but it's natural to want to blame someone when a tragedy occurs. It's a reminder of our humanity. I could tell Harvey thought I was at fault. My parents thought *he* was. Why? I don't know. Human nature. Personally, I don't think it was anyone's fault. It just wasn't time for that soul to come into this world."

The visitor responded to a text message and then returned the phone to the table.

"Harvey and I started to drift apart, which was okay with me. I was so weak from the loss, more spiritual than physical. Acceptance does that to you."

Sheila removed a small package of meat from the refrigerator, unwrapped it, and placed it in the crockpot, absentmindedly saying "A lovely roast for dinner tonight would be nice. Maybe add some brussels sprouts later."

Sheila looked over the bottles of spice. "I was never much for spirits." She sprinkled some garlic salt in the crock pot. "Not much for either type of spirits: liquid or religious. But I just knew such personages were here, with us."

Sheila heard but ignored the slight "woof" from her backyard.

"Harvey's descent seemed so quick, looking back on it," Sheila recalled, wiping a tear away. "His problems began a few years back."

Sheila rubbed her left wrist, grabbed a tissue from her sleeve and dabbed her nose, then tucked it back away.

"Arthritis first, then some swollen glands, then little polyps here and there. That was okay for Harvey, not too painful. But when they started removing this organ and that growth . . . well, that's when what little life he had in himself began to leave his body. No. Began to leave his soul. Finally, he told the doctor no. We were sitting in the doctor's office. The doc was jabbering away about this pre-operation stuff, the operation will do this and that and this to ease his pain. And Harvey looked at the doctor and said something. It was so quiet. I looked up, surprised that the doctor seemed to have stopped talking in mid-mumbo. Then I realized Harvey had spoken. The doctor was looking at Harvey and I was looking at the doctor looking at Harvey. So, I asked him.

"'What Harvey? Whadya' say?'

"I said *no*," Harvey said, raising his chin up off his sunken, hairless, and scarred chest. He quivered slightly but steeled himself, sure and confident, almost teenage-back-seat cocky.

"The doctor looked from him, to me, then back to Harvey. I knew what he was thinking: 'Another senile old fart gonna make me work today.'

"The doctor continued telling Harvey how this next operation would ease his aches and pains. Harvey only heard about half as much as the doctor wanted to say as he shuffled his feet in his decrepit shoes.

"Harvey stopped him," Sheila chuckled. "Doctors hate to be stopped in mid-mumbo jumbo. Think that's not true? Try it the next time some doctor's got you on an examination table, poking and prodding you, being Chatty Cathy.

"Harvey told the doctor, 'Doctor, I'm almost eighty years old, I've been in pain most of my life, it's getting worse. None of these operations can cure me. I know that and you know that. I just wanna, I need to . . . go home.'

"I looked at the doctor. He was stunned. First a patient interrupting him and then a patient saying no? What was the world coming to?

"I stood up and walked over to Harvey, put my hand on his shoulder, and told him 'Okay. Let's go home, Harvey.'

" 'Do you know what . . .' the doctor began before I cut him off. I kinda enjoyed it. 'Doctor, he knows.'"

Sheila watched as the lady visitor looked over her shoulder as other people now entered the living room, some peering into the kitchen. Concerned. But the lady waved her hand dismissively at them.

"Harvey and I walked out of the hospital. I drove him home, helped him walk into the house, and upstairs. Those old shoes have remained by the back door, untouched these many months. Harvey went to the bed that day, basically for the last time. We both knew he'd never get out of that bed short of death. We accepted it and that helps, the certainty of inevitability is quite calming.

"What was also inevitable was the mounting bills: hospital, doctor, medicines, and household expenses. We had no idea what to do about them. He had been receiving a small pension from Whirlpool and his Social Security. Some might say this was an opportunity, looking on the positive side. But living the rough life we've lived; we wanted no more opportunities. We needed a pot of gold, not the silver lining. Gradually we came to figure we could rent out a room, the one off the living room would work best. Living near the hospital we were pretty sure we could get a nice intern or resident to rent from us in order to beat down our hospital debt. Harvey especially liked this little poetic justice."

Sheila went to the coffee pot, topped off her cup at the counter, gave it a shot of creamer, and stirred in more sugar from the Paul Bunyan bowl when she returned to the table.

"Harvey's pain was constant. At times he would join me in this real world, maybe catching the *Wheel of Fortune* after the Channel 4 six o'clock news. But more and more he lapsed into a world filled with pain and anguish, torment and grief, as wave after wave of death cells attacked his task-torn body. Daylight hours forced him awake more due to his long-term body's clock than his conscious knowledge that dawn had arrived. And only late in the night would his body take a rest from its daily torture. Painkillers might have helped, but when Harvey left the hospital that last time, he left behind all his pills, ointments, and hopes. He was ready and when it came, he didn't want to be in a haze. He told me in the car on the way home he wanted to 'breathe the fresh spring breeze, hear the squirrels chatter, feel the seasons pass.'

"I cleaned up the spare bedroom, threw out a lot of junk which had suddenly lost importance, and placed a notice up on the board at the Red Owl supermarket. When I returned home from my errands the first day, there was a young man sitting on my front stoop with the notice in his hands. He was stocky, bright looking, dressed nice in clean slacks and a button-down shirt which flattered his just-scrubbed appearance. He looked directly in my eyes and they twinkled as we discussed the room. He didn't have much by way of references, said he was only passing through but offered to pay two months' rent up front. Fresh, crisp bills stretched out in front of him.

"Something calmed me when I talked with him, he was young, maybe naïve to the world but so friendly it seemed like I'd known him forever. We continued to talk about the room, Harvey, and the mount-ing bills while we prepared dinner, washed dishes, and had some fancy French coffee he had brought with him in his duffle bag. His only disturbing behavior was to incessantly tinkle his spoon in his mug like Harvey had done, irritatingly, for decades. He slept in his new room that first night. Harvey and I both slept well that night and for the next week. A certain calm seemed to come over the house."

Sheila placed a slice of bread in the toaster and depressed its plung-er, then refilled her coffee mug. She remained standing by the toaster.

"It was last Tuesday when Harvey woke up in the middle of the afternoon. He looked refreshed and was, surprisingly, not in pain. He wanted to talk with our renter, John. But I told Harvey, 'I think John's out' just as the closing of the front door told us John was back. I went downstairs to tell John of Harvey's request and let him know he didn't have to if he didn't want to. I figured it might be discomforting for him to see a man in such pain, so near death. John took my hand, and by his touch and words a calm overtook me.

"'Sheila, it's time that I talk with Harvey, it'll help both of us.' John told me.

"John walked up the stairs with a smooth gracefulness belying his young years. He gave a soft knock and then entered Harvey's bedroom. He was up there quite a while. Despite my best stretched-ear techniques, I couldn't hear anything. Near dinnertime John came down, sat in that very chair, and with a sigh containing the weight of the world's ills said, 'I wished I had known him many years ago, he must have been a very strong man. He doesn't have long now but he's at peace.'

"I smiled. 'Yes, he was a big man. Strong, stocky, and sure of himself. In many ways you remind me of him when he was your age. But as far as being at peace, he's ravaged by floods of bodily ills which make him thrash in his bed for hours each day. He only sleeps at night when his body just gives up the fight for a few hours. You're nice to be so considerate, John, but he's not at peace.'

"John took my hand, and again I experienced that cooling calmness. It sent shivers up my spine. *Had I met this person somewhere before?*

"John assured me, 'Sheila, you would have made a wonderful mom. Self-confident, diligent, hardworking, anticipating Harvey's needs before he realizes them. But Harvey will be in peace until he leaves this earth.'

"With that, John went to his room for the night. I checked on Harvey, to give him his nightly foot rub to break his torments. I found him sleeping, his skeleton chest rising to greet each new relaxing breath.

'John, who are you? I wondered as I went to bed that night, full of questions but not a whit of concern. I slept soundly that night and have every night that John has been here.

"John wasn't around much for a few days. I figured he was job hunting or checking on possible schooling. It was later that week that Harvey had a turn for the worse. I thought I'd lose him that night, but he hung on, still in pain but hanging by a thread. He wanted to talk with John. I had just got him shussed up when John came into the room."

"John walked over to Harvey, gripped his hand and said, 'It'll be soon, but not tonight. Sleep well, Dad.'

"I paid no attention at the time to the *Dad* part, figuring John was trying to compliment Harvey, helping him get some slumber, some peace.

"I had plenty of questions, but John would answer none of them as he walked me back to my bedroom. As he was leaving, he pressed a small vial into my hands." Sheila pointed to a clear two-inch long vial, half full with some white substance lying next to the Paul Bunyan and Babe the Blue Ox sugar bowl.

"I've thought for many hours about John's next words, as he closed my hands over that vial.

"*'Mom, you were too young to have a baby. I've come to see Dad before he dies. I need this vial to leave this world—to go back to my world after Dad dies. So please keep it for me. I'm having a hard time seeing Dad in this much pain. If you keep the vial, I'll know I can't leave early.'*"

A male police officer came to the kitchen and cleared his throat to interrupt. The female officer, who had been sitting quietly at the table, turned to talk with him. The toaster popped up. Sheila padded to the counter with her coffee cup. She plated her toast, gave her coffee cup a stir, and returned to the kitchen table with a butter knife.

The female officer returned her focus and noticed Sheila's cheeks glistened with tears, a few dripped on her toast. She brushed butter on the toast, cut it diagonally, and took a timid bite.

"See, that's how I knew this young man, John, our renter, is our baby. Our baby! Because he knew—*he knew*—what I said when I was moaning and thrashing on the lawn those decades ago."

Sheila looked at the nice female police officer, with her cell phone recording their conversation, and the two other officers now crowded into her kitchen, just watching her in silence. Sheila ignored another "woof" from outside and the paw scratches at the door.

"And," Sheila continued, "yesterday morning, when I grabbed Harvey's favorite coffee mug from the cupboard, poured coffee into it, and looked at that vial, I knew what John—our baby was telling me. How to ease his dad's pain. And how to keep my son here. I won't be cheated twice in one lifetime! Doesn't my boy deserve a life? Deserve to stay in this world?"

Sheila looked at them defiantly. "So I uncapped the vial and poured some of it into Harvey's coffee, gave it a stir, and walked upstairs. My son will have the life he was denied! Even if I'm not here for him."

The female police officer quickly looked down at the kitchen table. Paul Bunyan and Babe the Blue Ox stared back with vacant smiles.

Beside an empty vial.

Alarmed, her eyes raced back to Sheila.

Sheila Emerson's eyes, sad and wet like the first signs of a Minnesota spring, looked back at the panicked female officer. Sheila's hands shook as she took a small sip of her coffee, then a large gulp. Her next words were a whisper.

"It is, after all, the best decision for all concerned."

END

STEVEN G. HOFFMEYER has been writing his entire life: stories and articles (for himself, and newspapers in high school and college and ones he started in and after law school), legal briefs, numerous arbitration awards and fictions of mystery, capers, and adventure (although legal briefs may have edged into fiction). Hoffmeyer is a lifelong Minnesotan, a so-so attorney, a pretty good labor mediator, a successful arbitrator with cases across the country, and now with "The Best Decision For All Concerned," a widely successful published author of short story fiction of less than 4000 words, based in Minnesota, exhibiting bad behavior.

HELL WEEK
By Greg Dahlager

First, they had to remove the duct tape that bound their wrists behind their backs before they could do anything about the blindfolds. It would require teamwork, and overcoming a problematic amount of alcohol still coursing through their veins.

"Stop shaking," Nora Bauer said, now that she and Tiffany Martin blindly managed to arrange themselves back to back, Nora running her fingers along her pledge sister's tape, trying to find the seam.

"It's freaking cold!" Tiffany wailed.

"We're a bit underdressed tonight," Nora conceded, but Tiffany didn't laugh. Both wore nightgowns and slippers. Wherever they were, they could feel the November wind whipping.

Nora thought she might have found the seam but lost it because Tiffany couldn't stop twitching and shivering. When she located it again, she picked at it with a fingernail, finally gaining enough purchase to start peeling.

"Are they trying to kill us?" Tiffany cried.

Nora almost had it—it was peeling faster now and her left hand gathered the unraveling tape with each revolution around Tiffany's wrists. "There! You're free."

"Thank, God." Nora heard Tiffany rip her blindfold off and gasp. "Oh! We're in the middle of nowhere!"

"Can you take off my blindfold, pretty please?"

Tiffany complied, and Nora found herself standing in a shallow ditch between a gravel road and a frozen cornfield, with rows of dead, broken stalks jutting up through the snow at all angles like vandalized gravestones.

"We're gonna die out here," Tiffany said, sounding resigned to it already.

"We're in a farm field. That means there's a farm nearby. Probably just down this road. See where the streetlight is?"

"It's so far away! I'm freezing."

"Can you undo my tape?"

"My hands are too cold."

"Can you do it, anyway?"

"I'll try." Tiffany stumbled behind her, burping and slowly working the tape off with the marginal benefit of eyesight, and a three-quarters moon that was a shining piece of luck tonight.

Nora rubbed her wrists once freed, and then her bare arms, cursing Ashley Palmentere. Beyond the remote streetlight, some distance away, she saw a faint but sprawling glow. A town. "Let's go."

Running in slippers proved tricky, so Nora settled for a fast walk, but Tiffany couldn't keep up. Nora glanced back to find Tiffany down on her knees, vomiting on the gravel. In fairness, they'd made her drink more shots during lineup because she'd gotten the most answers wrong of all the pledges. Nora went back and helped her up and, together, they advanced more slowly down the road, having wrapped their arms around each other for warmth. Finally reaching the pool of mercury light cast from a pole opposite the darkened farm, they separated and hurried up a gravel driveway to a clapboard farmhouse. Nora rang the doorbell repeatedly, but the house remained still and silent. She then banged on the door with her raw, frozen fist, yelling "Help!" Tiffany banged her own fist on a window that looked like it belonged to a bedroom, and then on another. No lights came on. No sounds were heard. If anyone were home, they were either afraid to answer the pleas of midnight callers, or they slept the sleep of the dead.

✻

The Kappa Omicron pledge class at the University of Minnesota had numbered sixteen young women approaching initiation. Tonight was the fourth night of the week-long ritual known colloquially as Hell Week, where candidates proved themselves worthy of membership in

KO, or weeded themselves out if they weren't. Two by two, pledges had reunited at the chapter house, having survived their "wilderness adventure test," proving resolve, resourcefulness, and teamwork. Rachel Anderson and Daphne Matthias—numbers thirteen and fourteen—had just been welcomed home by their fellow pledges with jubilant squeals and exuberant hugs.

"Line up!" Ashley Catherine Palmentere, chapter president, called out in her most commanding voice, delighted to kill the pledges' short-lived elation. Paityn Ainsley, pledgemaster, had just built a roaring fire to heat the backsides of the pledges, who would have to stand before it in two straight rows, wearing their nightgowns, facing the darkened room that hid the wary, watchful eyes of four dozen actives, ready to drill them.

"Pledge Chlamydia!" Caitlyn Murphy, the rush chair, yelled.

"Ma'am, yes, ma'am!" Siobhan Landon stepped out of the front line, standing straight and tall, like a proper cadet.

"What is my name?"

"Caitlyn Brigid Murphy, ma'am."

"What is my hometown?"

"Minnetrista, Minnesota, ma'am."

The actives filling the darkened room snapped their fingers in approval.

"What is my major?"

"Business, ma'am."

"Can you be more specific, Pledge?"

"Um. Finance?"

The actives became a den of vipers, hissing in unison.

"Step back!"

"Pledge class," Paityn proclaimed, "due to your pledge sister's disregard for learning even the most superficial information about someone she claims to want to call her sister, you will all perform one hundred jumping jacks while reciting the Greek alphabet. I'll count for you. One . . ."

Kirstin Hartvigsen, social chair, poured the triple shot of Jägermeister into a Dixie cup that Siobhan had to slam while doing jumping jacks for her wrong answer, as Ashley Palmentere looked on with approval.

"It's after midnight," Brianna Jones, recording secretary, said to

Ashley, leaning in and reeking of Dior. "Where are Nora and Tiff? Where did you take them, anyway?"

"I don't know what their problem is," Ashley said, leaning away from Brianna. "Everyone else made it back."

"You were their driver. You dropped them somewhere on campus, right?"

"Maybe a bit off campus," Ashley said, priding herself in her mastery of understatement, and focusing again on the pledges who had made their way back.

"Pledges, switch lines!" Caitlyn commanded, and the two rows of women traded places, the ones closest to the fire getting a reprieve.

"Pledge Succubus!" Inga Lindgren, the chapter historian, yelled, rising from a couch across the darkened room.

Jen Jorgenson stepped forward. "Ma'am, yes, ma'am!"

"Where was Kappa Omicron founded?"

"College of William and Mary, ma'am."

Snaps all around.

"What year?"

"1897, ma'am."

More snaps.

"Who were the five founders?"

"Elizabeth Church. And—um . . ."

Vicious hisses teemed from every direction.

"Step back!"

Paityn shook her head. "Pledge class, your pledge sister's unwillingness to learn the most rudimentary history of our esteemed sorority betrays a character flaw that can only be remedied by more jumping jacks, while singing 'Bless My Sisters, Bless This Bond.' Sing well, or you'll do it all over again, and closer to the fire."

The pledges in their nightgowns did their jumping jacks and began to sing, while Kirstin prepared a Dixie cup for Jen's consumption.

"Seriously," Brianna continued, as she always seemed to do, "we should probably call the police. It's been four hours. It's, like, twenty degrees out there."

"And tell them what? We're hazing some pledges and lost a couple?"

"Fair point."

"You're soft, Brianna," Ashley said. "Yet you somehow manage to be an attacker on the Gopher lacrosse team with that bleeding heart of yours?"

"Not everyone has your killer instinct, Madam President," Brianna said curtly, finally leaning away, but without taking the lingering scent of her perfume with her.

Ashley leaned back against the couch, signaling for Kirstin to bring her a shot. If she couldn't hoover a couple of lines in the next two minutes, a shot would have to do. She swallowed, savoring the sweet licorice taste and the soothing warmth that came with it, crushing the Dixie cup in her fist, and hurling it at the closest pledge.

Danielle Durand parked herself on the arm of the couch beside her. "Where the hell is Tiffany?" She was a sophomore and Tiffany's sorority big sister, obligated to look out for her.

"I don't know. If she has any brains, she'll find her way back."

Claudia Barber, Nora's big sister, would probably make a similar demand of her once she arrived. She was bartending until close at the Improper Fraction tonight—hopefully making good tips because Ashley planned to fine her for missing tonight's affairs.

Of the sixteen young women who'd pledged Kappa Omicron in September, she expected two would wash out—or die trying not to. One was Nora Bauer, a sturdy girl from Two Harbors who was pretty in a certain kind of light, but wore too much flannel and not enough pearls or makeup, and talked in a dialect that betrayed her backwoods upbringing. Back home, Ashley imagined Nora splitting her own wood, rebuilding snowmobile engines, hunting elk. Ashley had long felt bidding this girl had been a capital mistake, and blamed her rush chair, Caitlyn, for thinking Nora was KO material when she clearly wasn't.

The fact that Nora had snooped her way into some financial matters that were none of her business may have also played a role in Ashley's haste to be rid of her.

The second one going down was Tiffany Martin. She came from Wayzata, and a good family that lived in a large home on Lake Minnetonka. She'd taken third in State 2A for singles tennis her senior year of high school, and was pretty enough to model skiwear and swimwear in ads for a local sporting goods retailer. Ashley could have been perfectly content to call Tiffany a sister but, alas, Tiffany was Nora's roommate, and roommates sometimes share gossip—so whatever happened to Nora had to happen to Tiffany, too. There was little sense in taking chances.

✵

They finally reached the blacktop road that led toward the glow of lights. "There's a town," Nora said, shivering. "Let's walk there."

"It's miles away!" Tiffany protested, teeth chattering. "We'll freeze to death before we make it there."

"People don't freeze to death, generally. They die of hypothermia."

"Was that meant to cheer me up?"

Nora saw a pair of lights moving in the distance, gradually getting bigger. "Tiff, look. Someone's coming!"

"Is it Death?"

"It's a car. Or truck." Nora started to run toward the approaching vehicle, but lost a slipper. Tiffany picked it up and brought it to her. "Hopefully, whoever this is will help us," Nora said, putting the slipper back on. "But if it's trouble, our code word is 'Sweetheart'."

"And what do I do if you use the code word?"

"Run like hell."

The two stood in the road, waving their arms and jumping up and down when the high-beams eventually reached them. A pickup truck slowed down, and they ran toward it.

The passenger window lowered. "Please, help us!" Nora said to a young guy in a Polaris cap with a cigarette jutting from the corner of a lopsided mouth.

"Are you prostitutes?" he asked, head tilted, one eye squinting at her.

"No! Why would you say that?" Nora rubbed her arms and made her shivering as obvious as possible.

"You're not wearing much."

"It's a long story. Will you give us a ride?"

"Where to?"

"Someplace warm?"

The guy nodded slowly. "I can think of a place."

He got out and held the door open, helping her step up onto the running board as she climbed in. It was a crew cab truck, and she thought it nice that he gave her the passenger seat, closer to the heater. When everyone settled, Tiffany was in the backseat behind the driver, with the cap-wearing guy next to her, foregoing his seatbelt and scooting close. Driving the truck was a shaggy-haired, bearded guy in a shearling jacket, wearing a roguish smile. On the radio, Hank Williams, Junior sang "Whiskey Bent and Hell Bound," as the driver shifted into gear and they started on their way. "I'm Cowboy. That's Gunner."

"Huh," Nora said, turning her heating vents toward her. "I'm Aspen, and she's Willow."

"What are your real names?"

"What are yours?"

"Told you. Cowboy. And that's Gunner."

"All right, Cowboy," Nora said, leaning closer to the heat. "Could you drive us to Minneapolis? It's probably not what you had planned for tonight but there's a cool two-hundred in it for you."

"Figured you chicks had to be from the Cities. You got no sense."

"How's that, Cowboy?"

"Look how you're dressed. Lucky you didn't freeze to death."

"More likely," Tiffany volunteered from the backseat, "it would be hypothermia."

Cowboy glanced into the rearview mirror, still grinning. "You chicks from the Cities are a hoot with your five-dollar words."

"Look, we're cold, and far from home," Nora said. "Will you help us?"

"Well, the money would be nice, wouldn't it, Gunner?"

"You betcha!" Gunner said, shifting closer to Tiffany in the backseat.

"But I can think of something that would be even nicer," Cowboy said. He leaned his head back on the headrest and glanced over at Nora, taking his eyes off the road and winking at her.

"Have you been drinking, Cowboy?" Nora asked, smiling while quickly formulating a Plan B in her head.

"Does a bear wear a funny hat?" Cowboy said, his smile spreading like a disease. "Does a pope shit in the woods?"

"Maybe I should drive."

"Maybe you should give me a kiss."

"Take us to Minneapolis, and we can talk about it," Nora said.

Cowboy pulled the truck off the blacktop onto a remote gravel road and stopped the truck, putting it in neutral and setting the brake, engine still running. "Kiss first. Cities later."

"Get off of me!" Tiffany shouted from the backseat, pushing Gunner away.

On the radio, Patsy Cline sang "So Wrong," as Cowboy reached over and played with Nora's hair. "Cowboy's been lonesome since his old lady took off."

"I'm sorry about that," Nora said, removing his hand from her head and placing it back on the gearshift. "You can tell me all about it if you like, on our way to Minneapolis."

"I don't like to play rough," Cowboy said, his smile looking ever-more sour. "But I still do, sometimes."

"Say, Cowboy," Nora said, her heart keeping the beat of a much faster song than what was playing on the radio. "Take a look at my friend. Isn't she pretty?" She undid her seatbelt. "Turn the light on."

Cowboy's smile faded ever so slightly. And then he put on the interior light, turned and looked at Tiffany, who squinted back, shrinking away from everybody.

"She's prettier than me, don't you think?" Nora said.

Cowboy scrutinized her with eyes that looked glassy in the dim light. "She's about as hot as Carolyn Moss. Gunner, isn't she about as hot as Carolyn Moss?"

"Hell, yeah," Gunner said, cracking his knuckles.

"And she's always talked about, you know, two guys," Nora said, smiling at Cowboy. "At once." She turned toward Tiffany in the backseat. "Haven't you, Sweetheart?"

Tiffany stared back at her in fear and revulsion for this sudden betrayal to save her own skin. And then something clicked, and she undid her seatbelt and scrambled out the door, running toward the tailgate of the truck.

"Get her!" Cowboy yelled.

Gunner jumped out and slipped into the darkness behind them.

"She's getting away," Nora said pleasantly, tipping her head in the direction of the action behind the truck.

"Shit." Cowboy threw his door open and leapt out, forgetting to kill the engine.

Nora climbed over the center console into the driver's seat, pulling the door shut and flooring the clutch with a slippered foot, putting the gearshift in reverse, releasing the brake. She eyed the mirrors, seeing nothing in the reverse lights behind the truck, but giving it some gas and rolling backward until she saw the backside of Cowboy, lurching into the darkness. She pushed her foot down hard and the truck sped up and there was a thump, and Cowboy appeared in the headlights now, laying on his side on the gravel. Nora slowed to a stop at the edge of the road, then made a three-point turn, heading back in the opposite direction, her headlights reaching Gunner on the verge of catching Tiffany. Nora gave the truck a little more gas, and gave him a glancing blow that threw him into the ditch. She slowed the truck as she reached Tiffany, lowering the passenger-side window. "Get in, Sister."

Tiffany climbed in, slamming the door.

"My God!" she screamed, breathlessly. "You killed them!"

"I did no such thing," Nora said, shifting, picking up speed. She turned onto the blacktop, heading south.

"You ran them down with this stupid truck!"

"I just gave them a bump."

"They're dead!"

"You don't know that. Maybe they're just sleeping off a dozen pitchers of Grain Belt." Nora shifted into fourth gear. "They'll be fine. Probably."

"You can drive a stick!" Tiffany exclaimed, in an abrupt change of subject.

"Can't you?"

"No!"

"Doesn't your dad have a Porsche 911?"

"Yeah, but—I'm not insured to drive it. I just get to ride along."

"Poor kid."

"Are you okay to drive, anyway?"

"More or less," Nora answered. She took the pack of Marlboro's from the dash and helped herself to one, pushing in the truck's lighter, and then getting her cigarette started.

"You don't smoke," Tiffany said, staring at her.

"No," Nora agreed, exhaling two plumes through her nostrils. "Under ordinary circumstances." She glanced at the fuel gauge. Nearly full.

"Why are they trying to kill us, anyway? The KO's."

Nora lowered her window and flicked ash out into the rural darkness. "They're not trying to kill you. You're collateral damage. It's me they're after. And I'm not sure it's anyone but Ashley that wants me dead."

"Why?"

"She knows that I know she's been embezzling from the chapter's parlor fees. And all that money we raised for the Animal Humane Society? They never got it."

"She's been stealing? But she's president! And she's richer than anyone!"

"She's a coke fiend with extravagant tastes whose daddy cut her allowance in half after the big divorce."

"Whoa!"

Nora changed the radio station to something playing pop music.

"This has been quite the night." Tiffany settled into the passenger seat and began a series of hiccups that would last until they reached Maple Grove.

At the darkened Kappa Omicron house, Nora dropped Tiffany off, telling her to wait in the living room. She parked the truck on a side street in Dinkytown, found a napkin in the center console, and used it to wipe down the steering wheel, gearshift, dash, lighter, vents, and door handles, including the ones Tiffany had used. She had thrown her cigarette butts out the window along their way, and now she swiped the rest of the pack, slipped out of the truck, and raced down University Avenue toward the KO house.

Inside, she found Tiffany curled up and dozing on a couch before a fireplace glowing faintly with dying embers. In the sunroom, fourteen of her pledge sisters lay sleeping on the tiled floor, their bodies tucked up to one another, blankets pulled close.

Nora shook Tiffany awake, and they went upstairs to get dressed.

On the top floor was Ashley's room. Being president, she got a private room, as luck would have it. They breached it quietly, and Nora sat on the edge of Ashley's bed, slapping her cheek to wake her up. "Surprised to see us?" she asked when she saw the whites of Ashley's eyes. But then she clapped her hand over the president's mouth. "Don't answer that." Ashley's eyes grew wider as Nora leaned in. "Time for *your* medicine. Let me know how it tastes."

Tiffany kneeled beside the bed next to Nora and held up her roll of duct tape, smiling.

Blindfolded, her hands bound behind her, Ashley rode in the backseat of a car being driven by Nora, who seemed to be smoking a cigarette, judging by the smell. This would ordinarily be another strike against her, except . . .

"You've already proven yourselves. You don't have to do this. Whatever it is."

"It's called the 'president purity ritual,'" Nora said. "If you're not the self-dealing sadist I think you are, you'll find your way back to the KO house alive."

"Yeah," Tiffany chimed in from the passenger seat. "Whatever happened to 'Subjugating the self to the sisterhood'?"

"Look. I know you two know certain things," Ashley said, refusing to let her voice quiver, though it wanted to. "So, I'll let you in on the—benefits. Even split. Three ways."

"Not interested," Nora said.

"Working class girl like you?"

"Working class girl like me earns her pay."

"And what about the funds we raised for the Animal Humane Society?" Tiffany demanded, sounding worked up about it. "Those poor cats and dogs need our money!"

Ashley bit her lip to keep from getting emotional. It worked every time, until now. "You don't have to do this," she repeated.

"You're probably right," Nora said. "But it's the middle of the night, and I'm not thinking straight."

"How *did* you get back, anyway?"

"We met a couple of nice gentlemen who loaned us their truck," Nora said.

Tiffany giggled for some reason.

"Maybe you'll have the same luck," Nora suggested.

Ashley sensed the car turning onto a gravel road. A minute later, it stopped. She felt the rush of cold as her door opened, someone grabbing her arm. "Let's go," Nora said.

She stumbled across the gravel on her blind journey, and then climbed what felt like a gradual hill. Nora let go, moving behind her. "Open your right hand." Ashley did as she was told, and felt something placed into her palm. "It's a pocketknife. You can use it to free your wrists once we're gone."

"I'm not like you," Ashley said. "I'm not good at these sorts of games."

She heard Nora take a deep breath and let it out. "I know."

"And yet, you're doing this to me."

"You tried to kill us."

"That's not true. I knew you'd make it."

A hopeful hesitation followed. But then: "Goodbye, Ash."

She heard footsteps receding through the snow. A car door shutting. A car leaving.

It was very cold, and she wore only her nightgown and slippers.

She rubbed her thumb along the edge of the pocketknife, trying to find the groove to open the blade and cut through the tape that bound her wrists together. But her hands grew cold, she began shivering, and the knife dropped from her hand. The wind howled and rushed right through her as she knelt to the cold ground, grabbing blindly behind her for her lost knife, but only finding twigs in the icy dirt and snow.

✳✲✳

The news of Ashley Palmentere's death from hypothermia came as a shock to nearly everyone in the Kappa Omicron sorority. In fact, her body's discovery in Mower County, blindfolded and bound, worried the entire state, dominating the news cycle for a week. Detectives interviewed every woman in KO individually, and received uniformly similar answers. Everyone had last seen Ms. Palmentere leading the pledge class as they studied the sorority's history in preparation for the final pledge exam, offering sisterly encouragement. No one had heard anyone break into the house and kidnap her. No one could think of anyone with a motive to do such a thing. When an investigator raised the possibility of a hazing rite gone wrong, pledgemaster Paityn Ainsley said emphatically, "Kappa Omicrons don't haze."

Meanwhile, up in Stearns County, a pair of hospitalized young men suffering various broken bones also made the news, claiming to have been attacked by a pair of prostitutes named after trees who tricked them, stole their truck, and ran them down. No fingerprints were lifted from the stolen truck, found four blocks from the Kappa Omicron house.

"What happens in KO, stays in KO," Claudia Barber reminded her little sister, Nora, hugging as they left the cemetery following Ashley's interment. National was sending someone to the house Monday to discuss their fate.

Nora glanced one last time over her shoulder at the gravesite surrounded by Ashley's grieving family. The setting sun's pale light silhouetted them, and the sixty solemn sorority sisters, clad in black, now dispersing. "Yeah, I've heard secret societies are like that," she said, slipping the last of Gunner's cigarettes between her lips.

End

GREG DAHLAGER is a *Writer's Digest* award winner, and his short fiction has appeared in the *Saturday Evening Post* and the anthology *Dark Side of the Loon: Where History Meets Mystery.* He is a graduate of West Hennepin Citizen's Police Academy and a member of the Twin Cities chapter of Sisters in Crime.

Other Anthologies
from Twin Cities Sisters in Crime

FESTIVAL OF CRIME

Minnesota, Land of 10,000 Lakes, and more annual festivals than you can shake a stick at. County fairs, arts and craft shows, music festivals—from Austin to International Falls, people flock to these events for food and fun. But a few festivalgoers have more devious intentions in mind.

DARK SIDE OF THE LOON:
WHERE HISTORY MEETS MYSTERY

Dark emotions and even darker thoughts seep from the murky depths inspired by moments in Minnesota history, from the days of the great bison hunts to the Hinckley Firestorm of 1894 to the 2005 theft of Dorothy's ruby red slippers from Grand Rapids, and more.

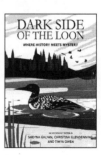